Huntress

Huntress

MALINDA LO

www.atombooks.net

ATOM

First published in the United States in 2011 by
Little, Brown and Company
First published in Great Britain in 2011 by Atom
Reprinted 2014

A CIP catalogue record for this book
is available from the British Library.

ISBN 978-1-907411-09-0

Printed and bound in Great Britain by
Clays Ltd, St Ives plc

Papers used by Atom are from well-managed forests
and other responsible sources.

MIX
Paper from
responsible sources
FSC® C104740

Atom
An imprint of
Little, Brown Book Group
100 Victoria Embankment
London EC4Y 0DY

An Hachette UK Company
www.hachette.co.uk

www.atombooks.net

To Amy Lovell

LONDON BOROUGH OF WANDSWORTH	
9030 00004 0440 5	
Askews & Holts	09-Oct-2014
JF TEENAGE 14+	£6.99
	WWX0012778/0003

Huntress is set in the same world as *Ash*, but it takes place many centuries earlier. There are some significant cultural differences between the time periods.

Pronunciation Guide

In multisyllabic names, the emphasis is on the italicized syllable. In some cases, both syllables should be given equal weight. In human names, the letters *ae* are pronounced like the *a* sound in *mate* and *skate*; the letters *ai* are pronounced like the *i* sound in *kite* and *site*. Xi names (designated with asterisks) have different pronunciation rules.

Ailan: *Eye*-lahn
Anmin: *Ahn*-min
Cai Simin Tan: Tsai Sih-*meen* Tan
Con Isae Tan: Con *Ee*-say Tan
Ealasaid*: *Ay*-lah-*sed*
Elowen*: *Ell*-oh-*when*
Farin: *Fahr*-in
Kaede: *Kay*-dee
Kaihan: *Kye*-hahn
Maesie: *May*-see
Maila: *My*-lah
Maire Morighan*: Mare *Mor*-ih-*gahn*
Mona: *Mo*-nah
Nara: *Nah*-rah
Niran: *Nee*-rahn
Noa: *No*-ah
Ota: *Oh*-tah
Parsa: *Par*-sah
Pol: Pole
Raesa: *Ray*-sah
Raiden: *Rye*-den
Shae: Shay
Sota: *So*-tah
Suri: *Soo*-ree
Taeko: *Tay*-ko
Taisin: *Tie*-sin
Tali: *Tah*-lee
Taninli*: *Tan*-in-*lee*
Tanis: *Tan*-is
Tulan: *Too*-lahn
Xi*: Shee
Yuna: *Yoo*-nah
Yuriya: *Yoo*-ree-ah

 # PART I

Clouds and thunder arise:
The sage brings order.
Those who chase deer without a hunter
Lose their way in the Wood.

—*Book of Changes*

Chapter I

She saw a beach made of ice, and she felt her heart breaking.

The ground where she stood was frozen white, but twenty feet away, cold blue ocean lapped at the jagged shore. Someone there was climbing into a rowboat, and she knew that she loved this person. She was certain of it in the same way that one is instantly aware of the taste of sweetness in a drop of honey. But she was afraid for this person's life, and the fear raised a cold sweat on her skin and caused a sick lurch in her stomach, as though she were on a ship during a violent storm.

She opened her mouth to call the rower back—she couldn't bear the loss; it would surely cripple her—and at that moment she realized she could hear nothing. All around her was an eerie, unnatural silence. There was no sound from the ocean. She could not even hear herself breathing. She felt her tongue shaping the syllables of the person's name, but she did not recognize what the name was until the rower turned to face her. *Kaede.*

The rower was Kaede, and she looked back with dark, troubled eyes. Loose strands of black hair whipped around her pale face; there were spots of red on her wind-roughened cheeks. Her lips parted as though she would speak. But then Kaede reached down into the boat and lifted out a long oar, dipping it into the azure sea to propel the small craft away from the shore. The droplets of water falling from the blade of the oar were tiny stars, extinguished as quickly as they burned into being. The boat cut through the water, leaving the shore behind, and just before the destination came into view, the vision ended.

She was wrenched out of the icy landscape and back into her body, where she was sitting in the empty practice hall, alone on her cushion.

She opened her eyes, blinking against the light of the single candle she had lit on the altar. Her heart was pounding, and there was an acrid taste in her mouth. Her hands, folded in her lap, were trembling and chilled. A trickle of sweat ran from her temple down her cheek.

She drew her knees up and hugged them close, burying her face in the crook of her elbow, and because there was no one to hear her, she let out the sob that reared up in her throat. The sound echoed in the vaulted ceiling of the practice room, and for once she gave in to the overwhelming feelings rushing through her. She felt gutted. She felt powerless.

She had never seen so clearly before, and her teachers would praise her for it. But she felt no satisfaction, for she could not rejoice in the vision of someone she apparently loved departing on a journey to her death.

4

Chapter II

aede was working in the cliff garden when she received the summons. This was her favorite part of the Academy—the crescent-shaped patch of earth carved out of the edge of the island, facing the mainland. On a clear day, she could see the brownish-green hills behind the crooked roofs of Seatown. But there had not been a clear day in a little over two months; only this constant gray light and scattered drizzle. Yet, as much as she hated it, it was better to be outside in the brisk sea air than trapped indoors behind the Academy's suffocating stone walls.

She continued down the row of stunted carrots, working in the rich fertilizer that Maesie, the Academy's cook, had given her at the start of her shift. A hard winter had been followed by no sign of spring, and Maesie had delayed planting at first, hoping for sunshine and warmth before she subjected her seedlings to the cold earth. But one morning she announced that she would wait no more, and the seeds went into the ground that day, followed by biweekly applications of the thick black fertilizer she concocted in the evenings. And despite the lack of sunlight, the seeds sprouted, though they were thinner and weaker than usual.

Kaede had just finished the row and was about to drag the jug of fertilizer to the next when Maesie came out of the kitchen, an odd look on her face. She held a wooden spoon in her hand as if she had come straight from the stove. Kaede straightened, brushing off her dirty hands on her cotton trousers. "What is it?"

"I've just had word from the Council," Maesie said. "They want to see you."

Kaede was puzzled. What would the Council of Sages want with her? She was hardly one of their favorite students. "What? When?"

"Now. You'd better leave your things there. I'll have someone else finish up for you."

She blinked at Maesie. "Now?" She wasn't sure she had heard correctly.

"Now. But you should clean up before you go—you don't want to track mud all over their chambers."

～

Kaede had not been to the Council chambers since her first visit to the Academy of Sages when she was eleven, to apply for admission. In the ensuing six years, there had never been a reason for her to make the long trek to the North Tower, for the only students invited into that inner sanctum were those who could perform the rituals they were taught. Although she had read the *Book of Rituals* several times, Kaede had never successfully completed even the simplest of blessings. She knew she had only been allowed to remain at the Academy because her father was the King's Chancellor, and her mother—before she married him—had been a sage. Now she wondered if her time at the Academy was finally coming to an end, for why else would the Mistress have called for her, if not to dismiss her at last?

To reach the Council chambers, she had to climb a lengthy, circular flight of stairs. Carved in every step were the words to a different verse from the *Book of Changes*. She knew that if she read each step in order from the ground floor up, she would find the entire first folio there, comprising the core teachings that every student was required to learn during her first year. But Kaede only glanced down at random, and the verses made little sense out of context.

In disorder, misfortune.
In sincerity, fear gives way.
Dragons battle on the plain: yellow and black blood spills.
Fire in the mountain lake: grace brings success.

The phrases irritated her, reminding her of countless hours spent huddled over her books, feeling as though they were only mocking her. By the time she reached the landing outside the iron doors to the Council chambers, she was eager to be done with it. Whatever form her dismissal might take, she would welcome it.

She reached for the rope hanging from the mouth of the iron dragon embedded in the stone wall, and pulled. Several minutes later the left-hand door was opened by Sister

Nara, the youngest of the three Council members. Her black hair, which was normally coiled in two careful braids tucked against the nape of her neck, was coming loose as though she had rushed through her morning rituals. Two small vertical lines appeared between her brown eyes as she said, "Come in."

Kaede followed Sister Nara through the circular antechamber to the inner redwood doors. Each was hung with a round gold shield. On the left was a phoenix, its tail feathers curling toward its beak, wings extended: the sign of harmony. On the right was a unicorn, the symbol of justice; its deerlike head was lowered so that its curving horn pointed down, while its goatlike tail curled up.

Sister Nara opened the doors, and the moment that Kaede entered the Council chamber, she knew something was wrong—she could not have been called there merely to be dismissed. For there were two men seated at the long wooden table along with the Council members and the Mistress of the Academy: One of them was her father, Lord Raiden, the King's Chancellor; the other was King Cai Simin Tan himself. What could have possibly brought him all the way from his palace to the isolated Academy?

Out of long habit, she folded her hands and bowed to the King, but she did not acknowledge her father. The last time they had spoken, they had argued heatedly, and the memory of it still made her face burn with suppressed anger.

At the head of the table, Maire Morighan, the Mistress of the Academy, said, "Kaede, please sit down."

As she walked to the table, her cloth shoes making no

8

sound on the cold stone floor, her pulse quickened with curiosity. She saw the three Council members: Sister Nara, who was just pulling out her chair; Sister Ailan; and Sister Yuna. She saw Maire Morighan, her hands clasped on the table before a small wooden box. And, unexpectedly, she saw another student seated beside Sister Ailan. Kaede recognized the girl's face, but she couldn't remember her name. They had arrived at the Academy the same year, but after that first year, they had never had any classes together. She was supposed to be extraordinarily gifted, and she took all her classes in private with Sister Ailan. Kaede had never given much thought to her, but now she wondered why she was here. The girl's cheeks darkened a little under Kaede's gaze, and she turned deliberately toward the Mistress. And then Kaede remembered: Her name was Taisin.

Maire Morighan said: "You must be wondering why you have been called here. But before we can tell you that, you should know a bit more about why His Majesty has visited us so unexpectedly." She inclined her head toward the King. "Would you like to tell the tale, Your Majesty?"

King Cai glanced at Lord Raiden before turning his attention to Lord Raiden's daughter. He had seen her before, of course, when the Chancellor brought his family to the palace, but the King had never done more than keep track of her as a potentially useful tool. She was not the beauty her mother was, though she resembled her in spirit, at least, for she raised her eyes to him boldly. He ran a hand over his triangular beard, considering where to begin.

"One month ago," the King said, "a visitor arrived at the palace in Cathair. He demanded an audience with me, but he was in a wretched state—looked as if he'd been traveling for months, clothing all torn up. I thought he might be mad. Of course, I refused to see him. I couldn't risk it. This year alone my guards have uncovered three assassination attempts—those southern lords are getting more brazen by the day. So I waited until Lord Raiden—until your father returned from his visit to the South. That was about two weeks ago."

Kaede finally let herself look at her father, whose face was carefully blank as he regarded the King. He was wearing the plain black cap and robes of his station, but they were made of the finest silk, embroidered all over with phoenixes in black thread. The last time she had been home in Cathair, her father had been preparing for the trip to the southern provinces that the King had mentioned. The past two years had delivered extremely harsh winters followed by particularly poor harvests, especially in the South. This year, the strange, lingering winter, combined with the unexpected spoilage of much of the Kingdom's food stores, had led to growing panic among the people. The Academy was largely insulated from such things, but Kaede knew that some in the Kingdom were already going hungry, and hunger led to unrest—especially when the wealthy continued to eat well.

The King continued: "Your father met with this visitor as soon as he returned. He—I could hardly believe this when I first heard it—the man claimed that he had been given something by the Fairy Queen, and she had ordered him to deliver it to me. We have heard nothing from her people, the Xi—at least nothing *official*—in generations." He leaned forward, stabbing a heavily ringed finger against the table to emphasize his point. His blue silk sleeves ballooned. "I thought it was a hoax at first."

Kaede asked, "What do you mean, nothing official?"

Irritated by the interruption, the King answered brusquely, "There have been some sightings—nothing definite, mind you—but it seems that some of the Xi have been coming across the borders into our lands."

"It may not be the Xi who are crossing over," Maire Morighan said.

"Then who—or what—are they?" the King snapped. "They're unnatural, these creatures, whatever they are, and they don't belong here."

Lord Raiden said mildly, "Your Majesty, perhaps we can discuss the identity of these creatures later. Let's continue."

The King relented. "The man brought a box with him; he said it had come from the Fairy Queen herself. Inside the box there was a medallion and a scroll. The scroll was written in the language of the Xi, which we could not read. Lord Raiden informed me that the scroll appeared to be genuine, and in that case, we had no choice but to bring it here. This morning, the Council deciphered it. It appears to be an invitation to me to attend the Fairy Queen at her palace in Taninli at midsummer."

"This is the box," Maire Morighan said, gesturing to the small rosewood container before her. She placed her finger in the center of it, and the top opened like the petals of a flower. From within, she removed a tiny scroll and a medallion on a long silver chain. "We have read the scroll, and it is indeed an invitation. It seems that the Fairy Queen, at least, still abides by the laws of our treaty."

Kaede was puzzled. "What treaty?"

"Many generations ago, our kingdom negotiated a treaty with the Fairy Queen that established the border between her lands and ours," said the Mistress. "It was also agreed that we would each keep to our side of the border, and that no one—human, Xi, or other races of fay—would cross it without an invitation from the other land's sovereign. It has been so long since the Borderlands Treaty was signed, and no invitations were ever issued, I believe, until now. So this is quite unexpected."

Everything Kaede had been taught led her to believe that the Xi had no interest in humans anymore. Some traces of them remained—especially here at the Academy, where each Mistress took on a name in the Xi language—but Kaede had always had the impression that the Kingdom was better off without the Xi. "Why do you think they're contacting the King now?" she asked.

The Mistress's eyes flickered to the gray sky outside the windows. "We believe that the unchanging seasons—and even those creatures who have been crossing into our lands— we believe that these are all connected. You have learned, in your lessons here, that we are all part of one vast motion of energies. Something is disrupting the natural flow of things. The meridians that run across our world have been…bent… somehow. We suspect that the Fairy Queen may be aware of this, too. It is very important that we accept her invitation." Maire Morighan's lips narrowed briefly, as if in disapproval. "However, the King is not able to go on the journey, for it will take many months and may be quite dangerous. He will send his son, Prince Con Isae Tan, in his stead."

"I remind you that my hands are full dealing with the chaos in the southern provinces," the King said defensively. "They're nearly ready to launch a civil war. I cannot leave my kingdom for months just to gallivant off on an invitation to the Fairy Queen's court—an invitation that says nothing about why she's inviting us after all this time, I might add."

"With all due respect, Your Majesty," Maire Morighan said, "it is the Council's strong belief that the Fairy Queen may know why the seasons haven't changed, and *I* remind *you* that all the storms and droughts and food spoilages have been the primary cause of all that unrest. We need to reestablish relations with the Xi; it is a matter of supreme importance."

"His Majesty and I agree that we must answer the Fairy Queen's invitation," Lord Raiden put in, trying to smooth both King Cai's and Maire Morighan's ruffled feathers. "But he cannot travel now. Not only are we on the verge of war, the Queen is pregnant."

"I dare not leave her," the King said stiffly. "She has had a difficult pregnancy." Kaede remembered that the King's first wife had died more than a decade ago, but he had not remarried until last year, when he chose a much younger bride. It had been something of a scandal, for the new Queen was the same age as Prince Con, the King's son from his first marriage.

"We understand," Maire Morighan said, as though they had argued over this many times already. She looked at Kaede. "We have also consulted the oracle stones about the invitation, and they called for Taisin, your classmate, to accompany the prince."

Kaede shifted in her seat, confused. "But what does this have to do with me?"

The Mistress leaned forward slightly, her dark eyes focused on Kaede. "You have been called, as well."

Kaede stared at her for a moment, dumbfounded. "Me?" It made no sense to her.

And then Taisin, who had been silent until now, said: "I had a vision. I had a vision, and you were in it."

Chapter III

ord Raiden watched his daughter's face as Taisin spoke. Kaede was startled, curious, but guarded. She lifted a hand to tuck a strand of hair behind her ear. He had noticed the minute she entered the Council chambers that she had cut off her hair at chin-level since the last time he had seen her. She should be wearing it in a cylindrical roll at the nape of her neck in the manner of a proper sage-in-training—like Taisin. It was a small rebellion, but an unmistakable one, and Lord Raiden felt a familiar frustration rising in him. He had thought the Academy would discipline his daughter, force her to act in accordance with her station. But instead, it seemed to have only encouraged her to run wild. He could see traces of dirt on her hands, and he frowned.

"Taisin is a true seer," Sister Ailan was saying, "and we consulted the oracle stones. They confirmed what she saw. Kaede must also go on this journey."

"But the stones are not always clear," Lord Raiden objected.

"There are hundreds of stones with thousands of marks on them. Perhaps they've been read incorrectly. And Taisin is so young—"

Sister Ailan said crisply, "I have not read them incorrectly, Lord Raiden. And Taisin may be young, but she is our most gifted student in a generation."

Lord Raiden looked pointedly away from Sister Ailan to Maire Morighan. "Mistress, I must question the wisdom of sending my daughter on such a mission. You yourself admitted it might be dangerous. I know the state of our kingdom right now, and I can assure you it is not a place of peace. I refuse to risk my daughter's life."

"Raiden," the King said, "you know we would send as many guards with them as necessary."

"Of course, Your Majesty, but you know as well as I do that Kaede is not gifted in the way that Taisin apparently is. Nor is she trained to defend herself as your son is. And Kaede is only a child; she is not yet eighteen." Lord Raiden glanced back at Maire Morighan. "You should be sending an experienced sage, not a couple of students. You heard my daughter—she isn't even familiar with the Borderlands Treaty."

Kaede's cheeks burned at the dismissive tone in her father's voice. Resentment seethed inside her, acidic and sour. She wanted to lash out at him, but Maire Morighan gave her a warning look, and Kaede reluctantly bit her tongue.

"Lord Chancellor," the Mistress said, "I understand your concern for your daughter's safety, but the matter is no longer in our hands. Taisin's vision was exceptionally clear, and when we consulted the oracle stones about Kaede, they were decisive. Kaede is meant to accompany Taisin, and no other sage may go. That is the word of the stones. Even if we don't always understand why the oracle stones say what they do, there is a reason. They have never steered us wrong. We must trust in them."

"Wait," Kaede interrupted, frustrated. She turned to Taisin, whose brown eyes were shadowed as though she had not slept well. "What was in this vision?" Kaede asked. "What was I doing there?"

Taisin glanced at Sister Ailan as if to ask permission, and when her teacher gave an almost imperceptible nod, she said haltingly, "I—I saw you on a beach—a beach made of ice." The memory of it washed through her; she felt the same loss and fear she had felt that night in the practice room, and beneath it all, she remembered the deep ache of love. It was disorienting, for in her life at the Academy, she had rarely noticed Kaede before, and now, sitting there across the table, Kaede was simply another girl in a black Academy robe, the plain stone buttons marching across her left shoulder as they did across her own. Taisin was sure she had no feelings for her—not here in the Council chambers. The emotions in the vision seemed to belong to someone else, and Taisin couldn't reconcile them with the present.

"What were we doing on this beach?" Kaede asked.

Taisin took a deep breath. "The vision was very clear, but it was also quite limited. I only saw the beach, and the ocean…and you. You were important." Taisin colored, and she lowered her eyes to her lap. "I had the vision the night

17

after the Council told me the oracle stones called for me to go to the Fairy Queen. I knew that the vision was about this journey, and I knew it was telling me that you must be a part of it."

"Kaede," Lord Raiden said, addressing his daughter for the first time that day. "You know that you have duties that you cannot shirk." Kaede's stomach dropped; she should have known he would bring that up. "This is not the best time for you to be absent."

"When would be the best time, Father?" Sarcasm twisted her words. "Should we ask the Fairy Queen to wait until you're finished with me?"

The Chancellor's face darkened with suppressed rage. "You disrespect your King, and I will not tolerate that," he snapped.

"I think you are the one who is disrespecting *me*," Kaede countered, hot with anger.

The King frowned, but before he could speak, Lord Raiden pushed his chair back from the table, the legs scraping loudly against the stone floor. He stood, towering over the table. "You are behaving like a spoiled child, Kaede, which only goes to show that you are not prepared to take on the responsibility that this journey would entail."

"If I'm so irresponsible, why do you want to marry me off to some lord from the South?" Kaede demanded. "Why would you trust me with a political alliance if you think I'm such a child?" The words seemed to echo in the room, and she heard her own heartbeat thudding in her chest. When her father had first presented her with his plan last winter, they had argued over it for hours. He wanted her to

18

marry a complete stranger just to keep the man's province under the control of the King's Guard. The idea of it sickened her.

"We are trying to prevent a *war*, Kaede," Lord Raiden said coldly. "Surely you are not so selfish that you would send your kingdom to war just because you don't wish to settle in the South?"

"It's not about where I wish to *settle*, and you know it. And who's the selfish one? You only want me to marry him because it would be good for *you*."

Maire Morighan rose abruptly, cutting into their argument. "Enough," she said. "Lord Raiden, please sit down."

"Mistress—"

"*Sit down*," the Mistress ordered. The Chancellor's face was nearly purple with frustration, but he sat, the chair legs scratching across the floor again. "Lord Raiden, with all due respect, this is not your decision to make."

For one brief, glorious moment, Kaede felt vindicated, but then her father said, "She is my daughter. She is not of age. She does not go where I do not permit."

Kaede fumed, but before she could rebut him, the Mistress said coolly, "Undoubtedly that is true. But this journey is every bit as important—perhaps even more important—than your plans for her. You must give her up to us. She has another duty that comes first now."

"Don't I have any say in this?" Kaede asked. She looked at Maire Morighan, who seemed exasperated with both her and her father. "Mistress, you can see that I have no desire to do what my father wants me to do. But you aren't giving me a choice, either." Maire Morighan frowned, but before she could speak, Kaede rushed on. "I have been a student here for almost six years. Not the best student, but I have paid attention. And the one thing that has always made sense to me is the teaching that every individual has the right to make choices about their lives. Every minute of every day, we make choices. Why would you take that away from me now?"

Kaede knew she was taking a risk by speaking so forcefully to the Mistress of the Academy. But the anger she felt at her father boiled within her, driving away any fear of offending Maire Morighan.

The Mistress was not surprised by Kaede's willfulness. That had always been the one quality that hampered Kaede's ability to work through the rituals. But she was taken aback by Kaede's appeal to the Academy's teachings. From across the table, Sister Yuna said softly, "She is right. She deserves to choose her own path."

Maire Morighan looked at Kaede, whose face was filled with desperate determination. At last the Mistress said, "All right. You have until the evening meal to make your decision."

Chapter IV

aede's entire body was tense as she hurried down the stairs away from the Council chambers. The unexpected encounter with her father had rattled her, and she needed to shake it off. Her teachers would have advised her to go to the practice hall, to sit quietly, but she wanted to go outside and breathe the fresh air.

She took the empty corridor behind the kitchens, avoiding the students at their work shifts. The kitchen cat, curled in his basket by the back door, stretched lazily as she unlatched the door and slipped outside. The rain had lightened to a drizzle, but the cobblestones of the path down to the beach were slick, and she walked carefully. The sea, visible ahead of her in a gray swathe only a few shades darker than the sky, moved in giant, undulating swells. She could hear the crash of the surf below.

When she reached the edge of the kitchen garden, she went down a narrow stone staircase toward the sand. A stream of smoke curled up from the groundskeeper's workshop huddled against the retaining wall ahead. Fin was in. Kaede hesitated only a moment before heading for the workshop. She knocked on the wooden door, and hearing a gruff answer from within, she pushed it open, the hinges creaking slightly.

Inside, the workshop was a warren of crates and sandbags, wood scraps and tools. A lamp was lit in the back, where Fin called out, "Who is it?"

"It's me," Kaede replied. She threaded her way through the shop toward the sound of Fin's voice.

Fin was seated on a stool at her workbench, mending a gardening tool. Her short gray hair curled over her ears and forehead, which was marked with black oil as if she had pushed her hair aside with dirtied fingers. She had once been tanned dark from the sun, but without a clear day in months, her skin had paled. She was still as vigorous as ever, though, despite the fact that she had celebrated her half-century mark the previous winter. She glanced at Kaede with quizzical brown eyes. "What are you doing down here? Your work shift with me isn't until tomorrow. Maesie has you today, doesn't she?"

Every student at the Academy spent several hours each day working in the kitchens or the library, cleaning the practice hall or sweeping the corridors. During Kaede's first year, she had been assigned a task suitable for a Chancellor's daughter: sitting in the library and marking down the names of every student who came and went. The duty had left her so restless that she had soon been reassigned to Fin, the Academy's groundskeeper, who set her to work sweeping the Seawalk or filling sandbags. On slow afternoons, Fin would take her out to the North Beach and set up a target, teaching her how to toss the knives she kept in a tooled leather case, evidence of her former life with the King's Guard.

Fin saw the nervous energy in Kaede's stance, and she asked, "What happened?"

Kaede took a deep, shaking breath. "My father is here. And the King. When did they arrive? Where is their ship?" She hadn't seen or heard any ship in the harbor that morning, and she knew it would have caused an uproar, for the only ships to come and go were scheduled months in advance.

Fin put down the tool, wiping her oily fingers on a rag. "They came in the middle of last night. The ship sailed back to Seatown as soon as the King disembarked. They wished to keep it secret." But there could be no secrets from Fin; she had been roused by Sister Nara herself, bearing a candle and urging her to come down to the dock. She looked at Kaede's agitated expression and said, "We should take a walk out to the North Beach."

Startled, Kaede said, "Now?"

"Now is as good a time as any. I could use a break." Fin levered herself up from the stool, reaching for a long leather case on the shelf bolted to the wall above her head. She slung the case over her shoulder. Her joints were a bit stiff from sitting still in the damp air, yet she moved with the measured gait of the former soldier she was.

Kaede followed Fin out into the misty afternoon. "Did you know they were coming?" she asked as they walked across the wet sand.

Fin shook her head. "I didn't. They sent word by carrier to the Council, but only an hour or so before they arrived. You've spoken to them?"

"Yes. The Mistress summoned me to the Council chambers."

"Ah. What did they want?"

Kaede explained what had happened, and recounting the argument with her father caused her anger to flare again. "I can't do what my father asks—I just can't," she said vehemently.

"Are you—" Fin hesitated, glancing sideways at Kaede, who had a fierce scowl on her face. "Are you in love with someone else? Is that why you refuse to marry this man?"

Kaede almost laughed. "No. I'm not in love with...anyone." She wasn't sure if she ever had been in love, although she remembered the rush of emotions that accompanied her first kiss, with her classmate Liya, up in the crescent garden. It had been almost two years ago, on a sunny early summer afternoon. They had been clumsy and shy at first, but the giddiness that flooded through her after the kiss had plowed through all those nerves. She had felt exhilarated—free. But had she been in love? She didn't think so. There was no heartache on either side when their little romance ended a few months later.

Kaede and Fin rounded an outcropping of rock that jutted from beneath the Academy's iron foundation and stepped onto the North Beach, a crescent of unmarked, light brown sand cradling the sea. About a hundred feet out, waves crashed against submerged rocks that created a breakwater. When it had been warm, Kaede had often come here with classmates to swim in the sheltered cove. Fin set the case down on the sand and unlatched it, asking, "Who does your father want you to marry?"

Kaede paced back and forth, her footprints sending long trails across the sand. "One of the lords in the South. Someone named Lord Win."

"Is it a political alliance?"

"Yes."

"Your older brother made a political marriage, didn't he?" Fin unfolded the wings of the leather case; within it were about a dozen knives. The smallest—an ornately jeweled dagger—could fit into an ankle holster; the largest was more accurately a small sword.

"Kaihan? Yes. He married the King's niece."

"And how is that marriage working out?" Fin straightened, carrying a square target toward the stony cliff wall that sheltered the cove. Years ago, she had affixed hooks into the wall and punctured holes in the target to hang it.

"I don't know. I haven't heard anything out of the ordinary." Kaede stopped pacing and squatted down by the knife case. She was about to select her favorite throwing knife—a bright steel dagger with a black leather grip—but Fin bent down and pointed to a different one.

"Why don't you try this one today?" Fin suggested.

Kaede was surprised. "Why?"

Fin shrugged and moved off. "It's time for a change, I think."

So Kaede picked up the dagger that Fin had pointed out. The blade was just shorter than the length of her forearm, and though it was made of a darker metal than the other knives, it was simple, straightforward, and ground very sharp. Her fingers slid over the nubbly surface of the grip, and it fit comfortably enough in her hand.

She rose, counted out twenty paces from the target, and shifted the hilt in her hand so that the blade was pointing backward toward the sea. Then she flung it, extending her arm in the direction of the target. This dagger flew differently than the ones she was accustomed to. It was heavier, and she hadn't adjusted her technique to the weight yet, so it struck the very edge of the target and tumbled to the sand.

Fin went to pick it up and asked, "Do you think Kaihan objected to his marriage?"

"I don't think so. His wife—we've known her since we were children. But even if he did object, it wouldn't have made a difference. My father doesn't take no for an answer."

Fin handed the dagger back to her. "Again. The flight of the blade was unsteady last time. Be centered in your body when you throw it."

Kaede curled her fingers around the grip again, and this time, she felt the core of her belly engaged in the movement of her arm. When the knife left her hand, she felt her fingers reaching after it, and the dagger struck the center of the target.

"Good. It's not so different from the other knives, you see."

Kaede sighed. "I can't marry this Lord Win."

"Why not?" Fin's expression was blandly curious.

Kaede pulled a face. "Fin, I could never marry any man, you know that."

Fin gave her the dagger again. "Kaede, you should realize that the chances of your making a political marriage with another woman are—well, it is unlikely. It has happened before, but you know that it's rare."

Kaede reddened. "I don't want to make any political marriages with anyone."

"That is your birthright, and it is your burden." Fin stepped out of the way. "Try it again."

The dagger clanged against the cliff, several inches off the target.

Fin asked, "Did you talk to your mother about it?"

Kaede grimaced. "Yes. She said that I should be open to the possibility that I could love a man. That I was being too narrow-minded." She pushed her hair behind her ears as the wind came up, blowing a salty, wet breath across her face. "And beyond that, she said that plenty of married women have lovers—and sometimes their husbands die young, especially in a time of war. Can you believe that?"

"Well, your mother is a politician's wife," Fin said, smiling slightly.

"Yes. But I don't want to be a politician's wife."

"What do you want to do, then?"

Kaede held the knife in her hand again, feeling the weight of it. It was made of iron, she realized. Solid iron. "I don't know," she said slowly. "I don't want to be a politician, either. Marrying this man is just a way for me to establish myself at court. It cements an alliance, and I would be expected to do my best to make sure it stays strong. I'd have to be pregnant within a year. I don't want that. I want to do something else with my life. I'm not like Kaihan, who just wants to have a family and stay in Cathair. I want to see the world."

"You could see it. If you go with Taisin to answer the invitation of the Fairy Queen."

Kaede had never even considered the possibility of seeing Taninli, the Fairy Queen's city. It was only a legend to her. A thrill ran through her as she thought about it: What would it be like to set foot on those streets? They were supposedly built of diamonds. But a nagging worry tugged at her. "Fin, I don't understand something. Yes, the idea of going on this journey—it's exciting. At the very least, if I go I can put off the marriage my father wants to arrange. But the vision that Taisin had ..." She trailed off, struggling to put her finger on what was bothering her. "I think she's hiding something," Kaede said at last. "I have no talents as a sage, but Taisin said that I'm important. Why? It doesn't make sense to me. But visions—I don't think they can be avoided. I'm not even sure if I truly have a choice."

Fin studied her student, with her serious expression and windblown hair. She noticed Kaede's fingers cradling the hilt of the iron dagger as if it had always been hers. After a long moment, Fin said, "The teachers here know much more about visions and fate than I do. But what I know is that in every moment of your life, you have a choice. Every choice leads to another, and another after that. You can only make a decision based on what you know now."

Kaede laughed. "That's almost exactly what I said to Maire Morighan. But what if what I know now is not enough?"

"Making a decision isn't about knowing every potential consequence. It's about knowing what you want and choosing a path that takes you in that direction."

Kaede shifted the knife from her right hand to her left,

and back again. "I guess I know what I want, then." She lifted the knife; it was heavy, dependable. She felt every muscle in her arm engage as she threw it. The dagger struck the very edge of the target and clung there, quivering slightly. She sighed, opening and closing her fingers. "At least, I know what I don't want. And I'll delay that marriage as long as I can."

Fin put her hand on Kaede's shoulder and squeezed it gently. Then she went back to the target and retrieved the knife, bringing it to Kaede. "This is for you," Fin said. "It's forged from one piece of iron. I have had it since I left my mother's home; it used to be my father's dagger. It will now be yours."

"I can't take your father's dagger," Kaede objected, trying to give it back to Fin.

"Yes, you can. This dagger is as powerful a thing as I have ever had." Reluctantly, Kaede took it. "If you go on this journey, you're likely to encounter the Xi. They don't like iron. Most blades these days are made of steel, but this one is all iron. And it has survived for many generations. You should keep it on you."

"I thought the idea that the Xi don't like iron was only an old wives' tale. Is it true?"

"This Academy would not be built on iron if it were only a tall tale. Do you realize how much effort—how much magic it took to raise this place?"

Kaede looked at the Academy's iron foundation, sunken into the top of the rocky cliff. Above the dark gray iron, stone walls formed the North Tower.

"No Xi will ever set foot on this island," Fin said. "That's proof enough for me."

"Have you ever seen the Xi?"

Fin nodded. "When I was with the King's Guard in the Northerness. I was young. The Xi came out of the Great Wood one afternoon while we were securing one of the villages up in the hills, and they watched us." Fin voice was urgent. "You keep an eye out, Kaede. They're not like you and me. Bear that in mind."

Her words reminded Kaede of something else the King had said. "Have you heard the news of creatures coming out of the Wood in recent months? The King spoke of them, but Maire Morighan did not explain. Is it the Xi?"

Fin furrowed her brow. "I don't know. Your teachers have told you nothing about it?"

Kaede shook her head.

"What I know is only hearsay," Fin said. "Some strange bodies have been found in the villages bordering the Wood. Some folk have said they're the bodies of monsters. All I know is that the Xi don't look like monsters, and that's why they're so dangerous. If you're going into the Wood, it won't be an easy journey. You must keep that dagger with you at all times."

The intensity in Fin's tone was sobering, and Kaede said, "I will."

She stepped back, lifting her arm, and threw the knife again and again, until all she could hear was the iron ringing as it flew through the air, the sharp strike as it hit the wall, and behind her, the rising-and-falling groan of the sea.

Chapter V

aisin saw Kaede arrive late at the dining hall for the evening meal, and she knew it meant that Kaede had just come from Maire Morighan's chambers. They did not speak, for all meals were taken in silence, but they looked at each other from their opposite corners of the sixth-form students' table. There was a new sense of intention in Kaede's demeanor, and Taisin was certain that Kaede would be coming on the journey. It made her nervous all over, anxiety and anticipation prickling across her skin.

After the meal, a servant was waiting for her in the corridor with a message: Sister Ailan wished to see her in her study. Taisin went immediately, hoping to avoid Kaede for as long as possible. She didn't know what to say to her; she didn't know what she *could* say to her.

She had barely knocked on Sister Ailan's door before it opened. Her teacher ushered her into a beautifully appointed room lit with two globe-shaped oil lamps, one on the desk, one resting on a dark wooden stand carved with lotus flowers. One wall of the rectangular room was lined with windows, but umber-colored curtains were pulled across them to block out the night. Beside the windows, two simple, elegant armchairs faced each other across a low round table on which a tea tray rested. A black earthenware pot of tea steamed there, and Sister Ailan gestured to Taisin to take a seat while she poured the tea.

"Tomorrow morning, you will depart," Sister Ailan said.

Taisin lifted the warm teacup in her hands, inhaling the scent of jasmine flowers. It had been many months since she had smelled such fragrance; the jasmine, these days, was reserved for special occasions.

"I have one item to give to you before you go," her teacher said, and she went to retrieve something from top drawer of her desk. She placed it on the table before Taisin: the wooden box that had come from the Fairy Queen. "Go ahead and open it."

Taisin set down her teacup and leaned forward to look at the box. The carving was exquisite; the lid looked exactly like a chrysanthemum. She had never touched anything made by the Xi before. Until the King's arrival she had never thought the Xi would come into her life at all, except through the pages of history books. The idea of going to their land was strange and wonderful—and frightening, if her vision was true.

As Maire Morighan had done, Taisin placed her fingertip in the center of the carved chrysanthemum and felt the wood give slightly, like a bed of moss. She lifted her hand away and the petals folded back smoothly. Within the box she saw the scroll and a black velvet pouch.

32

"That is the medallion," said Sister Ailan. "Take it out."

Taisin emptied the pouch into her hand, and the medallion tumbled into her palm. The links of the chain gleamed in the lamplight. There were faint colors in it: slight streaks of azure and emerald coiling through the silver. The same colors were repeated, though faintly, like a watercolor, in the silver metal that held the stone, and symbols were engraved around the rim. When she touched the symbols, the stone seemed to shimmer as if there were something living within its depths. "What do these symbols mean?" she asked in a hushed voice.

"We are not sure. It is not the language of the Xi—or if it is, it is something more ancient than we can read. But you shall take it with you."

Taisin was surprised. "Me?"

"Yes. It will be entrusted to you. It may be a talisman of some sort—to mark you as a proper guest of the Xi."

Taisin slid the chain around her neck, and when it touched her skin it was cold for only an instant, and then it felt as though she had always worn it. She cupped her hand around it in astonishment, and looked at her teacher. "It feels like it's mine."

Sister Ailan's brow wrinkled just slightly. "You must keep it safe, Taisin."

"I will."

Sister Ailan sat back in her chair, lifting her own teacup. As her right arm rose, the dark green silk of her robe's wide sleeve fell back, exposing the sage's mark on her forearm. Every sage who took the vows was given a mark just above her wrist: a stylized symbol slightly larger than a gold coin.

Though it was tattooed in black ink, Taisin had always seen colors in it, as she did now in the lamplight—shadow colors, as indistinct and shifting as dusk over the sea.

She had looked forward to receiving the sage's mark on her own skin since she was a child, but remembering her vision, her face burned. "Teacher," she began in a hesitant voice, "I must ask you something." When she had first told Sister Ailan about her vision, she omitted the feelings that had been so upsetting, fearing they were a sign of weakness or inexperience. But they had come back to her again and again, and now she could not ignore them.

Sister Ailan regarded her gravely. "Yes?"

"In my vision, I felt something." Taisin clutched the tea-cup with both hands, as if that might hide her self-consciousness, but she was afraid it was written plainly on her face.

"What did you feel?"

"I felt—I think that I"—she looked away, biting her lip, and finally she blurted it out quickly—"I think that I was in love with Kaede. In my vision. But that is—that can't happen, can it? I want to be a sage, and I know that all sages take vows of—of celibacy. Does this mean that I—that I will never become a sage?"

Sister Ailan heard the anxiety in Taisin's voice. She answered carefully: "Your vision is not the same as a fortune foretold by a traveling mystic. It is not a prediction of the future, Taisin."

"No, but visions—the one I had—isn't it a glimpse of the truth? A truth that exists already within the energies of the world? Everything I do—everything that Kaede does—will bring those energies into the form they took in my vision. Isn't that what you taught me?"

"You are thinking about this too analytically. Your vision is the truth, but it is not the future. It may be that you don't yet understand what you saw."

Taisin put down the teacup, curling her fingers into fists. "Teacher, I want to be a sage more than anything I've ever wanted in this world. I don't want to jeopardize that by falling in love with anyone."

Sister Ailan considered Taisin's flushed face, her renitent posture. She asked, "How did it make you feel, this . . . love?"

Taisin was taken aback by the question. "I—I have been trying to forget it."

"Why?"

"Because it can't happen," she said miserably. "It can't. If Kaede comes on this journey—if my vision comes true—then—" She broke off, remembering the dreadful fear roiling in the pit of her stomach when she saw Kaede leaving the beach behind. At last she said, "I don't want her to die."

Sister Ailan leaned forward and took Taisin's hands in her own, curving her warm, dry fingers over Taisin's fists. She looked into her student's dark brown eyes. "Love is not what you fear, is it? You fear the loss of it."

Taisin's eyes filled with tears; she was mortally embarrassed. She should not cry in front of her teacher. She wanted to pull her hands away, but Sister Ailan held them fast.

"It is true," her teacher said in a low voice, "that sages

35

take a vow of celibacy. If you wish to be a sage, you will have to walk that path alone. It is a wondrous path, Taisin, and I know that you wish to follow it. That is a choice you will make later, when you are ready. You are not a full sage yet. Now you have a different path to take. Don't let your fear of the future overshadow your decisions in the present. You must remember that."

She let go of Taisin's hands, and Taisin folded her arms across her stomach, looking uncertain. "What should I tell Kaede, then?" she asked in a small voice. "How can I tell her what I felt?"

"Why do you need to tell her?"

Taisin shrugged. "I don't know. I thought—she is the only other person in my vision. Shouldn't she know?"

Sister Ailan leaned back in her chair, running her hands along the armrests. "Taisin, sometimes it is better for others to not know what we have seen in our visions. You see how much it has distracted you. Think of how much it will distract Kaede."

"Then you think I should not tell her?"

"You must determine that on your own. Just know that whatever is meant to happen will happen, whether she knows what you saw or not. It might be better for her to make her decisions without the additional...suggestions that your vision would give her."

Taisin nodded. "I understand."

"Good." Sister Ailan gave her a rare smile. "Then shall we continue? I have a few other things to tell you."

"All right." Taisin listened as Sister Ailan gave her instructions on what she would need to do when she reached

Cathair, but beneath it all she felt an upwelling of emotions that threatened to engulf her. How could she keep her feelings secret? Was there any way to prevent what she had seen from happening?

She resolved, at least, to try.

 # PART II

A tree grows on the mountain.
The wild goose flies near:
It seeks the flat branch.

—Book of Changes

Chapter VI

he next morning, the King's ship came to ferry Kaede, Taisin, the King, and his Chancellor to Seatown. Kaede remained out on the deck for the three-hour crossing, preferring the salty sting of the wind in her face to the cramped warmth down below. The spray soaked through her cloak, but she didn't mind. She wanted to remember this day: when she left behind the life her parents had built for her. She watched the Academy diminishing as they sailed away until it was only a small gray speck, indistinguishable from the vast dark sea.

In Seatown, a contingent of the King's Guard was waiting to escort them through the crowded, noisy wharves. It stank of fish and seawater, but all Kaede saw were the black uniforms of the guards around her, their thick leather boots splashing through slimy puddles. They soon arrived at two black carriages, their doors emblazoned with the mark of the King, and Kaede and Taisin were quickly ushered into the second one. The carriage lurched as it turned away from the wharves and began the ascent up the steep road into Seatown proper.

Kaede watched out the window as they drove past an open-air kitchen with an old woman ladling out steaming broth to a line of young men—sailors, with their hair tightly plaited in single braids. They passed long brick walls dividing the compounds of Seatown's wealthy traders from the common folk who did the work of the city. And soon enough, they left Seatown behind and struck out onto the King's Highway.

ॐ

The journey to Cathair would take a little over a week, and every mile of it was carefully scripted. Every place they stayed was first secured by the King's Guard, and every meal they ate was first tasted by the King's chief taster to ensure that the food was not poisoned. Kaede and Taisin rode in the fifth black coach in a line of eight. Lord Raiden and the King rode separately in the third and fourth carriages; two were reserved for the King's servants and were loaded with his wardrobe trunks; and they were all preceded and followed by guards.

Neither Kaede nor Taisin had traveled with the King before, and at first all of it was strange and overwhelming: the guards who rode with their hands on their swords; the rituals of greeting each evening when their hosts prostrated themselves before the King, holding their empty hands out to him for his blessing. And they ate better than they had in years, for no landlord would serve the King anything less than his finest offerings, even if that meant butchering a tenant farmer's last suckling pig. The King, who wore a different silk robe to each meal, ate it all with gusto, but Kaede, who had grown accustomed to the simpler food at the Academy, found all the rich sauces and succulent meats to be excessive. The King's appetite turned her stomach.

During the day, she and Taisin sat mostly in silence within the cushioned confines of their carriage, each staring out her window at the countryside. They passed a farmhouse burned to the ground, its roof about to collapse. They drove through a village that was empty but for a few hollow-eyed beggars lurking in the abandoned market street. And they passed many people in torn cloaks walking down the side of the road toward Cathair. Sometimes the travelers ran after the coaches for a short distance, but the caravan stopped for no one.

"Where are they going?" Kaede wondered aloud.

"To search for food," Taisin answered, startling Kaede. Taisin rarely spoke, and Kaede had not yet determined whether it was because she was disinterested in conversation or merely shy.

"How do you know?" Kaede watched Taisin struggle to contain some kind of emotion, fidgeting with the edges of her cloak.

"It has been a difficult year. Two difficult years. My family's farm—we have done better than some. My family has received travelers for some time now, seeking food. We send them on to Cathair, for we have heard that there are provisions there for the needy."

"Your family has a farm?"

Pink crept up the curve of Taisin's cheeks. "Yes."

Kaede realized that Taisin was self-conscious about it,

and that made Kaede feel tactless, clumsy. She changed the subject awkwardly. "Do you have any brothers or sisters? I have three brothers. They're all older than me."

Taisin seemed surprised by the question. "I have a younger sister, Suri. She is twelve."

"Is she as gifted as you are?"

Taisin turned red, the color streaking across her throat and face, and she stammered, "M-my sister is gifted in her own way."

Kaede was taken aback by Taisin's reaction. She wanted to tell her she hadn't meant to embarrass her, but her classmate had turned away to stare out the window, her eyes fixed on the changing landscape. Kaede didn't understand why Taisin seemed so uncomfortable around her. Had she done something wrong? She tried to find something to distract herself in the carriage, but there was nothing new to see in that small, dark space. She suppressed a sigh. It might be a very long journey indeed.

❧

On the fourth day, it rained. It was a heavy, unwelcome downpour that turned the dirt road into a muddy mess. At a crossroads that had seen better days, the caravan had to stop entirely while the drivers climbed down and dug the first carriage out of a rut that had trapped the wheels in several inches of sludge. Taisin had almost nodded off to sleep in her seat, the sound of the rain soothing away the bumpy discomfort of the King's Highway. When Kaede cried out in alarm, Taisin jerked awake, her head knocking against the window.

There against the glass was a man's angry face, his mouth

open as he shouted at them, raising his fist to bang against the door.

Taisin screamed; she scrambled back as the force of his blows caused the coach to sway. Her shoulder slammed against Kaede, who was also pushing herself away from the door. In their haste they tumbled onto the floor, their bodies pressed together in the narrow space between the seats.

The man outside raised his hand again, and this time there was a rock in it, and it smashed against the glass so hard that it cracked. But before he could strike again, a guard grabbed him, pulling him away with a force that yanked his shoulder back at an unnatural angle. Another guard joined the first, who pinned the struggling man's head in the crook of his leather-armored elbow, and the second guard struck him full in the face, blood flying out as the man's nose was crushed. A third guard appeared, and the man, who was thin and weak from hunger, had no chance at all. One of the guards drew his sword, and before the man could take another breath, the guard slit his throat. He doubled over, his life spilling down his chest, mingling with the rain that still fell, unceasingly, from the sky.

It was a crime punishable by death to attack the King, and the royal mark was painted on every one of the coaches in that caravan.

Inside the battered carriage, huddled on the floor, Taisin felt her heart pound from shock. Kaede was crowded so close to her that Taisin could feel the other girl's muscles as tense as a drawn bowstring. Suddenly the door was wrenched open, and Kaede's father was standing outside, the rain running down his face. He hadn't bothered to put on a cloak. "Are you all right?" His voice was rough with panic. Behind him three guards stood with their swords drawn, and beyond them the body of the attacker was slumped on the muddy road.

"We're fine," Kaede said, her voice shaking.

"Blasted idiots!" Lord Raiden shouted, and spun toward the guards. "You paid no attention!" he snarled. "This cannot happen again. Next time it will be one of you who is dead." He slammed the door of the carriage shut, and the cracked glass shattered completely, letting in the rain. Lord Raiden threw up his hands and ordered, "Fix this!"

Kaede began to get up, and Taisin realized that she was gripping Kaede's hand with white fingers. Heat rushed through her and she dropped Kaede's hand as if it were a live coal. Kaede turned to her, a strange look on her face, and then the guards came to sweep the glass out of the carriage. Taisin pulled herself onto her seat, avoiding Kaede's eyes. A man had just been killed scarcely ten feet away, and yet all she could think of was the jolt that went through her when she felt Kaede's hand in hers. She had reached for her without any awareness of what she was doing. Was it already happening? Was her vision already coming true?

Taisin set her jaw stubbornly to prevent it from trembling. She deliberately gazed out the broken window, where the guards were carrying the body of the dead man toward the side of the road. Others approached with shovels, and they began to dig a grave in the soft ground. None of them had any idea who he was, and they would never find out. After the guards rolled him into the earth, they marked the grave with a circle of stones, and the caravan departed.

Eight days after they left the Academy, the road widened and flat paving stones replaced hard-packed dirt. The coaches picked up their pace, and the King's guards were able to relax just slightly. After the attack, there had been repercussions all around. The guards had been ordered to increase their vigilance, and now no one was allowed to leave the caravan unprotected. Kaede and Taisin were sent off with two female guards if they needed to stop at the side of the road, and though the guards turned their backs, Taisin especially chafed at the indignity of it. Kaede, who was more accustomed to being followed by servants, still had never experienced this level of interference in her daily life. She did her best to pretend as though it was entirely ordinary: traveling with the King, being surrounded by armed guards at every moment, riding in a carriage with a window covered by an oilcloth where it had been broken by a starving bandit. If she paused to think about it too closely, the significance of it all frightened her, and she would rather go blindly forward than dwell on what it all meant.

By the time they saw the stone walls of Cathair in the distance, Kaede had almost convinced herself that this new existence was normal. After all, the crenellated guard towers of the city were as tall and warlike as ever. Nothing had disturbed them, so far. But then they encountered a sight that she had not anticipated: a growing collection of tents pitched on the barren fields on either side of the road. As they drew closer to the city walls, the tents appeared more and more like permanent fixtures, the canvas walls dirtied with grime from fires burning in hastily dug pits. Kaede realized that the people camped closest to Cathair had been there the longest. They stood up as the King's caravan passed, but though some children ran toward the coaches, most remained still, gaunt as specters, knowing that nothing would come their way.

The sight of all these desperate people overwhelmed Kaede. The world had changed so much since she had last been outside the Academy walls six months ago. She hardly recognized this city that she had grown up in. The streets were thick with guards, and all the guards carried weapons. Half the shops seemed closed; the ones that remained open had new bars over their windows. When the carriage rolled to a halt outside her family's compound, Kaede was absurdly relieved to see that her home was the same as ever—red gates and dark red tiled roofs rising behind the wall.

Taisin was continuing on to the palace, where she would stay until they departed a week from now. Kaede looked back at her before she exited the carriage, feeling oddly reluctant to leave her. She said, "You can send word if you need anything."

Taisin was surprised by the offer, but also a tiny bit pleased, and it was the pleasure that made her feel awkward. "Thank you," she said formally.

Then Kaede heard the red gates open, and her mother's voice calling her. Giving Taisin a small smile, she climbed out of the carriage, carefully closing the door with the oil-cloth tacked over the broken window.

Chapter VII

here was a strange man in her father's study. Kaede paused in the doorway, her hand on the latch. He was tall, and he wore an uncommonly fine dark blue silk tunic embroidered with white-capped waves, but his hair was as short as a guard's. He turned at the slight creak of the door that Kaede pushed open, and broke into a smile. A single dimple creased his left cheek.

"Kaede," he exclaimed. "It's good to see you."

"Con?" she said, recognizing him at last. He had been a regular guest in her parents' home when she was a child, for he was close in age to her brothers Taeko and Tanis. She bowed to him. "What did you do to your hair?" The last time she had seen him had been at Kaihan's wedding last year, and Prince Con Isae Tan—like all young men of rank—had worn his long black hair in a topknot.

The prince grinned, running a hand over the prickly ends of his black hair, now barely half an inch long. "I cut it off."

She laughed. "Why?"

He shrugged. "I wanted to look ordinary."

Behind her, Kaede's father said, "Ordinary? What did your father think of that?"

Kaede stepped aside as Lord Raiden entered his study, carrying an account book under one arm. He set it down on his desk and took his seat behind it, flicking back the wide sleeves of his black robe. "Kaede," he said, glancing perfunctorily at his daughter, "the prince and I have business to attend to. You may leave us."

The smile that had lit Kaede's face upon seeing Con disappeared. The prince glanced from father to daughter and said, "Lord Raiden, perhaps Kaede might join us."

"What? I don't think so."

"Lord Raiden, she is part of this business." The prince's voice was gentle but firm.

Lord Raiden met the prince's gaze. There was a brief silence. "Fine," he said gruffly. "Kaede, close the door when you come in." He did not wait for her to sit down before opening the account book and paging through to a section marked with a ribbon. "As I was saying earlier, the King has ordered a contingent of guards to accompany you, as well as several wagonloads of supplies. I've no idea how long this trip will take; all the maps are confoundedly inaccurate."

Kaede realized they were discussing the journey she was about to embark on—and that her father had had no intention of telling her anything about it. She bit back the flaring anger inside her and sat down in the empty chair next to Con. The prince said, "Lord Raiden, I know that my father always travels with a large number of guards, but I think we would be better served by a smaller party."

"It is dangerous out there, Your Highness. The people are restless. Our caravan was attacked on the way back from the Academy."

Con nodded. "I know. But I think we would be more likely to slip by, unnoticed, if we were fewer in number. Consider this: If we travel with one guard each, we can stay at inns along the way instead of requiring shelter from my father's loyalists. It will allow us to gain information, as well. I can send word to you by carrier or messenger if necessary."

Lord Raiden frowned. "One guard each is not much. The King will not support it."

Con leaned forward, putting a flattering smile on his face. "Lord Raiden, my father will support anything that you recommend."

Kaede's eyes flickered from Con to her father. She could see that he wanted to believe what the prince said.

"Your Highness, that is kind of you to say, but I'm afraid it will be too dangerous." Lord Raiden glanced at his daughter, who was watching him with a stony expression. "And besides, my daughter is traveling with you. I want her to be safe."

Kaede choked back a laugh; he had never been so concerned for her safety before she was called to go on this journey. When she was a child, he had rarely seemed to notice her at all. She was convinced that his worry, now, was only a pretense; he was just frustrated that she was not doing what he wanted. When her father saw the disbelief on her face, he glared at her, and she glared back.

Con saw the exchange but made no mention of it. "No one will know who we are if we travel lightly, Lord Raiden. But if we travel with a caravan of guards, we will be a slow-moving target."

"What about the Xi? They aren't to be trusted. It would be better to send more guards with you."

"The more people we send, the more the Xi can turn with their glamours. We should bring only the guards we can trust."

Lord Raiden tapped the tips of his fingers together. "Whom would you propose to take with you? Which guards?"

Con relaxed a bit. He could sense that Lord Raiden was about to give in. "Tali, of course," Con said. Tali had been his personal guard since he was a boy, and he was trusted by both the Chancellor and the King. "He is completely loyal to me."

Lord Raiden nodded. "Tali would be going with you anyway. I agree he is a good choice. Who else?"

Con had already consulted with Tali on this, and he had two names ready. "Pol should go. He is one of Tali's favorites and has been in the King's Guard for ten years now. He is from the Northerness, and he is a skilled hunter. He would be a valuable asset. And I think we should also bring Shae, from the Third Division, though she is fairly new to the Guard." Tali had suggested the woman, who had only been a guard for two years. "She's from the village of Jilin;

grew up near the Great Wood. She'll know it better than any of the other guards."

"So there would be six of you," Lord Raiden said. "You, Taisin, Kaede, and three guards."

"Yes."

"You'll need six horses?"

"I would suggest four riding horses, and two to pull the supply wagon."

"No servants?"

"Tali will do the cooking," Con said with a grin.

Lord Raiden let out a short laugh. "You won't eat well."

"We don't need to eat well. We just need to survive the journey."

Lord Raiden nodded slowly. "All right. I'll speak to the King about your wishes."

"Thank you." Con looked over at Kaede, who had listened to their conversation in silence, and asked, "Does that sound all right with you?"

Kaede blinked. "With me?" She hesitated. Her father was watching her. Hearing the prince and her father discuss the details of the journey had made her feel largely irrelevant. Six years at the Academy behind her, and she was utterly unprepared for this sort of thing. She felt both useless and irritated by the uselessness. But she would never allow her father to see her misgivings, so she said nonchalantly, "Of course. It all sounds fine." But the palms of her hands were clammy, and Con's words rang in her ears: *We just need to survive the journey.* What was he expecting? She began to wonder, seriously, what she had gotten herself into.

The night before their departure, the King hosted a private banquet in their honor, and even Queen Yuriya, her belly swollen in the seventh month of pregnancy, joined them in the dining room. In addition to the King and Queen, Taisin's family was present: her father and mother, with somewhat awed expressions on their faces; and her sister, Suri, with large dark eyes that seemed to look right through a person.

Kaede's family had been invited, as well. Her mother, her hair twisted into the shape of a spiraling shell, sat at the King's right hand. Her father sat next to Prince Con, who suffered the good-natured ribbing of Kaede's three brothers for cutting off his hair. Kaede was between the prince and her middle brother, Tanis, who had recently returned from the South and only wished to discuss politics with the prince. Caught between them, Kaede fell silent, watching Taisin across the table. She was seated next to Kaede's brother Taeko, who was the closest to her in age and had become something of a flirt in the last few years. Taisin had a small smirk on her face as Taeko attempted to impress her, and Kaede liked Taisin the better for it, as few were immune to Taeko's charms.

The broad, circular table was laid with a cloth of pale gold silk printed with twining crimson and green flowers, and there were eight courses. There was cold salad and clear soup, with translucent mushrooms floating within the broth in cloudlike clusters. There was roast duck and sweet, brined pork and tender, spiced lamb. There were tender cabbage leaves sautéed with ginger; there was an entire river fish with its mouth propped open on a carrot; and at the end there were bowls of sweet bean soup, with candied plums sinking to the bottom like treasure. Kaede couldn't help but feel as though it were a last meal of sorts, and the forced joviality of it all made her uneasy. It seemed wrong to eat like this when people were going hungry in that tattered tent city outside Cathair's walls.

At the end of the evening, the King stood up and toasted them as if they were about to depart on a holiday, and Kaede almost winced as she was forced to raise her glass along with everyone else. When she glanced at Con and Taisin, she saw that they, too, had sober looks on their faces as they listened to the King's booming, slightly drunken voice. She was relieved when the toast was over. She did not know what lay ahead, but she was ready to find out.

Chapter VIII

aisin lay awake on the platform bed, gazing up at the wooden canopy. The silk sheets were cool and slippery beneath her, and when she shifted, her skin slid across them with a whispering noise that sounded abnormally loud in the hush of her chamber. Her family had been given rooms adjoining hers, but the palace was so large that she could hardly believe they were sleeping under the same roof. The last few days with them had been precious, though. She would see them in the morning once more, but she already missed them.

She tried to relax; she knew she should get as much sleep as possible, because tomorrow would be a long day. But she was anxious and unsettled, and the palace was too grand to be comfortable. When she first arrived, she had stared wide-eyed at everything. She had never seen furniture as fine as the dark red lacquered armchairs and tables in these rooms; she had never slept in a bed as magnificent as this one, with a frame carved into the shapes of singing birds on branches. At night, there had been a phalanx of servants to bathe her in jasmine-scented water, and in the morning, more servants came to dress her in clothing so exquisite she was almost afraid wear it.

But all the luxury in the palace did nothing to dull the sharp clarity of the emotions that gripped her every time she remembered her vision.

Since the first time she had envisioned that beach of ice, she had seen it twice more in dreams. Each time she awoke feeling torn up with loss, the sight of Kaede departing as painful as a fresh wound. Tonight in the palace, she was still awake when the vision began to pull at her, like fingers gently tugging her toward a deep blue pool. Part of her did not want to go, but part of her experienced this tugging with a kind of intellectual detachment. She had never encountered this kind of Sight before; it was like there was someone or something leading her forward. It was not unpleasant or frightening; it was merely quietly insistent. She knew it would win eventually, and so she gave in, allowing her mind to open up to what it wanted to show her—and then she was there: standing on the beach as always, her feet planted on the snow, looking out at the boat that Kaede rowed away from the shore.

For the first time, she sensed another person with her. She knew, somehow, that if she turned around, Con would be standing behind her. And she realized that she could feel some of what he was feeling: pain, physical pain, and beneath that a knotted rope of worry. He was moving toward her, and his fingers wrapped around her shoulder as if to restrain her. She saw Kaede leaving; her stomach twisted with dread.

But this time there was more: a hot wash of guilt, spreading a bitter taste in her mouth.

The Taisin lying beneath silk sheets in the palace twisted her body, curving it as though she were running after Kaede, but the one standing on the beach did not move beneath the press of Con's hand. Instead she looked up, past Kaede's receding figure, and there she saw something that took her breath away. In Cathair she gasped out loud, crumpling the sheets into her fisted hands. There before her in her mind's eye was a fortress rising up from the frigid sea like a mountain of snow. It was as though an iceberg had been carved with a giant knife, shaped into towers and walls; and cut into those walls were glass windows that winked in the brilliant sunlight like a thousand sparkling diamonds.

The fortress was on an island—or perhaps it was simply a particularly large ice floe—and Kaede was rowing toward it. Each stroke took her farther from the beach Taisin stood on, her feet growing colder by the second, and now she heard a sound for the first time: Con speaking in her ear, an urgent tone in his voice. *Come back*, he was saying to her. *Come back.*

Taisin awoke well before dawn, the vision still clear in her mind, her nightgown soaked with sweat. She shivered; the silk sheets held no warmth. She sat up, shaking, and climbed down from the platform bed to retrieve her knapsack. She pulled it open and rifled through it in the dark until she found her woolen traveling cloak. It had been laundered by the palace servants, and now she wrapped it around herself, the scratchy fabric a welcome contrast to the cold silk.

What had Con meant? Come back from what? The image of the ice fortress loomed in her memory, monstrous and beautiful. Who—or what—could have built that? The only thing she was sure of was the way her heart constricted every time Kaede left, and every time she felt it, she was more determined to make sure it never happened. But now the guilt confused her. Why hadn't she felt it before? She was bewildered; she was frustrated. She didn't understand the version of herself in the vision. That Taisin had emotions that the present-day Taisin—the one clutching her cloak to her chest in the King's palace—couldn't relate to. Was she fated to become that other Taisin?

Restless, she went to the windows overlooking the courtyard and unlatched them, curling up on the window seat. She tried to remind herself who she was right now, at midnight, in this grand, noiseless palace. She was a student at the Academy of Sages; she was in her sixth year, nearly ready to receive the mark. She was the daughter of two farmers; she was an older sister to Suri. She was not in love with the daughter of the King's Chancellor.

She repeated these facts to herself over and over as if they were a mantra until she fell asleep, her head leaning against the window frame.

Chapter IX

aede awoke the morning after the banquet
with a thrill of excitement inside her:
Today was the day. She couldn't wait to
leave Cathair behind. Her earlier misgivings were forgotten; now she tasted the
allure of adventure.

Three guards were waiting with Con and Taisin in the
palace stable's south courtyard when Kaede and her father
arrived. Though a few stable hands were standing nearby
with the horses, no one else had come to see them off, and
the small group was dwarfed by the vast expanse of carefully raked gravel around them. Even Taisin had arrived
alone, having already said good-bye to her family. Kaede
supposed they were already following Con's plan to draw
as little attention to themselves as possible.

The prince introduced Kaede to Tali, a burly guard with
a salt-and-pepper beard and hair shot through with gray.
The second guard, Pol, moved with the stealthy grace of a
dancer. He was older than Con but younger than Tali, and

he spoke with a northern accent. The third guard, Shae, was Con's age or perhaps a year or two older, and like the other guards and Con, she wore her black hair cut very short. She had expressive dark brown eyes, and there was a liveliness in her that Kaede liked immediately.

There were four riding horses, and two hitched to a supply wagon. Taisin would ride with Pol on the wagon seat; Con, Tali, and Shae would ride their own horses; and Tali led a chestnut mare to Kaede. "Con tells me you can keep up with us," the guard said.

She had to crane her neck to look up at him. "I can."

"Good." Tali gave her an unexpectedly encouraging smile. "The mare's name is Maila." He left her with the horse and went to talk to her father and Con.

When everything had been checked one last time, Kaede's father came to kiss her formally on both cheeks. The press of his lips was so dry and light that she might have imagined them. "Go safely," he said.

She felt a twinge of disappointment at how distant he was. She did not see that he turned his face away to hide the worry that lined his forehead.

They exited Cathair through the North Gate, passing a short line of travelers waiting to be admitted into the city. There was no encampment outside this gate, only brown fields with patches of moss growing over the ground. Every so often they passed a family walking toward Cathair, their belongings dragged behind them on a handcart or piled onto their backs. At noon they stopped by the side of the road to eat steamed bread stuffed with salty pork.

"From the palace kitchens this morning," Tali said as he

passed around the buns. "We won't get much of this from now on, so enjoy it while it lasts."

Kaede took a bite as a gust of wind blew around them. The horses stamped. In the distance she saw smoke rising from a farmhouse chimney, and two figures moved slowly in the empty field as if cataloguing their losses. "The road wasn't so empty south of Cathair," she observed.

"The winter was much harder north of the city," Tali said. "I think that those who wished to seek shelter in Cathair have already come; most of the rest refuse to leave their villages."

Con squinted up at the sky. "It's going to rain." He looked at Kaede. "North of here is the Great Wood. People believe that the trouble comes from that direction—I don't think anyone wishes to seek it out. With few people coming or going, it makes for an empty road."

"Then won't we be highly noticeable?" Kaede said. "What about maintaining some secrecy?"

Tali frowned. "We'll be all right. There are travelers on the road—just not many. And we're such a small group that we shouldn't attract too much attention."

"What will we say is our purpose?" Taisin asked. The damp wind whipped back loose strands of her hair.

"Sir," Shae said to Tali, "if I might make a suggestion?"

Tali gestured with his half-eaten bun. "Go ahead."

"If we are asked, we could say that we're going to visit my family. That will take us to Jilin, and beyond that is the Wood itself—we won't need a story then."

"It's a good idea," Tali said. "We can do that if we need to, but I don't think we'll need to tell much of a story." He turned to Con and added, "Let me do the talking, Your Highness, and no one will ask."

"All right," Con said. "But you don't need to address me so formally. None of you do—in fact, you shouldn't while we're on the road. What happens to one of us happens to us all. We are all equal in this."

As if to underscore his words, at that moment the sky opened, and Kaede stuffed the last bite of her bun into her mouth as they all scrambled for their rain gear.

⁓

It rained for little more than an hour—not heavily but steadily, sliding down their oil-slicked cloaks and dripping onto chilled hands. When it stopped, there was no sun to dry them off, and they were still damp when they arrived at the hostel they planned to sleep at that night.

It was in a small village built right up to the road, a way station for merchants. The hostel itself was tiny, and all but two of its half-dozen rooms were taken. After a supper cooked over the shared stove in the courtyard, they separated to go to their rooms for the night, Kaede with Taisin and Shae, Con with Tali and Pol. Each room had a single platform bed that looked particularly hard and unyielding.

"There's not much space," Kaede said. Gauging the width of the bed, she judged that there was just enough room for the three of them. She guessed that in Con's room, one of the men would have to sleep on the floor.

Shae lit the murky oil lamp on the wobbly bedside table and said, "There's no heater, either. We may as well get to know one another."

Kaede laughed. "I'll take the side closest to the wall." She began to spread her blankets out.

"I'll be closest to the door," Taisin said quickly.

Shae shrugged. "That's fine with me—I'll be the warmest one." She and Kaede grinned at each other, but Taisin seemed to color a little and would not meet their eyes. She turned her back on them to unlace her boots and pull off her outer tunic. As Taisin lifted her hands to her hair to unpin her braids, Kaede caught herself watching. She looked away and saw Shae observing her with a small smile. Kaede flushed. "So," Shae said, "you have brothers. Three of them, I understand?"

Grateful for the change of subject, Kaede answered, "Yes. All older than I am."

"I have an older brother myself, and an older sister."

"Are they both still in Jilin?"

"Yes. My entire family is."

Taisin tried to ignore them, setting up her bedroll on the edge of the platform. Kaede asked Shae, "Did you grow up there, then? What was it like?"

Shae pulled a leather-bound flask from her knapsack and sat down on the dusty wooden floor, cross-legged. "It was a good childhood," she answered, taking a swig from the flask and offering it to Kaede. "You're not too young for this, are you?"

Out of the corner of her eye, Taisin saw Kaede sit down, leaning her back against the cold wall. "Do you think I'm too young?" Kaede said.

"One never knows. Would you like some?"

"Not for me. At the Academy, we don't indulge."

"You're not at the Academy anymore."

"True," Kaede agreed, but she did not take it.

"Taisin," Shae called. "None for you, either, I imagine?"

"No, thank you," Taisin answered, feeling uncomfortable. She didn't know what to make of Shae. They had said very little to each other all day, and they didn't seem to have much in common. But she could tell that Kaede liked her, and that made Taisin feel oddly jealous of the guard. Annoyed at herself, Taisin pulled out the *Book of Rituals* from her knapsack, telling herself that she should review it. She climbed onto the bed and opened the book in her lap, squinting at the page in the dim light.

"There are stories about the Great Wood," Kaede was saying.

"What have you heard?" Shae asked.

"I've heard that things work differently in the Great Wood. That people get lost, even if they have a map. That magic goes awry there; rituals go bad. That sort of thing."

"I've heard those things, too."

"Are they true?"

Shae did not answer immediately, and when she did speak, her words were measured. "Every story, I think, has a grain of truth to it. But sometimes, people are misled by what they believe, and they see what they think they should see, not what is actually there."

"That could be said of almost anything in life."

"That doesn't mean it's not true." Shae paused for a moment. "I'll tell you this much. The Wood is a special place. It was difficult for me to leave it. Every day I spend away from it, I miss it. For me—for my family—things make more sense when we are at home there beneath the trees."

"Then why did you leave?"

"There was nothing for me to do at home. My family is not rich, and King Cai offers a steady wage to his guards."

There was no shame in her voice, only a matter-of-factness that made Taisin wish she could be as easy about her own family background as Shae was about hers. But Shae was a guard in service to the King; it didn't matter who her parents were. Taisin wanted to be a sage, and few of them were lowborn. Taisin knew she was lucky that the Academy had taken her, for her family could not afford to pay for her education. It was a compliment to her talent, yes, but it was also a reminder that she owed the Academy a great debt.

"Why did you decide to become a guard?" Kaede said.

"I like action," Shae said, a smile in her voice. "I had no talent for the sagehood, and besides, the King makes it easy to join his Guard. When the recruiters came to Jilin two years ago, it seemed like a good thing to do." Shae shrugged. "I've liked it well enough so far, though I didn't think I'd be away from home for so long." There was a pause, and Taisin heard Shae putting the flask away, lacing shut her knapsack. "How old are you, then?" the guard asked.

"I will be eighteen at midsummer," Kaede replied.

"You'll celebrate your birthday at the Fairy Queen's palace."

"I suppose so."

Shae yawned. "I'm exhausted. There are many nights ahead of us; we can talk more later. I'm going to sleep."

"Would you like me to turn down the lamp?" asked Taisin, blushing when she realized her question showed that she had been listening.

Shae smiled at her, and it was such a friendly smile that Taisin was ashamed for feeling jealous. "I can sleep in broad daylight," Shae said, getting up and gathering her bedroll. "Don't bother to stop your reading for me. But perhaps Kaede has a preference?"

Kaede shook her head. "Stay up as late as you like," she said, and stood to change out of her traveling clothes.

Taisin looked away, trying to focus on her book. She shifted over to make room as Shae and Kaede climbed onto the creaking platform and settled in for the night. At home, Taisin always shared her sister Suri's small bed; indeed, she probably had less space there than she did tonight, but it was not the same. She could have curled up against Suri's back, sharing her warmth. Here, her body was tense, trying to avoid inching too close to Shae's slumbering form.

Taisin sat up past midnight, feeling awkward and self-conscious, staring at the page before her but not reading a word. Her ears rang with the sound of Shae's and Kaede's breathing in that small room, and beneath it, the flutter of her heartbeat seemed as loud as a drum.

❧

Kaede awoke very early, eager to get back on the road. Her eyes opened to dim light coming through the small window, and beside her she felt the warmth of Shae's body. She sat up too quickly and winced; she was not used to riding a horse all day, and her muscles were paying for it. The hard

68

bed hadn't helped, either, and she gingerly eased herself out of it, trying to avoid waking Shae and Taisin. She dressed as quietly as she could, and after a moment's hesitation she buckled the dagger that Fin had given her onto her belt. It made her feel a little self-conscious to wear a weapon like that, but the guards—and Con, too—were all armed. Feeling the hilt pressing gently at her ribs, she picked up her boots and took them outside to put them on. It was chilly in the courtyard, and from the color of the sky above she could tell that it was just barely after dawn. She decided to head to the stable and look for breakfast among their provisions instead of waiting for the others to wake up.

Just as she was rounding the corner of the hostel she heard the swift passage of an arrow followed by a thud as it struck its target. She flinched. Pol was standing in the stable yard and shooting at a tree. He looked over his shoulder at her and said, "You're up early."

"So are you."

He went to pull the arrows out of the tree. "It's too cramped in that room. Tali's a big man."

She smiled. He shot again and again, sending a series of arrows fleet and sure to the center of the trunk, just below a branching limb. She marveled at the way he made it seem so effortless: lifting the long bow, nocking the arrow, loosing the string so that his right hand arched back gracefully, echoing the flight of the arrow itself. She wanted to be able to do that.

"Will you show me how to shoot?" she asked.

He looked at her as if gauging her potential. "The bow is a bit long for you."

"Let me try. At least it'll be something to do while we wait for the others to wake up."

"All right."

The bow, made of a springy, yellowish-brown wood, was as tall as she was. Pol took off his shooting glove—an odd, three-fingered leather glove with a bulging, padded thumb—and showed her how to strap it onto her right hand. The first time she tried to pull back on the string, she could feel the muscles of her neck and shoulder straining at the effort. The arrow she had nocked slipped and fell, flailing like a downed bird, to the ground at her feet. It was not, she realized quickly, like throwing a knife. Pol seemed amused by her attempt, but said kindly, "My father gave me my first bow when I was a boy of six. It'll take some time before you get the hang of it."

He corrected her stance and told her to breathe in as she raised the bow; to press that breath down within herself as she stretched the string; to allow the arrow and her breath to loosen simultaneously. But the more she tried, the less she succeeded, and she began to sweat from the effort.

"You are too willful," Pol said, observing her latest failed attempt. She reminded him of a young bird flapping her wings, unable to gain the lift needed to take off.

"What do you mean?" Kaede's arm and shoulder ached, and the bowstring had snapped loudly and painfully against her left forearm enough times that she was sure it would leave a red welt there.

"If you think about it too closely, you will choke the energy of the arrow. Your body—and your thoughts—are

70

getting in the way. Try to let go of your thoughts when you shoot. You do not have to force the arrow to fly; it wants to fly."

His words reminded Kaede of her teachers' instructions at the Academy, but hearing them applied to archery was like hearing those lessons in a different language—one that was maddeningly familiar but as elusive as a slippery fish.

Pol saw the growing frustration on her face, and he took the bow from her and showed her, again, the smooth rhythm of the draw, the arrow in flight, his hand in the air. "Stand like this," he told her, spreading his feet wider. "Put your hand here." He moved her left hand down on the grip.

Bit by bit, the bow began to seem less foreign to her, though she knew she was far from being as skilled as Pol was. By the time Tali came out to the stable yard to fetch their breakfast supplies, Kaede was sweating and famished, her right shoulder aching, and still the arrow had not struck the target.

Pol said, "We'll practice every morning—how about that?" He seemed excited by the prospect.

"Delightful," she said, smiling weakly, and he laughed at her. But she handed the bow back to him with some reluctance.

Before she left the stable yard, she couldn't resist unsheathing her dagger and tossing it at the tree, just to remind herself that she wasn't completely inept. It flew out of her hand so easily—she didn't have to think about it—

and struck the tree with a solid thunk. She flexed her fingers thoughtfully. Her hand knew what it was doing. Perhaps it was her body that needed to learn this new language, not her mind.

She went to retrieve the dagger from the scarred tree trunk and went inside for breakfast.

Chapter X

wo days after they left Cathair, the road curved east as it followed the bend in the river Nir. In better times, fishing vessels trawled the river, but now there was little to catch, and what could be caught was better left uneaten. Word had spread through the roadside hostels of a fisherman who had brought in a giant carp—a rarity in any season, but especially abnormal now—only to discover that the fish's belly housed hundreds of tiny stinging eels.

There were other rumors, too. One traveler, a thin man with a nervous black horse, told them he had seen a strange creature lurking behind one of the riverside taverns: half woman, half animal, with a fox's red-gold tail and sharp teeth. A young man had been found dead nearby, his body bruised and bitten.

"All of this trouble comes from upriver," the thin man said, jerking his thumb toward the Nir. He ran his eyes over the group of travelers and their gear—their wagon still full of supplies, the fine workmanship on their horses' saddles—and suspicion flickered over his face. He glanced at the burly, gray-haired man, who was clearly their leader, and asked, "Where are you headed?"

"To Jilin," Tali answered, his tone not inviting further questions. Jilin was at the southwestern edge of the Great Wood, where the Nir originated.

The thin man eyed the group's wagon; the wheels were especially well made. There weren't many travelers heading north, and even fewer who were so well outfitted. But a kind of unspoken camaraderie had developed among travelers on the King's Highway in the last two years, for dark times gave cover to dark deeds, and it was better to pass on one's news without learning too much about anyone else. So the thin man said only, "I've heard that something's not quite right at Ento. I haven't been there recently, but as you're headed in that direction, you might ask about it."

Tali said, "We will."

❦

Two nights later, they lodged in a tiny village perched on the banks of the Nir, and Ento was the only subject of conversation in the village's lone tavern. Crowded with out-of-work fishermen, the dark, low-ceilinged room smelled of river water and spirits. The locals had glanced at the six travelers when they first entered, but made no effort to lower their voices to keep their gossip private.

"A man came through the other day," a fisherman was saying. "He told me people are deserting the place as quick as they can."

Built on an old crossroads, Ento had once been home to

a major marketplace. But now there was little to sell, and the town had fallen on hard times.

"That family who was here last week said the same thing," said another man.

"I hope whatever's happened in Ento doesn't move south to us."

"Not likely to be so lucky," said one man bitterly. "Wind blows south from the Great Wood—we're right in the line of it."

Tali turned in his seat and said casually, "We're headed in that direction. What happened?"

Taisin kept her eyes down, but she was curious, too. The more they heard about Ento, the more she was convinced there was something there that she should see. Her instincts were tugging on her in a way she had never experienced before. She turned slightly toward Tali, hoping he would ask the right questions. Earlier in the day, he had told them he would find out as much as he could about what was going on in Ento, and Taisin twitched with impatience.

The fishermen all swiveled around to stare at Tali, and one of them—a man with a long, scraggly gray beard—said, "You'd be better off avoiding that place."

"Why?"

The fishermen looked at one another uneasily before one of them spoke, his missing front tooth flashing like a dark eye. "It was little things at first—goats gone dry, wells turning bad."

"Same things have been happening all over the Kingdom," said the gray-bearded man.

"That was bad enough, but now folks are saying that the Xi are taking our children," said the man with the missing tooth. His voice was harsh and loud, and the common room fell silent.

Taisin glanced up in surprise; she had never heard of the Xi having much interest in human children before. Across the table, Tali just barely shook his head at her, and she swallowed her question.

"It's only one child, and no one knows if it's true," objected a man from across the room.

"Has a child been taken or not?" Tali asked bluntly.

The man with the missing tooth scowled. "The mother says it's still her babe, but the father came through here just yesterday. Looked as though he'd lost everything. He said the child is a monster, and his wife has gone mad."

"It's dark magic," said the graybeard. "If you can avoid Ento, you should. Take an alternate route."

The room erupted with men arguing whether the town was safe to travel through. "Thank you for the information," Tali said, his voice nearly drowned by the din.

Taisin tried to focus on her meal, but the fisherman's words rang in her mind. What kind of dark magic? Her pulse raced. She wanted to know.

∽

The rumors came more quickly as they approached Ento. The child was one of the Xi, cursed to inhabit the body of a human to atone for a crime; the child was the reincarnation of a legendary sorcerer; the child was a demon who had eaten the human child. After hearing the tale of the demon, Tali suggested, "Perhaps we should bypass Ento altogether." They were in the stable yard of another inn in another fishing village, unpacking their gear for the night.

"It will lengthen our journey by several days," Pol said.

Taisin, who had just finished feeding the horses, came around the corner of the wagon. "I think..." She hesitated as they all turned to look at her. She took a breath and said: "I think we should continue the way we planned. The rumors are...they're just rumors."

"They're rumors, yes," Con said, "but, Taisin, I traveled north with Tali last fall, before the worst of the winter storms. The things we saw there were—well, they make me inclined to believe these rumors."

"Nobody seems to have been hurt by this child," she said with studied nonchalance.

"That's true," Tali agreed.

"Then we might as well travel through Ento," Taisin said. "It will be inconvenient to avoid it, and there is no guaranteed benefit." She saw Kaede watching her with interest. She could tell that Kaede wondered why she was so adamant about this, for she had never indicated her opinion on their route before. She still couldn't explain it; she only knew that she needed to see this creature, whatever it was. She lowered her eyes, trying to hide her excitement. Tali would be suspicious if she appeared too eager.

Shae said: "She has a point, Tali. And we'll only be there one night."

He relented. "All right. Ento it is."

❧

A little over two weeks into the journey, the rhythms of travel had settled into Kaede's body. She woke early, met Pol in a stable yard or at an empty patch of dirt near their hostel, raised the bow, and loosed arrows until breakfast. Her arms and shoulders grew stronger, but still she could not strike the target. They rode all day, stopping only for a noon meal at the side of the road, eaten cold. She came to know her horse, Maila, who was both sweet-tempered and energetic. She grew accustomed to falling asleep with the sound of others breathing nearby, and at times she wondered how she had ever lived another way. She thought of her small chamber in that great stony Academy, and her parents' luxurious Cathair home, where she had entire assortments of rooms to herself, but she did not miss them. She realized that she loved the road: Every day was new and unexplored.

Kaede especially enjoyed talking to Shae, who told stories about her training as a guard; about learning to fight and to ride with a sword. Her life was so different from Kaede's years at the Academy that she was always eager to hear more. She began to wonder if she could join the King's Guard when she returned from this journey. Then she would never have to face the dreary politics of court life; she could be on a horse all day, going to places she had never been before.

Shae always included Taisin when she told her tales, even if Taisin was pretending to study, as she often did. It was noticing Shae's kindness that caused Kaede to gradually become aware that Taisin watched her, often, with hooded eyes. She would look away as soon as Kaede glanced at her, so initially Kaede wondered if she were imagining things. But as the days passed, she began to watch Taisin, too. Her classmate was quiet, reserved; she spoke when spoken to, but rarely entered into any conversations on her own. Con tried to draw her out by joking with her, and sometimes Taisin seemed to appreciate it, but she quickly retreated back into a state that seemed to hover between anxiety and frustration. Once, when Kaede caught Taisin looking at her, she had the odd impression that Taisin thought of her as a problem to solve, but she did not know how to do it.

The day they were due to reach Ento, Kaede spent nearly the whole afternoon puzzling over the enigma of her classmate. She had just resolved to speak to Taisin about it directly when they caught sight of the town gates in the distance. They hung open as though abandoned, and as they approached they saw there was no one in the gatehouse.

"You're sure you want to stay here tonight?" Pol said from his perch on the wagon seat.

Tali said: "We'll just sleep here and make an early start in the morning. Let's go."

They were the only guests at the hostel that night, which meant that, for once, there were enough vacant rooms for each of them to sleep alone. After supper, Tali, Con, Pol, and Shae went upstairs, but Kaede lingered behind in the common room waiting for Taisin, who had taken their empty bowls to the innkeeper in the kitchen. When Taisin returned several minutes later, she was startled to see Kaede still there.

"I thought you went upstairs," Taisin said, picking up her cloak from where she had left it, slung over a chair.

"I wanted to talk to you." Kaede stood up, but hesitated. What should she say? All her words seemed to flee from her; she felt awkward.

Taisin suddenly looked nervous. "Now? Now is not—I can't talk now."

"Why?" Kaede eyed Taisin's cloak. "Where are you going?"

"I'm going to see the child."

A chill rushed through her as Kaede realized which child Taisin meant. "The child—the one they say is a monster?"

Taisin began to move toward the door, pulling the cloak over her shoulders. "The innkeeper told me where the mother lives."

"You're going now?"

"Yes."

Fear prickled across Kaede's skin. "I don't think that's a good idea. Tali wouldn't like it."

Taisin stopped and looked back at Kaede. "I haven't yet seen any of these strange creatures that people keep telling us about. Don't you want to see what we're dealing with?"

"What do you mean, 'what we're dealing with'? Why are you so eager to go?"

"It's all related," Taisin insisted. "The weather. The

80

rumors we've been hearing about these...creatures. The Fairy Queen's invitation."

Kaede remembered Maire Morighan's theory that these disparate events were all connected, but Taisin spoke with an assurance that was surprising. "How do you know?" Kaede asked.

"I can feel it. Every day on the road—I feel something pulling me. I don't know what it is, but I have to find out. I know it's important."

Kaede was doubtful. "I don't think you should go alone. Let me get Tali, or Pol—"

"They won't let me go," Taisin objected. "They barely even agreed to stay in Ento for one night. They certainly won't let me go look for the child. You can't tell them."

"But—"

"I have to go. Now." Taisin's hand was on the doorknob as she added, "Do you want to come with me?"

Kaede glanced at the empty stairs uneasily. She knew she should tell the others, but Taisin was right. Tali would never allow her—or Kaede—to go, and Taisin's urgency had sparked Kaede's own curiosity. She wanted an adventure. Perhaps now was the time to get it.

Just as Taisin was pulling the door open Kaede said, "Wait. All right. I'm coming with you." She ran back to grab her own cloak from where she had left it at the table, and pulled it on as they left the hostel.

Chapter XI

hey took the lantern hanging at the entrance to the hostel courtyard, and it shed a small pool of light as they went down the road. "The innkeeper told me that she lives in a house on the edge of town," Taisin said, but beneath her briskness was a note of trepidation.

The buildings they passed on either side were dark, and some of their courtyard gates were wide open. There would be nothing inside to tempt any thieves; Ento had been deserted as if it were the host of a plague. At the end of the paved road they turned left down a rutted dirt lane; only the last house seemed to be occupied. A dim glow emanated from a curtained window, and from within they heard a baby crying.

Taisin strode up to the front door and raised her hand to knock, her knuckles ringing on the wood. The door was pulled open by a woman with haunted eyes and thin, oily black hair. "What do you want?" she asked defensively.

"May I see your child?" Taisin asked.

The woman's eyes flicked back to Kaede, who was standing behind Taisin. "Who are you?"

"I may be able to help," Taisin said. "Please, let me see your child."

"I won't let you take him away from me," the woman warned her.

"We are not here to take him," Taisin reassured her.

"What can you do? You're only a girl."

For a moment Taisin wavered. What exactly was she planning to do, anyway? The baby cried again, and the sound of it jerked at her gut. She forced down her self-doubt and said: "I am training to be a sage. Please—I've come a long way, and I want to help you."

The woman eyed the two girls on her doorstep. They were both young and obviously inexperienced. The girl who had spoken was so eager to prove herself, while her silent companion seemed reluctant to be there at all. These days, the woman was suspicious of almost everyone who came to her door, but these two girls, with their artless faces, made her feel hopeful for the first time in weeks. Perhaps this girl really was a sage in training, but even if she was lying, what harm could a couple of girls do? She stepped back and allowed them to come inside.

The house, consisting of one room, was small but clean. A fire burned on the stone hearth, and nearby was a rocking chair and a cradle. There was a platform bed against the far wall, its blankets mussed as though someone had slept there recently. A little shrine was built into the corner;

84

Taisin saw the scroll listing ancestors' names, a spray of dried flowers, a small pot of incense. It did not look like the house of a madwoman.

"When was your baby born?" Taisin asked.

"Three months ago." The woman's eyes darted toward Kaede, who said nothing. "He is healthy," she insisted.

"Where is your husband?" Taisin asked.

Tears filled the woman's eyes, and she began to rub her left arm nervously, as if it were a lucky stone. "He has gone," she answered, and her voice broke. "He has gone."

"Why?" Taisin asked.

"He—he believes I have betrayed him." She rubbed her arm more quickly.

"Why would he think that?"

"He says the baby is not his." As she spoke, the baby opened his mouth and wailed. She knelt down and picked him up, rocking him in her arms until he quieted. "But I never betrayed my husband. I was with him every night. This is our baby." Tears trickled out of her eyes, leaving shining rivulets on her cheeks.

Taisin walked to the woman and put her hand on the baby's blanket. "Let me see him."

At first the woman clutched her baby closer, but as Taisin waited calmly, she slowly relaxed and allowed Taisin to pull back the blanket. The child looked perfectly normal: a sleeping baby boy, fine new hair in a black cap over his head, a small nose, a bow of a mouth.

Kaede approached them, unease rising in her. The mother's eyes were skipping about the room, looking everywhere but at Taisin or her son. The boy let out a small coo as he awoke, reaching for Taisin's hand. He wrapped his little fingers around her thumb and tugged. Taisin's eyes widened; a shudder went through her.

"What is it?" Kaede asked. This did not feel right.

"How wondrous," Taisin breathed. The baby's eyes were black as coal, without a glint of light in them. They were unnatural.

"Taisin," Kaede said warningly. She could see the boy's eyes now, and a knot of horror clenched in her belly. No human had eyes like that.

"It's all right," Taisin said, but Kaede didn't know if she was talking to the baby, his mother, or herself. Taisin seemed entranced by him.

He let go of her thumb and reached up with chubby fists, trying to grab the strands of Taisin's hair that had come loose from her braids. She leaned closer, and the medallion that Sister Ailan had entrusted her with tumbled out over the collar of her tunic, as if it had been pulled. It was shiny and bright, and the stone was like a magnet to the child's hands. When he touched it, he and his mother and Taisin shone for an instant as long as one blink—and then Taisin was clutching at the child's fists, which were firmly clasped around the medallion.

"Let go," Taisin hissed, and the child would not obey. There was an eerie smile on his face as if he were mocking her, his black eyes wide and staring.

"What are you doing to him?" the mother demanded,

trying to back away, but he would not let go of the medallion, and it tethered the both of them to Taisin.

"Let go!"

"He doesn't understand you. He's only a baby!" the mother pleaded.

"He understands," Taisin said, and the baby's mouth yawned open in a soundless cry.

Kaede wanted to intervene, but she didn't know what to do. Panic raced through her frozen body.

Taisin put her hands on the baby's forehead and said, "Reveal your true spirit—I command you to come forth!" The baby let out a growl, raising the hairs on Kaede's neck.

The child strained toward Taisin while his mother tried to pull him back, and it was almost as though he was suspended in the air between the two of them. Kaede wondered if her eyes were playing tricks on her, for he seemed to be lengthening. Taisin said again, her voice harsh and deep, "Reveal your true spirit! I command you to come forth."

And then the child began to change. His hands were growing, his head was enlarging, and where baby fuzz had once covered a pale new scalp, now long tentacles were emerging. Parts of his body were dissolving into mist and then re-forming into a greater thing: a creature made of scales and feathers both, as if it could not decide exactly what kind of being it should be. Its hands were still pulling on the medallion around Taisin's neck, and the woman was still trying to hold this creature that had moments

87

before been her baby but was now kicking back at her with clawed feet that tore gashes into her arms. Blood erupted on the woman's skin, and the creature screamed, fury distorting its face.

Kaede was rooted to the spot, stunned by what was happening in front of her. She felt useless; her limbs would not obey her. She saw the creature's taloned hands stretch toward Taisin's throat. Kaede realized that it was going to rip that medallion from Taisin's neck, and her neck would come with it. Instinctually, Kaede felt for the dagger that Fin had given her. The touch of the iron hilt seemed to unstick her feet from the floor at last, and she moved through what felt like thick mud toward the monstrous child.

The woman was clinging to the thing that had erupted from her baby; she was screaming at Taisin; Taisin was still trying to pull the medallion out of the creature's hands; and Kaede took the last few steps, her muscles straining against unseen weights, and plunged the iron into the monster's chest.

After the viscous density of the air, there was little resistance; it was suddenly like carving through fog or mist. But the monster felt it. It turned its horrible black eyes toward her, and for a moment, Kaede lost her breath looking into those bottomless depths. They were as dark as a thousand starless midnights, and she was dragged down with despair; she was sure that she would sink so far into the earth that her body would be crushed at any moment by the mass of the world above it.

And then she felt something give. Warmth seeped over

her skin, and time sped up again with a great whoosh like a blast of winter wind, and the monster shriveled up until there, in the woman's bloody arms, was a baby with an iron knife protruding from its still belly.

Along the side of the baby's face was an iridescent fringe of feathers, grown out of its skin like a strange mane, the only sign that it had ever been anything other than a plump little boy.

Chapter XII

The woman collapsed onto the floor, and the lifeless creature rolled out of her arms, leaving a glistening crimson trail down the front of her dress.

Taisin's body hummed with a jumble of emotions—awe at witnessing the child's frightening transformation; terror that it was going to kill her. But Kaede had saved her. She was alive. And then the full force of what had just happened—what she had barely avoided—swept through her.

She sank to her knees, taking a deep, ragged breath. She was as cold as if she had been submerged in icy water. She wrapped her arms around herself; she was shaking. She became gradually aware of the heart-wrenching sound of the mother's sobs: She was crying. And Kaede stood as still as stone, her face ashen, her right hand streaked with the creature's blood.

Taisin pushed herself up; her knees wobbled. She touched Kaede's arm. "Kaede, it's over."

Kaede's dazed eyes flickered to Taisin. As if she were coming awake after a disorienting dream, awareness flooded into her. She saw Taisin's face, drained of color; her dark, anxious eyes. Taisin could have been killed. Kaede reached for her, cupping Taisin's face in her hands, pulling her closer as her thumbs pressed into Taisin's cheeks. "Are you all right?" she asked urgently.

Taken aback, Taisin said, "Yes."

"It didn't hurt you?"

"No."

Kaede's face was tight with worry, and Taisin realized that the worry was for her. All at once, she wasn't cold anymore. She backed away, flustered, and Kaede's hand left a smear of red on her left cheek.

They heard a voice behind them: "What's going on?"

They spun around to see Con standing in the open doorway.

"Are you all right?" he asked, taking in the sight of Taisin and Kaede, the queer little body on the floor, the keening mother.

Taisin swallowed; she tried to gather herself together. The strange pull she had felt before was gone. Had the child been the source of it? Had it called to her? And what was that creature? She had certainly never heard of anything like it at the Academy, and her lack of knowledge frightened her.

She saw Con still watching her, waiting for an answer. "The child that we have been hearing about—it was not human," she said. Her voice was steadier than she expected it would be. "We must destroy it." Saying the words turned the horror into a task, an assignment.

"Why?" Kaede asked. She still felt a bit muddled, and seeing the iron dagger still protruding from the creature's belly made her shudder. She went to it and pulled the dagger out. The blood was bright on the blade, and it made her stomach clench. She could have thrown the weapon into the fire, never to see it again, but Taisin came to her side and held out a torn rag.

"Use this," Taisin said. Kaede hesitated, but finally took the rag and ran it over the edge of the blade. The blood came off in long dark streaks. Taisin knelt down beside the tiny body. The eyes were still open, reflecting the firelight with an eerie liveliness. She shivered. "We must burn the body."

"Can't we just bury it?" Kaede asked.

"I don't know what kind of magic created it. Burial will only allow it to take root and spring up again."

Kaede imagined tiny, gnarled fingers reaching up through the soil like a strange new plant. "Fire, then," she agreed quickly. "Where?"

They wrapped the body in a canvas cloth that had been discarded in the corner, and Kaede tucked the bloodied rag inside. The mother lay like a broken doll on the floor, paying no attention to them. Con saw Kaede's worried expression and said, "We won't leave her alone; I'll tell the innkeeper about her."

Behind the woman's small house there was a bare dirt yard, and in the light of the lantern that Con held, they found the woodshed. He helped Kaede assemble the funeral pyre, and then they laid the small, wrapped body on top of it. It was light as a feather.

Kaede had taken flint from inside the house and was about to light the fire when Taisin said, "Wait. Let me bind the body to the earth first." She went back inside and returned a few minutes later carrying a saltcellar.

Con saw her fingers tremble as she fumbled with the coarse white grains. "Have you done this before?" he asked, not unkindly.

She wouldn't let herself look at him; she didn't want to see the doubt that must be in his eyes. "I know how it is done," she said. At the Academy she had learned about the appropriate rituals for a funeral, but only from books. And her knowledge of binding a malevolent being to the earth was entirely theoretical; she had never before encountered such a creature. She began to circle the funeral pyre three times clockwise, trying to quell the apprehension bubbling inside her. She didn't want to think about what could go wrong if she performed this ritual incorrectly.

She sprinkled the salt on the earth; she breathed deep into her belly. The night smelled of dampness, mud, and smoke from the small house's chimney. She halted at the head of the shrouded body, completing her three circles, and set the saltcellar down on the ground at her feet. She folded her hands together just below her breastbone and felt the rapid thrumming of her pulse, her whole body taut with nerves. She tried to slow down her breathing, to calm herself, but her voice still shook a little as she said, "As earth calls to earth, we bind you here: May you rest in peace and disturb us no more." She repeated it twice, then stepped back and said to Kaede, "You can light the fire."

The wood was slightly damp from the rain, and Kaede had to kneel down to blow on the spark until the kindling caught fire. Ever since she was a child, she loved to watch the flames dance; she and her brothers would build giant bonfires on the beach outside Seatown in the summer, adding driftwood until the fire roared like a dragon. But as these flames licked at the shrouded body, it turned her stomach to see it eat away the cloth. When the creature's skin began to catch fire, she turned away, pressing her hand over her nose to block out the smell. She felt a deep pain within her. Even if that creature had been a monster when she killed it, she had still killed it. The knowledge of it was oppressive; her heart felt like iron.

~

It was past midnight before the fire consumed all the remains. Taisin's eyes stung from the heat, and she felt weak, exhausted—as though something wild had been dragged through her body. "When the ashes have cooled, we'll have to bury them," she said.

"I'll stay," Con said. He saw the weariness on Taisin's face and the dull remains of shock on Kaede's. "You're both worn out. You should go back to the hostel and sleep if you can."

"Are you sure?" Taisin asked.

He squeezed her shoulder. "Yes."

Kaede rubbed at her eyes and asked, "What about the mother?" They hadn't heard her crying in some time.

"I'll bring her back with me if I can," Con said. "Just go back with Taisin. You look as if—well, you need some rest."

Kaede blinked. Her eyelashes felt clogged with smoke. "How did you know where to find us, Con?"

He seemed surprised by her question. "I noticed when you didn't come upstairs—I promised your father I'd look out for you. So I asked the innkeeper if he knew where you'd gone, and he told me."

Taisin touch Kaede's elbow. "Come on. Let's go."

Con's brown eyes reflected the embers of the funeral pyre. He nodded at her gently. "You should go. I'll see you in the morning."

Kaede and Taisin walked back to the hostel in the dark, having forgotten to bring the lantern with them. Kaede felt confused and tired; she felt guilty. Whenever the dagger at her side brushed against her thigh, it sent a shock through her.

She was startled when Taisin spoke, her voice only slightly louder than the sound of their footsteps on the dusty road. "Thank you. I owe you my life."

"You don't owe me anything." Kaede was overcome by a wave of despondency. If the night were not so black already, she would have closed her eyes to block out any light. The smell of the funeral pyre seemed to be burned into her nostrils.

"Kaede, you did the right thing—you did the only thing you could."

She knew that Taisin was trying to comfort her, but it only made her feel worse. "Let's just go back. I'm tired."

They walked the rest of the way in silence.

~

Kaede could not fall asleep. The bed was hard and cold, and she missed the sound of Shae and Taisin breathing nearby. All she could see, over and over in her mind's eye, was the hilt of her iron dagger protruding from the still form of that creature. It looked disturbingly like a human baby. She wondered if she would be haunted by that image forever.

After what seemed like hours, she threw off her blankets and packed up her bedroll, dressing quickly. She went downstairs and out to the stable. It was still dark. She rifled through the wagon until she found Pol's bow, taking it out to the courtyard. She nocked an arrow and let it fly at the wooden hitching post.

She missed.

It made her angry. Her skin flushed at her own incompetence. What good was she? She would never be a sage, and she had no other skills. Why was she even trying to shoot a bow? Did she actually expect to become a guard like Pol or Tali or Shae? Her father would never allow it. And she couldn't even kill a monster—a *monster*, she told herself—without feeling like a monster herself.

She jerked the iron dagger out of its sheath at her waist and threw it savagely at the post, but as soon as it left her hand, she knew it was a bad throw. She heard it clanging to the ground beyond the post. She let out a frustrated groan and stalked across the dirt yard to retrieve it. Her knees shook when she squatted down to pick it up. Her whole body was worn out, but she was too tightly wound to rest. She shoved the dagger into its sheath and went back to the bow.

When she had shot all the arrows, she went to where they lay and picked them up, stuffing them back into the quiver. Then she returned to where she had been standing at the opposite side of the courtyard and raised the bow again. She couldn't keep feeling this way. It would drive her mad. She breathed in, trying to loosen the knot of frustration and self-loathing inside herself.

The arrow's feathers brushed against her gloved hand as she pulled back on the string. She told herself that the only thing in the world was this arrow. There was no stable yard; there was no village of Ento; there was no Kaede, even. Everything melted away like fog in sunlight. She was riding on the sharp point of the arrowhead itself; she was flying through the predawn stillness.

The thud as it struck the hitching post surprised her.

She pulled another arrow, and another, and sent them all, more or less, into the post. Some shivered a bit before tumbling down, not having been sent with enough force. When she saw one fall, she pulled back harder on the next one. She felt emptied of everything; she only existed to hold the bow and to ready the arrow for its task.

She did this repeatedly until the sky brightened into gray. She did it until her shoulders and arms were aching and her eyes stung from staring so fixedly at the target. She did it until the gate to the stable yard opened behind her and she heard Con's voice say, "You're getting pretty good at that."

She turned to look at him, and it all came back to her: the woman, the child, the dagger in its belly. "My father asked you to look out for me," she said.

He was taken aback by the sharpness in her tone. "Yes. And your mother. And your brothers."

"They think I'm incapable of taking care of myself," she said bitterly. "They must think I'm a child." Her arms burned from holding the string taut, and the bow that had felt so light moments before now became heavy in her hands.

He frowned, shaking his head. "That's not it. They want you to be safe."

She looked down at the ground. The numbness inside her was being pushed away by hot emotion: resentment at her father, a sudden ache for her family—she missed them, she realized. There was a sludgy black sadness at the bottom of it all. She yearned for the clarity, the nothingness that had flooded her when she was shooting. She tried to draw some memory of that into her now, to smooth away the rawness. She remembered the creature's human mother. She asked: "What happened to the mother?"

"I brought her back with me. She inside. She's—she's had a shock." When Kaede only stared morosely at the arrow clutched in her hand, he said, "Come inside and eat some breakfast."

She nodded. There was an emptiness inside her, but she did not think it was due to hunger.

Chapter XIII

veryone told Kaede that she had done the right thing, but she felt hollow inside. When Fin had given her that dagger, it had been like a toy to her. Now she knew what a weapon was.

Two days after leaving Ento, the road narrowed and became packed dirt instead of paving stones. They had reached the end of most of the farmland, and now low hills began to rise in the distance. They were far from Cathair, and yet they still had more than a week of travel before they would reach Jilin and the Great Wood. Kaede felt the lack of sun with a brutal sense of futility: The whole world was gray, colorless. Her fingers were cold where they gripped the reins, and though she rode beside Con, who had been trying all morning to engage her in conversation, she felt alone. She knew he meant well, but he had no idea what she was going through. In the distance the road curved around a hill, and she was overcome by the desire to run, to leave them all behind.

She leaned over the neck of her horse and urged her into

a gallop, pushing past Shae and Pol. She heard them calling after her, but she didn't answer. On the left the road sloped down toward the river Nir; on the right it curved up a brown hillside. She caught sight of a lone tree at the top, stripped bare of its leaves, and then she was rounding the hill and there was only more road.

She loved the whip of the wind in her face. It was cool and faintly wet. She remembered the first time she had ridden a galloping horse: She had been a child, barely eight or nine, trying to keep up with her older brothers. They were at a family friend's country home, and her brothers had taken their host's horses out for a run in the morning. Her mother had told her she was too young to go with them, but she hated being left behind. She had sneaked down to the stables and taken out a fat little pony and somehow forced him into a gallop, chasing those boys down to the riverbank. When she arrived, flushed and proud of herself, only their host's son was surprised; her brothers laughed and chided her for taking so long.

Now she let her horse gallop at full speed until she felt her begin to tire, and then she gently slowed her down to a walk. When the road curved close to the river, she turned Maila toward the water, leaning back in the saddle as they went downhill the short distance. She dismounted at the riverbank and watched as Maila lowered her head to the water. The Nir was wide and deep here, sliding with a dim roar south toward Cathair. At this time of year, it should have been full of fishing vessels and ships carrying goods from the north—woolens, lumber, stone from mountain quarries. But the river was empty. Not even a waterbird floated on its surface. Trade had halted last fall when the storms began, and business had not returned to normal. The empty river should have been a peaceful sight, but instead it drove home something that Kaede hadn't fully understood until now: The Kingdom would die if the seasons did not change.

She sucked her breath in sharply. This was why she was here, standing on the banks of the Nir so far from the protection of the Academy walls and her family's influence. She was here because the Council of Sages believed the Fairy Queen knew something about why their kingdom was turning into a wasteland—a place where crops spoiled overnight, where farmers couldn't replant because there was no sunlight. Where monsters crawled out of their dark places and were found dead in northern villages, or were somehow reborn in the soft little bodies of human babies. She was here because the oracle stones said she was part of this journey to discover what the Fairy Queen knew. Did that mean that what she had done in Ento was meant to be?

Behind her she heard a horse on the road. When it began to descend the hillside to join her, she turned to see that the rider was Shae.

"Did they send you to bring me back?" Kaede asked.

"No." Shae dismounted and came to stand beside her. "To keep you safe."

"Safe. I don't think we've been safe for a long time."

"Does that worry you?"

"Should it?"

Shae shrugged. "I don't believe in worrying. It's a waste of energy."

They stood for a while in silence, gazing out over the river. Dried grasses rustled as a wind gusted down the barren slope, raising several strands of Kaede's hair. She tucked the ends behind her ears and looked at Shae, whose face was open, waiting. "Shae," Kaede said, and she felt the words come tumbling out of her: "When I chose to come on this journey, I thought—I thought it was going to be an adventure." Kaede grimaced at her own foolishness, but Shae gave her an encouraging smile.

"I like a good adventure myself," Shae said. "Why else do you think I wanted to join the King's Guard? I needed a living, yes, but I could have done something less...life-threatening. Some of us need adventures."

"But in Ento—" Kaede stopped, rubbed her hands over her face as though she could wipe the memory away. "It's not an adventure anymore. If it ever was."

Shae reached out and squeezed Kaede's shoulder. Several heartbeats later, she bent down, pulled up a dry stalk of grass, and began to shred it with her fingers. "I killed someone once," she said in a low voice.

"As a guard?"

"Yes. It was in one of the southern provinces, my first year as a member of the King's Guard. There was trouble at a border village, and I was sent with a contingent of guards to...to quell the resistance." Though her tone was calm, there was an undercurrent of tension in her words. It was clear that the memory was not an easy one. "At first it seemed as though the villagers would comply with our orders. Everyone was obeying. But then several men attacked us just as we were preparing to depart, and there was a—a scuffle. It turned out later they were sent by a neighboring lord to protect his stores, and they had been given the order to keep us out of the village for fear that we would take his grain." She paused, and plucked another long brown blade of grass from the ground. "Grain was never on our list."

"What were you sent to do?"

"We were supposed to make sure that the people of that village accepted the lord whom King Cai had instated as governor of that province. Because they were complying, there was no need to use force."

"But you did."

"Ultimately, yes. The men who attacked us were well armed and strong, and they took one of our guards quickly. I saw him beheaded not a foot in front of me. That's not a sight I'll ever forget." Shae let go of the torn shreds of grass. They fluttered out over the hillside like dandelion blossoms on the wind. "After that, the men who attacked us smelled a potential victory, and they—they charged us. I reacted before I could think." Her eyes were fixed on the distance as though she were seeing that day again. "One of them came at me, and all I knew was that if I did not kill him first, he was going to kill me. So I did."

"You were defending yourself."

"Does that make it all right?" They looked at each other, and the guard's dark brown eyes were troubled. "I knew that to be one of the King's Guard meant that I might have to kill. But I wasn't prepared for it when it happened. I wasn't prepared for the way it changed me. It was weeks before I could talk about it, though all my fellow guards praised me for what I had done. On the battlefield, they said, there is no time for anything but instinct. And yet, I can't help but wonder if perhaps our instincts are sometimes wrong."

"Do you regret it?"

Shae sighed and looked away. "How can I regret what I did, when it kept me alive?"

Chapter XIV

hat night, they camped on the side of the road for the first time. There would be no hostel for another two days' journey. Taisin and Shae tended to the horses as usual, rubbing them down and feeding them. Taisin enjoyed the work; it reminded her of home. When she was a little girl, her father had given her the task of brushing down the farm horses at the end of the day, and she had loved being in the barn at twilight, the smell of hay and horses all around her. Those were things she had truly missed at the Academy: the warmth of animals, and the simple honesty of their energies.

Focused on the horses, the feel of their muscles beneath her hands, she was startled when Kaede appeared by her side, a cup of tea in her hand. "Tali says supper will be ready soon," Kaede said, offering her the warm drink. Kaede seemed more relaxed now than she had been earlier in the day; Taisin wondered what had soothed her.

"Thank you," Taisin said. She began to tuck the brush under her arm, but then Kaede held out her hand.

"I'll trade you," Kaede said, smiling.

The smile made Taisin's cheeks burn. She was glad it was dark. "All right." She handed the brush over in exchange for the tea. It smelled of barley, nutty and hot, and it tasted wonderful.

"It's the last of it. I didn't want you to miss out." Kaede tilted her head briefly at the campfire, where Con and Pol were sitting on their bedrolls, joking with Tali as he prepared whatever concoction they would be eating tonight.

"What about Shae?" Taisin looked at the guard, who was working on the wagon horses several feet away.

"I already brought her a cup."

"Oh." Taisin raised the tea to her lips again, the steam wafting into her eyes. It reminded her of wintry nights at the Academy, curled up in her tiny room with her bed strewn with books. She felt a deep tug of homesickness inside her.

"I wanted to tell you something."

"You did?" Taisin's stomach fluttered. She often felt nervous around Kaede. It frustrated her, but she didn't know what to do about it. She was doing everything she could, she told herself, to avoid the fate in her vision—but she was afraid she was losing that battle.

"Yes." Kaede took a deep breath, steeling herself. "I didn't really understand, until today, even, what was at stake on this journey. Now I do. You were right, in Ento— we need to know what we're dealing with, or as much as we can know. So I have to ask you: What did you see in your vision, Taisin? You haven't told me—not exactly. But the way you look at me sometimes, I have to know: What did you see me doing?"

Taisin clutched the battered metal teacup with both hands and swallowed. All she could think was that Kaede had caught her staring at her. She was mortified that she had been so obvious; she was terrified that she would have to tell her the whole truth.

Kaede saw Taisin's distress. Even in the dark, the way her shoulders had stiffened betrayed her. "Is it so bad?" Kaede's own anxiety began to rise. "What did you see me do?"

Taisin shook her head swiftly. "No—no, it's not anything—you didn't do anything awful. That's not what I saw."

"Please. Please just tell me."

She knew she had to tell her something. "I saw you—and I—we were on a beach. An icy beach." Her voice shook a little, remembering. "You stepped into a rowboat, and you rowed away. I saw you leaving." She stopped, hoping that Kaede would ask for nothing more.

"A rowboat?" Kaede was puzzled. "And I was leaving? That's all?"

"Yes," Taisin said, and pressed her lips together.

As Kaede mulled over her words, Taisin saw that she didn't seem to realize that anything had been held back. But why should she? Taisin knew she had done her best to keep her emotions hidden. She had even tried to keep them hidden from herself, though it was becoming increasingly difficult.

Kaede asked, "Where is this beach?"

Taisin was startled. It had never occurred to her to won-der about that at all. "I don't know. I just saw it. It's part of this journey—that's all I know."

They heard Tali calling to them; supper was ready.

"You go ahead," Taisin said, taking the opportunity to change the subject. "I'll be there in a minute. I just want to put away the brushes." She held her hand out for the brush Kaede had taken from her, and for a moment Kaede didn't seem to want to give it to her. She was looking at Taisin closely, searching her face. Taisin tried to school her expres-sion into one of calm blankness; she had the irrational fear that Kaede could see right through her.

But Kaede only said, "All right," and handed over the brush. "Don't be long. The food will get cold."

Taisin clutched the brush with one hand, the teacup with the other, and told herself that she shouldn't be so silly. It was dark, and besides, Kaede couldn't read her mind.

❧

Around the campfire that night, they told stories. What had happened in Ento had left them all unsettled, and tale-telling was a welcome distraction. Con, it seemed, had heard every story ever told, and he regaled them with the legend-ary exploits of King Rin Tai, who traveled to the clouded mountain to face the sinuous green dragon who had terror-ized the people of six provinces.

"And when he returned, I suppose he married the most beautiful highborn lady in the land and had a dozen chil-dren," Shae said drily.

Con shrugged. "You object to a happy ending?"

Shae leaned forward, poking at the fire with a stick. The flames roared. "I'd like to hear a tale about an ordinary person for once. Not all of us are born princes." She softened the sharpness of her words with a smile, but Con was chagrined.

Tali laughed. "She has a point. Do you have a story in your head for us common folk?"

"Is that a challenge?" Con asked.

"Yes," Tali said. "A challenge."

"All right, then." Con flexed his fingers and thought for a moment. "Have you heard the tale of Farin and Anmin?"

Taisin smiled. "I have."

"Good. Then you can correct me if I get it wrong. Farin was a blacksmith—a noble enough profession, to be sure, but one that kept him hard at work day and night. His village was located near the King's Highway, and his smithy was adjacent to the town's best inn, which was always busy with travelers. One autumn, a wealthy merchant and his family were passing through Farin's village and boarded at the inn. The merchant had a daughter, whose name was Anmin. She, they say, was as beautiful as a spring morning."

Tali whistled. "I haven't seen one of those in a while."

Con gave him a stern look. "Anmin, as I was saying, was a beautiful girl. Her father had aspirations for her. He was a merchant, but he hoped to marry her to a wealthy lord and thereby increase his standing in the court."

"Here come the nobles," Shae said.

"Wait until you hear the whole story," Con objected. "Anmin was more than beautiful; she was also intelligent, and she knew what her father's plans were. But she had other goals in life. She had heard from her father that there were other lands across the sea, and she wanted to explore them. She knew that to become an explorer she would have to learn how to ride and defend herself—talents that no lord's wife needed—so every chance she had, she would practice swordplay or horsemanship. One afternoon while she was in the village, she discovered that her sword had a knick in it, and she decided to bring it to the blacksmith nearby. When she and Farin saw each other, they knew immediately that they had found their one true love."

"How did they know?" Shae asked. "Sparks flew from the anvil?"

Con grinned at her. "Don't you have any faith in the power of love?"

"Do you, Prince Con?" she teased him, and the tone in her voice made a tingle run through him. She was watching him with her head half-cocked, and he noticed a sly smile turning up the corners of her mouth.

He responded, "You're avoiding the question." The expression on Shae's face changed just slightly—he wondered if it was self-consciousness—and she ducked her head and poked at the fire again.

"Tell the story, Con," she said lightly, but she avoided his gaze.

"As you wish," he said, feeling a little surge of anticipation. Shae had always been friendly with him, never anything more or less, and for the first time Con became aware that he might like it if there was something more. While she prodded at the burning coals, he continued: "As I was saying, when Farin and Anmin first saw each other, they fell in love. They resolved to marry as soon as possible, but when Anmin told her father of her intentions, he flew into a rage and told her he had already arranged her marriage to the King's nephew. When she saw that he had no intention of backing down, she decided to elope with the blacksmith. However, the following morning, she awoke to discover that her father had been robbed during the night. All of the goods he had been transporting to Cathair had been stolen, and because soot had been found in the room where the goods had been stored, her father believed that Farin was the thief.

"Farin was brought to the village magistrate, who listened to the merchant's suspicions and found Farin guilty. But Farin insisted he was no thief, and he also knew that the magistrate could be easily bribed. With Anmin's help, Farin appealed to the provincial magistrate, who also sided with the merchant. Farin was about to be thrown into prison when the King's Magistrate agreed to hear his case—thanks to Anmin's hard work—and Farin was so convincing that the King's Magistrate told him that if he could face the judgment of the unicorn and survive, then he would be set free. Of course, if the unicorn found him guilty, he would be gored by the beast and die."

"No one ever survives the judgment of the unicorn," Pol said. "We are all guilty of something; the unicorn never finds anyone innocent."

"In some of the tales they survive," Taisin put in.

"Really? Which ones?" Pol asked.

"Hang on," Con said. "Let me finish this tale first. So: Farin was taken into the Wood to seek out the unicorn."

"In the version I heard, the unicorns were kept in a special enclosure at the palace," Taisin said.

Con blinked. "An enclosure?"

"Yes. There was an enclosure, adjacent to the King's Magistrate's office," she said. "The accused would be brought there and judged."

"I can't imagine the creatures would submit to being enclosed," Pol said.

"Because you've seen them before?" Tali said skeptically.

"No, but they're not horses to be trained. You might as well keep a phoenix as a songbird."

"I'm sure that's been attempted by some king or another," Shae said. "Con, please continue."

When she spoke his name her eyes flickered to him, and warmth spread over his skin. He swallowed. "All right. So, Farin was taken to the unicorn to face his judgment. Of course, Farin was innocent, but his heart was so pure and his love for Anmin so true that the unicorn not only let him live, he showed him who the real thief was: Anmin's own father, who had sought to incriminate the blacksmith to prevent him from marrying his daughter. When Farin returned to his village, he immediately told the merchant that he knew his secret, and he threatened to tell Anmin as well. But the merchant knew that if his daughter found out, she would never again acknowledge him as her father. Faced with the loss of his only daughter, he agreed to drop his accusations, and Farin and Anmin were soon married. Afterward, they both became explorers and lived long and happy lives."

Tali clapped, and the others laughed and joined in. Shae said, "That is a sweet tale, Con. But what's the moral of the story?" She watched him, her face half in shadow.

"Magistrates are generally corrupt," Pol quipped.

"Fathers shouldn't attempt to marry their daughters off to noblemen when there's a handsome blacksmith nearby," Kaede said, pulling a face.

Con smiled. "Those are a couple of ways to think about it." He looked at Shae as he said, "Or, perhaps the lesson is that true love will always prevail."

"How romantic of you," Shae said, and she might have meant for her words to sound wry, but Con heard a thread of wistfulness in her voice.

"I think it's true," he said. "Love knows no limits; it sees no distinctions based on birth or any other characteristic. A prince may love a seamstress as much as any princess."

"But would the seamstress be allowed to love the prince?" Shae asked.

"Love will always prevail," Con said. He thought he saw the hint of a blush on her face, though he couldn't be sure, for she stirred the embers in the campfire again, and the light flared reddish-gold over her skin.

❧

They sat up late telling stories, and by the time Taisin rolled into her blankets by the fire, she was so tired she fell asleep immediately. She didn't know how much later the vision came, but when it began, she could still feel the hard ground beneath her body, softened only slightly by the blankets she had folded into a thin pallet. But she could also feel the cold breath of winter on her face, and she could see the fortress of ice again. This time, she had left the beach behind entirely; she was floating, hovering up high, ascending toward the glass windows set into thick, frozen walls. She had never known that ice could take on so many shades of blue: sharp lines of indigo like the deepest sea, aquamarine shadows, even the glint of blue-green where the sun struck just so.

For the first time, she realized the significance of that. The sun shone here. Wherever *here* was, it was not locked in the unchanging clouded gray that blanketed the Kingdom. She wanted to look up at the sky, to gaze into the sun's brilliant white-gold eye, but she had no control over her movements, and she had arrived at one of the windows. The glass was like a mirror reflecting the light, and what she saw in the window made her jerk in surprise. A tiny person was hovering there on little feathered wings, like a hummingbird, and Taisin heard the creature speaking some kind of language she did not understand.

A moment later the window opened, and the creature fluttered inside. Taisin was pulled along with her, as if riding in the draft of her wings. The creature flew so quickly that all Taisin could do was follow. She only caught glimpses of what passed: walls of white, glacial floors, and every once in a while, a torch burning with a cold blue flame. She became aware, slowly, that the flying creature's heart was beating as quickly as a tiny war drum, urgent with some kind of duty. And then all of a sudden the way opened wide, and Taisin now understood that they had been flying down a corridor and had just emerged into a great, echoing space. She heard more sounds like the words that the winged creature had spoken. She could not make out the distinct syllables, but they made her heart ache, for they were all sounds of yearning—each being who cried out was crying out for freedom.

Taisin saw the creature's bright orange and emerald wings flutter as she twisted in midair to look down, and Taisin reeled at the sight below her. There were cages, hundreds of them, stacked like crates. She saw golden bars; she saw eyes of different colors peering up at her. The voices she had heard came from within those cages.

The flying creature turned to look back, but she did not seem to see Taisin. She had a tiny, delicate, girl's face, and she wore an expression of dread. Her glittering golden eyes widened with alarm, and then Taisin was thrust out of the vision as though someone had pushed her aside, and she was lying on her back on the hard ground beside a fire that sent golden sparks up into the black night sky. She saw Pol sitting up nearby; he had taken the second watch that night.

Her breath came as quick as that creature's wings had been beating. She knew she had been close to seeing something important. What had pushed her aside? Who was trapped in those cages? The memory of the imprisoned voices made her shiver. Who, she wondered, was their jailer?

PART III

Dragons battle on the plain:
Yellow and black blood spills.
Where frost is underfoot,
Ice cannot be far.

—Book of Changes

Chapter XV

heir first glimpse of the Great Wood came nearly three weeks after leaving Cathair. It was a dark smudge against the distant hills that blinked in and out of sight as the road curved. And then one afternoon as they rounded another bend, there it was, spreading its fingers out into the valley below, brushing up close to the river, extending to the horizon in waves of brown and green. Kaede had never before seen so many trees.

They camped within a copse of oaks that night. The weather had turned the leaves brown, even though it was midsummer, and a cold wind gusted through the gnarled branches, making the dried leaves rattle.

"We should get to Jilin sometime tomorrow," Shae said, squatting down to warm her hands at the fire while Tali cooked the rice. "Hopefully before dark."

"When was the last time you were there?" Con asked, sitting down beside her.

"Two years, one month ago," Shae answered. "It's been too long."

Shae's eagerness to reach Jilin caused them to push the horses hard the next day. The road took them through the outer reaches of the Great Wood, winding through clumps of oaks and bay trees. As dusk fell, shadows deepened beneath the branches. The road widened ahead, but the murky twilight made it difficult to see.

Shae, who was riding in the lead, called them to a halt. "Something's wrong," she said in a low voice. Beside her, Tali drew his sword.

Kaede felt a prickle of apprehension run down the back of her neck. It was too quiet; they couldn't even hear the sound of insects.

Suddenly a torch flared twenty feet ahead of them, and behind that torch, a half-dozen more burned into life. In the smoky light, Kaede saw men and women approaching with weapons in their hands; some held swords, while others carried long wooden staffs or axes. Fear raced through her. She heard the loud, ringing scrape as Con drew his sword, and she reached for her own iron dagger.

A man stepped out of the crowd of torchbearers, his black beard obscuring half his face, his eyes glittering in the torchlight. "Who goes there?" he called out in a harsh voice.

Shae had drawn her sword as well, and Tali and Pol flanked her. "Noa, is that you?" Shae called out. "What is going on? It's me, Shae."

The bearded man took a step forward, but he still brandished his sword before him. "Shae? Niran's sister?"

"Yes! Don't you recognize me?" She dismounted and sheathed her sword, approaching him with her hands outstretched. "Noa, I'm back. It's me."

For a long, tense moment, Kaede was sure the man was going to deny that he had any idea who Shae was and strike her down, but then he lowered his sword and closed the gap between them, crushing Shae into an embrace. "Shae," he said, his voice heavy with relief. "Why didn't you send word in advance?"

The other torchbearers gathered around Noa and Shae, their voices rising as they pelted Shae with questions about why she was back. She answered with rising concern in her voice: "I will tell you all—I will tell you everything, but where is Niran? Where is my brother? Why isn't he with you?" The crowd fell silent, and Shae turned to Noa and demanded, "Tell me, Noa. What has happened?"

"Your brother, Niran, is fine," he said, but his tone suggested that he was holding something back.

"Noa," Shae said. "What do you mean?"

"I'll take you to him. He's fine," Noa said again.

"Now," Shae said firmly, and Noa nodded.

೧

The village of Jilin was surrounded by trees, and trees marched down Jilin's few streets. The buildings seemed to have been situated to make room for giant trunks and root systems, and in the wavering torchlight, they looked almost as if they had grown out of the trees themselves.

Noa led them to a massive oak outside a long dark

building and said, "You should leave your horses here. It'll be easier."

Shae knew the village of Jilin intimately, and she knew immediately that Noa was not taking her to her brother's home. "Where are we going?" she asked him.

"Into the Wood." Most of the other villagers had returned to their homes, but two remained behind, carrying torches. "Let's go," Noa said, and struck off down a small trail.

In the daylight, the path would have been an easy walk, but in the dusk—brightened only by the flickering torches— it was an obstacle course. Even Tali tripped once, cursing under his breath. Kaede kept her eyes on Noa's torch ahead, trying to ignore the strange sensation that there was something out in the dark, watching her. It made the hairs on her neck stand on end, but she told herself she was imagining things.

After they had walked for about a quarter of an hour, Noa paused and called out, "Niran!"

Moments later a man came running down the path; behind him someone followed more slowly, bearing a torch. "Shae?" the man cried. "Is that you?" Niran was a tall man with a closely cropped black beard; his hands and face were streaked with dirt, but it could not disguise his surprise and joy at seeing Shae. He crushed her in an embrace, asking, "What are you doing here? Why didn't you tell us you were coming?"

"I'll tell you everything later," Shae said. "But why are you out here? What's going on?"

"We've found something," Niran said.

The torchbearer who had followed Niran came forward;

she was a woman, her black hair hanging in a long braid over her shoulder. "Shae?"

"Parsa," Shae said, and threw her arms around her brother's wife. When they parted, Shae asked, "What have you found?"

"Come and see for yourself," Niran said, and stood aside. There was a clearing just past him, and a long rectangular hole gaped open in the ground. Shovels were leaning against a nearby pine tree, and Kaede realized that she was looking at a grave. A chill ran through her. Beside the grave was a shape wrapped in a sheet. A body.

Niran bent down and pulled back the sheet. They saw the corpse of an inhuman creature, its arms wrapped around bended knees, its head lolling sideways onto the ground. It had long hair that resembled hundreds of tiny vines, some of them smashed and brown. The eyes had been covered by a torn piece of cloth, like a blindfold, and the mouth was stuffed with a black stone. From its fingertips, nails like long green blades of grass extended, curling over mottled, barklike skin. They were the only living things on the creature: It was as if the grasslike nails had sprouted out of a seed and were determined to make a new life out of what had already expired.

Taisin edged past Niran to take a closer look, curiosity vying with aversion. She wondered if it was some kind of fay. There were fay races other than the Xi—she thought the winged girl she saw in her vision must be fay—but she knew little about them. This one looked like it could have grown from a tree. She asked, "When did you find it?"

"Yesterday morning," Niran said.

"Did you place the stone in its mouth?" Taisin asked. It was traditional to put a stone in the mouth of a person who had been murdered, to prevent him from speaking to the living if he returned as a ghost.

"I did," Parsa said. "It is marked with the sign for peaceful rest."

Taisin couldn't see the mark; the stone was wedged in too deeply. The creature's lips were cracked and dry, reminding her of parched earth after a drought. "You were going to bury it?"

"Yes," Niran said.

"It should—it would be better if it were burned," Taisin said.

"We can't burn it," Niran objected. "We would set the Wood on fire."

"And we won't carry it into Jilin; it is polluted with death," Parsa said. Her eyes narrowed on Taisin. "Who are you? What would you know about this?"

Taisin shrank back, feeling stung. Shae said quickly, "We're here for a reason. I didn't send word because, well, our reasons mustn't become widely known. But I will tell you the truth." She glanced uneasily from the body to Taisin. "First, though, I think we should finish what you have started here."

Shae's brother looked them over skeptically, but he nodded. "All right."

He bent down to pull the shroud over the face of the dead creature again. Taisin said nothing. She hoped that the stone and the blindfold would do their jobs and take the place of a funeral pyre. She told herself that if the ghost of

126

the creature could not speak or see, then no real harm could be done. But still, she was uneasy. She had no idea if those traditions would work on something so clearly inhuman. She wanted to know more about it: How had it died? And where had it come from?

Niran and Parsa picked up their shovels, levered them under the body, and tipped it over the edge of the grave, where it fell with a dull thump. Taisin flinched. Beneath her breath, she muttered a blessing ritual meant to keep a body in its grave.

Niran, like his father and grandfather before him, was a blacksmith, and his family's home had been built adjacent to the smithy over the course of many generations. Kaede had the impression that additional wings had been added at random, creating a maze of connecting rooms that opened here and there into sky wells and broader courtyards. Niran led them through the main gate and past the smithy, the forge still smoldering, and then into the main hall, next to a kitchen where a fire burned in an open pit.

Shae's older sister, Raesa, who had heard news of Shae's arrival, greeted them warmly. "The children are asleep," she said. "You must come and eat."

Raesa's husband, Tulan, had brought back two hares from his traps that afternoon, and the rich fragrance of braised meat made Kaede's mouth water. They gathered together in the hall, sitting around two square tables pushed together, and ate salty flat bread and rabbit stewed with aromatic spices. A brown-and-black hound nosed his way around their feet, sniffing for fallen scraps. Raesa poured them hot, bitter tea in small earthenware cups, and Shae told her brother and sister why she had brought five strangers with her to Jilin.

"Please, don't tell anyone else what I've told you," Shae said when she finished.

Niran nodded, and glanced around the table at her companions. "How long do you plan to stay?"

"Not long," Tali answered. "I'm sorry."

"Stay through tomorrow," Parsa insisted. "You have to at least give us time to welcome you back."

"All right," Shae assented with a smile. "As long as nobody else objects."

"I'm happy to have a roof over my head for one more night," Con said, and no one disagreed with him.

"You're traveling into the Wood?" Raesa asked.

"Yes," Tali said. "We're headed north of the river Kell."

Raesa glanced at her husband, who had been mostly silent. But now he said, "When I was a boy, my uncle said he traveled that far, but when he returned there was something off about him. I never could get the whole story out of him."

Tali had brought their map case inside, and now he opened it, pushing aside empty bowls to unroll a map of the Wood onto the table. Kaede scooted her chair closer, wanting to get a better look. Tali had never shared them with her, though she had heard him discussing their route with Pol and Shae. Jilin was clearly noted on the map, and trails splintered off from the village and led into the Wood. Some of them ended abruptly only a few miles in; the longest followed the river Nir north, and then ended just south of where the Nir intersected with the Kell, which flowed east. Above the Kell, the Great Wood continued unabated to the northernmost edge of the map, which was marked with mountains: the Northerness. Tali looked at Tulan and asked, "Is there a way to cross the Kell? A bridge? It is unmarked."

Tulan leaned over the map to examine it, but he shook his head. "Not that I've heard of. I suppose there are stories of folks who have crossed the Kell."

"Where did they cross it?" Tali asked.

"They're stories, not directions," he said mildly.

Tali seemed disappointed.

"I think this map is as good as you're going to get," Tulan said. "It's accurate enough around here. I don't know about the northern part; I imagine that's all a guessing game."

"So how would you advise that we find our way to the Kell?" Shae asked.

"Follow the Nir. I'm fairly certain it does meet the Kell. You'll find it that way. That's as best as I can tell you." Tulan frowned, tugging at his beard. "You're going off the map. No one knows what's up there."

Chapter XVI

They slept in their bedrolls on the floor of the main hall, pushing the table and chairs to one side, next to the family shrine, to make room. Kaede found the stone floor as comfortable as a feather bed after days of sleeping on lumpy ground, and she fell asleep so quickly she barely had time to enjoy the flatness beneath her back. She was awakened in the morning by the shrill voices of children—Shae's nieces and nephew—who ran into the room and pounced on Shae's sleeping form, startling a yelp out of her.

At breakfast, Raesa and Tulan announced that they were going hunting, for they planned a celebration that night and hoped to bring back a deer. Pol volunteered to go with them, and when he asked Kaede if she'd like to come along—"You should see the bow in its natural environment," he said—she was surprised but pleased, and said yes.

The hound, whose name was Ota, came with them, his ears perking forward as they left Jilin behind and entered the Wood. It was another cool morning, but the Wood held none of the menace it had the night before, and Kaede wondered if she had imagined the sensation of something watching her. Now there were only trees, their gray-brown trunks scaled with lichen, and every so often the sound of a squirrel or rabbit bounding through the underbrush. Raesa and Tulan, like Pol, had quivers strapped to their backs and hunting knives at their waists; they carried their bows and moved with a stealth that Kaede knew she could not match. Her footsteps sounded like a herd of giants compared to theirs, and she feared that Pol had been wrong to invite her. She didn't want to scare away their supper.

But as they walked, Tulan said to her, "Raesa is a much better shot than I. When we find the deer it would be best if she and Pol move downwind, and then you and I can nudge the deer toward them."

"So you'll take advantage of my clumsy footsteps," Kaede said, smiling.

"You'll get better," Raesa said.

Kaede tried to limit the noise she made. She set her feet down as lightly as she could, imagining that she was a cloud, a mist, snaking slowly but surely around the gnarled oak trees. The Wood smelled of damp things: rainwater soaking into fallen logs, softening the bark until it crumbled back into the ground. In the distance, she heard the caw of a crow, over and over.

It was nearly an hour before Ota scented the deer; when he did, his entire body pointed northwest, his legs quivering in excitement. They had long ago left the well-maintained paths behind and were now picking their way down a tiny deer trail. As soon as Ota gave the signal, Raesa and Pol melted into the trees, moving as quietly as they could to avoid startling the deer. Ota vanished after them, and Tulan and Kaede continued on. Soon afterward Kaede saw the flash of a white tail just off to her left. All her senses came alive, and a thrill rippled through her. It was awe-inspiring to be so near to this animal. And yet—her breath caught in her throat—they were going to kill him. Her knowledge of the buck's imminent death seemed to magnify everything: the beauty of the animal, the smell of the forest, the beating of her heart. Time seemed to slow down. The caw of the crow echoed through the trees like a bell.

Beside her, Tulan crept forward, and the deer began to back away from them. Kaede followed, her pulse racing, and they pushed the deer ahead for some time, always moving in the direction that Pol and Raesa had gone in. With every careful step, Kaede was aware that death was coming closer, and she began to wonder if the buck knew it, too.

And then an arrow struck the deer in his side, and he bolted.

Ota leapt after him, baying, his nose soon dropping to the ground to follow the scent of spilled blood. The deer had been wounded, but it would run in panic for some distance. They could only hope that the arrow had landed deep enough, or else it would be a long and potentially fruitless chase.

Pol and Raesa came out from their cover, and Tulan asked, "Who sent the arrow?"

"Raesa did," Pol said. "You're right—she's a good shot."

"Don't speak too soon," she cautioned him, and they began to follow Ota on a jagged path through the trees.

But they were lucky; the arrow had been true, and it was only another half mile before they found the deer collapsed on the ground, his flanks heaving. Tulan unsheathed his long hunting knife and went to the deer, and before Kaede could catch her breath, he slit the buck's throat.

Raesa held Ota back from the stream of blood while the deer died.

Kaede halted several feet away. The sight of the dying animal brought back the memory of the creature she had killed in Ento, and for a moment she thought her stomach would turn itself inside out. Cold sweat beaded her forehead. Pol saw the expression on her face and said, "The buck will feed many of us tonight, and more tomorrow. It was a necessary death."

She swallowed. She knew that Pol was right. But never had the word *necessary* seemed so cold.

They strapped the deer's legs to a long fallen branch and hoisted it up on their shoulders, each taking turns to bear the weight on the way back to Jilin. Ota ran between their legs excitedly; he had been given a piece of the warm liver, but he smelled the meat and was eager for more.

When they reached Niran's home, Kaede slipped away. She felt bruised somehow, as though someone had smashed a fist into an old wound, and she wanted to be alone. There was a garden behind the smithy, and when she saw the rows of low green shoots, a pang went through her as she remembered working with Maesie. There were some things she missed from the Academy: the sea, and Maesie and Fin, and her friends. Beyond the garden, a small path led into the Wood, weaving between bay trees. It was gloomy now, but seeing the way the branches arched overhead, Kaede suspected it would be beautiful beneath the sunlight. She imagined a green tunnel, the leaves whispering in a warm breeze. She ached for the warmth of summer. Though it was now nearly midsummer, it was still as cool as late winter.

The path ended in a small clearing with a stone bench. Opposite the bench was a statue that appeared to have been shaped out of the oak stump rooted there in the ground: a deer's head. She sat on the bench and stared at it, wondering who had made it, who had imbued such life into the way the ears tilted.

She heard the footsteps some time later, and glanced up to see Taisin coming down the path. She looked a bit nervous, and she held out something wrapped in a white cloth. "I brought you some bread," she said tentatively.

"Thank you," Kaede said. It was flat bread fresh from the pan, still warm.

Taisin sat on the far edge of the bench beside her. "They're eating, if you want to go back."

The flat bread was good, slightly charred and salty. "I'll go back in a little while," she said between bites.

"They're butchering the deer. I think that Parsa intends to invite all of Jilin here tonight." Taisin glanced sideways at Kaede. "How was the hunt?"

Kaede's fingers were smeared with salt and lightly greased

with oil from the bread. She wanted to lick them, but thought it might be impolite. She scrubbed them on the cloth and said, "It was successful. No help from me." She grinned, but there was no joy behind it. "I just followed."

Taisin could feel the forced cheer coming from Kaede, who regarded her with serious brown eyes, her mouth slowly turning down at the corners as the grin faded. Taisin asked, "Are you all right?"

The question caught Kaede off guard. "All right? I'm—" She hesitated, the words stuck in her throat, and she looked down at her hands, twisting the cloth into a knot. "I didn't like seeing the deer die," she said at last. "It is—I thought hunting would be…normal, somehow. But something has to die."

Taisin wasn't sure what to say. She thought about telling Kaede that she had seen her first pig butchered when she was a baby; that she had helped every autumn—until she went to the Academy—when her father harvested their meat for the winter. She could say that the deer had died so that they might live, or that its spirit had been released into the world and it would return, again and again, transformed each time into a different being. But it did not change the fact that death came and took things that were not yet ready to leave the world of the living.

She reached out and covered Kaede's hands with her own, and Kaede looked at her in surprise. Taisin felt Kaede's fingers loosen on the cloth; her hand turned upward into Taisin's. Their fingers interlaced. Taisin's heartbeat quickened; a flush crept across her neck. She saw, as if from a distance, that her feelings were changing whether she wanted them to or not. She sensed that she was about to tip over the edge, and at some point, she wouldn't care if she was doing the right thing anymore.

But today, she was still in control. She pulled her hand away, taking a quick, determined breath. "We should go back. I told Parsa I would help her."

Kaede nodded, seemingly unfazed. "Yes. Shae's family has been very kind to us." They stood, and Kaede pocketed the cloth. "I don't think we'll eat so well once we leave."

"We should enjoy it while we can," Taisin said, and immediately felt ridiculous trying to make small talk about surviving the next leg of their journey. But Kaede didn't seem to notice her discomfort. She had started back down the path and turned to wait for her. Kaede was always polite; she was the daughter of the King's Chancellor, after all. Taisin suddenly felt every inch the farmer's daughter—clumsy and foolish.

Taisin balled her hands into fists at her side and followed, keeping her eyes on the ground to avoid betraying her self-consciousness. The path was well maintained, though narrow; the dirt was hard packed in the center, and tufts of brown grasses grew along the edges. And then she saw something that made her stop and turn back. She knelt down on the trail. There was a limp flower bud there, tucked behind a clump of grass—the only splash of purple anywhere in sight. Normally at this time of year, the Wood should be dotted with them, and the sight of this solitary blossom was almost as saddening as it was miraculous.

"Look at that," Taisin whispered. Kaede turned to see what she had found.

Taisin stroked the flower with one finger and bent her

head down close to it, trying to breathe in the air around the tiny growing thing. For as long as she could remember, she had been sensitive to all the shifting meridians of energy around her, and her years at the Academy had sharpened and honed her awareness of them. The last two years, with their summer droughts and winter storms, and now the unending grayness, had been heartbreaking. Before, she had been able to sense the life all around her—in the waving sea grasses that grew on the beach below the Academy; in the oak trees that climbed so slowly toward the sky on her parents' farm. It had been a steady hum underlying everything; a feeling of constant renewal. But in the last two years, the hum had faded; the lines of energy had become increasingly sluggish. Even the plants in the ground seemed to have given up. It was like seeing all the color leeched out of the world bit by bit. So, given the faintest whiff of rebirth in the form of these wilted, half-opened petals, Taisin could not resist.

She cupped the flower in her hand and called to it, and as Kaede stood over her, watching, the flower grew plump; the stalk lifted itself from the earth as though sunlight poured from Taisin's breath into its green leaves. The petals opened one by one, each a perfect violet teardrop, and at the center, the flower's black eye gazed unblinkingly up at Taisin, whose face glowed with the energy unfurling through her.

Kaede could have chastised her, for their teachers at the Academy had taught them from day one that such a display of power was reckless. It was the equivalent of lighting a signal fire on the tallest mountain to announce one's presence during a war. But at the same time, Kaede understood why Taisin had done it, for it was written clear as day on her face: It made her whole.

Afterward, when Taisin was too weakened to walk back immediately, Kaede sat with her on the forest floor, watching as the purple flower, gloriously open to the air, bobbed in the wind.

～

That night it seemed as though everyone in Jilin stopped by Shae's family home. Parsa and Niran seared thin slices of venison and served it with onions cooked until they were sweet. Other villagers brought more of the flat bread, some stuffed with pickled greens or mushrooms culled from the Wood; and one family brought two jugs of home-brewed spirits. Kaede avoided them, for the fumes alone made her eyes water. There was no talk of bad harvests or strange creatures; it was as if everyone had tacitly agreed to pretend that nothing was wrong, and the only thing on their minds was celebrating Shae's brief return home.

Kaede was grateful for the holiday feel; it drove away the shadows that had clung to her since Ento. She played a game of tacks with Shae's nephew; she joked with Tali about how much venison he could eat; she watched Con flirting shamelessly with Shae, who laughed at him and said loudly—so that everyone could hear—that he had no chance with her. But the way she turned her eyes back to him gave a different impression, and Kaede suddenly wondered whether there was something between them. The thought was surprising to her, but also a bit funny. Kaede simply couldn't imagine Shae in court dress at the palace with Con. She grinned to herself and glanced around the room, taking in Pol talking with Tulan, Parsa's two daughters racing out the door with rock sugar in their fists. Taisin was seated at the table chatting to Raesa, a smile on her face. The smile transformed her. Her cheeks were pink from the warmth of the room; her eyes were shining. She was a young woman still unaware of her own beauty, and Kaede could not look away.

Con pushed his way onto the bench beside Kaede and said, "She's lovely, isn't she?" He threw his arm around her shoulders with a brotherly squeeze.

"What?" she said, startled.

"Shae," he whispered in her ear. "Look at her!"

Kaede gave him a sidelong glance. "Are you being serious?"

"I'm always serious," he said, ruffling her hair. It had grown long enough now that she usually tied it back, but tonight she had had the opportunity to bathe, and it fell loose, still slightly damp, to her shoulders.

"Stop it," Kaede said, swatting his hands away and tucking the ends behind her ears. He reminded her of her brothers, and all of a sudden she missed them fiercely.

"Do you think I have a chance with her?" Con asked.

It took a moment for Kaede to remember what he was talking about: Shae. She tried to swallow her homesickness and said with forced lightness, "You have every advantage. Who wouldn't fall in love with you?"

His eyes sparkled as he gave her a mischievous grin. "Do

I detect a hint of jealousy? Are you going to fight me for Shae's love?"

Kaede gaped at him. "Now you truly must be joking. Why would I do that?"

"You don't want her for yourself?" He elbowed her. "I know you enjoy her company."

Kaede shook her head. "I take it back," she said, laughing. "You're too much of a fool—Shae will never love you."

He pulled an exaggerated frown. "You wound me, Kaede. Your brothers told me I could trust you—I shouldn't have believed them."

"That's good. I never believe them, either." They laughed together, and Kaede felt the tightness within her relaxing. She would see her brothers when she returned, she told herself.

Con's arm was still around her shoulders, and he whispered in her ear, "I saw you looking at Taisin. She's especially pretty tonight."

A flush spread over her face. "You must have been looking at her, too, then," she said, and Con raised his eyebrows at her in a sly smile.

She glanced away, her eyes seeking out Taisin almost automatically. Taisin was watching them, a thoughtful look on her face. When Kaede's gaze met hers, Taisin colored as though she had been caught stealing sweets. Kaede broke into a smile, and Taisin quickly turned away, ducking her head as if she wanted to hide. But scarcely a moment later she glanced back as though she couldn't help it, and Kaede felt a tremor inside herself as the blush on Taisin's cheeks deepened.

Con squeezed her shoulder. "I see I won't have to fight you for Shae," he said in an amused tone.

She gave him an exasperated look. "She's not going to fall in love with you if you stay here all night with *me*."

He grinned at her. "Good point." He stood up and straightened his tunic. "We must take advantage of tonight, for who knows what shall come tomorrow?"

Kaede watched him head toward Shae, but she did not make a move to go to Taisin. She finished her tea, one ear tuned to the conversations around her, occasionally glancing out of the corner of her eye at Taisin, who had pulled a little boy onto her lap to play a game of peekaboo with a red wooden ball. Kaede hadn't felt that tug toward another person in a long time. She certainly hadn't expected to feel it for Taisin, who was usually so distant and self-contained that any possibility of a deeper connection had seemed impossible from the beginning. But this afternoon, the sight of Taisin's face after she urged that flower to bloom— she had been luminous. It was as if a door had briefly opened, and behind it there was sunlight, warm and rich and seductive.

But Taisin was going to be a sage, and sages made vows of celibacy. Kaede had learned this in her earliest days at the Academy. Students were not permitted to form romantic attachments to each other—at least not officially, though Kaede had not been the only one to break the rules. But Taisin had always adhered to those guidelines. No one had even whispered about her in the dormitory.

Kaede told herself that what she felt was only a little seed; she would simply not water it. It wouldn't grow any larger than this tiny prickle of attraction. She wouldn't let it.

But that night after everyone had left, and they had all spread their blankets on the floor of the hall, Kaede lay awake for some time, trying to make out the sound of Taisin's breathing in the dark.

Chapter XVII

t began to rain scarcely an hour after they left Jilin. They pulled out their oilskin cloaks, but as the day wore on with no sign that it would let up, Kaede began to feel the wet weight of it like a burden on her back. That morning, Shae's family had seen them off with as much good cheer as they could muster, but it was obvious they had a difficult time fighting their fear that Shae would never return.

Niran had convinced Tali that their wagon would never make it through the narrow trails carved into the Wood, and he traded them two sturdy packhorses for the wagon itself. Pol and Taisin rode the two wagon horses, outfitted with saddles that Tali bought from one of Niran's neighbors. As they picked their way through the dim, drenched Wood, Kaede peered out from beneath the hood of her cloak at the surrounding trees. She felt, again, the eerie sensation of another presence. The farther they rode into the Wood, the more she noticed that there was a peculiar awareness to this place. The oaks might be half dead, but something else was distinctly alive out there.

When it began to grow dark, they set up camp just off the trail; downhill, the river Nir was pregnant with rain. Tali and Pol struggled to set up their tents in the downpour, staking them out between trees as best they could, while Shae and Con took the empty water skins down to the river to be filled. Taisin volunteered to search for bits of dry wood, and Pol called, "You'd better take Kaede with you." He stuck his head out from one of the half-constructed tents. "I don't have a good feeling about this place."

Even though the day had been one long, wet slog through an increasingly muddy forest, Kaede was absurdly pleased about the prospect of taking a walk through the Wood with Taisin. Taisin herself looked momentarily alarmed at the prospect of Kaede accompanying her, but the expression vanished almost instantly, making Kaede wonder if she had imagined it. As they struck off down the trail, Kaede glanced at Taisin, but Taisin kept her eyes to the ground, seeking out sheltered places that might have kept fallen wood dry.

They found a few branches here and there, and piled them into their arms beneath their oilskin cloaks. As Taisin pushed her way through thickets and into hollows, Kaede was surprised by her classmate's apparent disregard for mud. Taisin had always seemed so neat and orderly, not a hair out of place. Now she pushed back a stray lock with dirty fingers, leaving a dark streak on her face.

They came to a clump of hollyberry trees sheltered by a giant overhanging oak, and they bumped shoulders and hips as they reached for kindling beneath the brush. Taisin backed out a bit breathlessly. "You go first," she said, her face flushed. Kaede tried to stuff down the warmth that flared in her when Taisin's body had snaked past hers, and she began to haul out handfuls of twigs, handing them to Taisin.

When their arms were full, they headed back to the camp, and Kaede said with a grin, "You're covered in mud."

Taisin pointed out, "So are you."

Kaede glanced down at herself and laughed; the entire front of her, from her chest down to her knees, was smeared with dark brown. Taisin began to giggle, and then they were both bent over double, clutching the twigs and branches to their chests as they guffawed, their voices ringing in the twilight Wood. Kaede felt a little delirious; she was soaked through, muddy, and darkness was falling. The whole situation should be terrifying, but she felt a kind of helpless surrender to it. Here she was on this journey to a place that didn't exist on their maps, and all around unseen things seemed to stare out at them day and night. But there, not two feet away from her, was a girl who made her feel light-headed.

As their laughter faded they looked at each other, and there was an openness in Taisin's face—a kind of camaraderie—that Kaede had not seen before. It made her skin tingle. She did not think she was doing a good job of letting the seed die.

✺

The rain clung to them for several days. Sometimes there would be a break in the middle of the afternoon, or the rain would turn to mist for a while, but their belongings began to have an exasperating dampness that could not be burned off by their smoky campfire.

On the morning the rain finally stopped, they awoke to a world covered in fog so thick it was difficult to find one another in their small camp. It curled around the trees in ghostly white, seeping through their clothes and into their bones with its chill. But the fire burned hot that morning, and they drank their tea standing up, turning around slowly to warm their backsides. The fog clung to the river Nir all morning, making the trail difficult to see, and it did not burn off until afternoon. That evening, her teeth chattering from cold, Kaede stood so close to the campfire that when the wind gusted, it sent flames dangerously close to her face. She jumped back in alarm, and Tali laughed at her as he eased the iron kettle into the fire.

"Watch out," he warned her. "This wind is not like any I've encountered before. Sometimes it seems to have a mind of its own." The two of them had stayed to set up camp while the others went to gather more wood and refill their water skins.

Shae and Con returned from the river as Tali spoke, and Shae set her heavy water skin down on the ground and sighed, stretching her arms. "I'll take the wind over the rain any day—or night."

"At least the rain drowns out the sound of the wind," Tali said. "Sometimes I swear I hear it calling my name." He shuddered. "I don't like it."

Con looked at him curiously. "What do you mean? Are you hearing things, Tali?"

The guard squatted down and stirred the pot with a long-handled wooden spoon. "I must be. This Wood gets to me; I don't think it wants me here."

"Don't be ridiculous," Shae said. As if her words were an invitation to prove her wrong, the wind whipped around them, ruffling Shae's short hair and making the flames roar.

Kaede felt it like a silken scarf sliding quickly around her neck. She shivered.

Shae glanced at her sharply. "Did you feel something?"

Kaede put her hand to her throat, touching her skin with cold fingers. "I don't know. It was so fast."

They didn't notice, at first, that Tali had cocked his head a little, as if he were listening to someone whisper in his ear. His eyes were slightly glazed, and his entire body seemed pulled in a direction even he was not aware of.

"Tali!" Con called, alarmed.

Tali blinked and let go of the wooden spoon in surprise, and it fell into the fire. "Blast," he said, standing up. "I don't have another one."

"What did you just hear?" Kaede asked.

He looked confused. "Just now—did you hear it as well?"

"I don't know," Kaede said, disquieted. "I felt something, though." She looked at Shae and Con. "Did you hear anything?"

"No," Con answered.

Shae seemed worried. "Not really. The wind seemed a little...odd, but I don't know why."

Tali said grimly, "It's only talking to me, then."

"Who's talking to you?" Taisin asked. She was coming

back toward the fire, Pol following her. She dropped an armful of wood on the ground.

"The wind," Tali said. His broad shoulders were stiff with tension as he added, "The Wood itself."

Taisin's eyes widened. "You must not listen. Do you understand? Whatever you hear—whatever they tell you—you must not listen to them."

Tali was taken aback by her intensity. Pol, laying his firewood down, asked, "What's going on?"

Tali said gruffly, "We're just hearing noises in the dark."

Taisin's forehead wrinkled. "Has anyone else heard anything?"

They all looked at one another, anxious faces turned gold by the firelight. The black night beyond the camp had never felt so heavy; the branches of the trees leaned above them like ghosts. For a moment, the only sound was the crackle of the fire. The strange wind had left them.

Kaede finally said, "I felt something."

"What?"

"It—it felt like the wind was tightening around my neck."

Taisin stared at her, fear plain in her eyes. She turned to Tali. "Tell me what you heard."

"It wasn't speaking our language," Tali said, scrubbing a hand through his gray hair. "But it wanted—it wanted me to follow it." He had broken into a nervous sweat, and he wiped his forehead on his sleeve.

"You mustn't follow it," Taisin said.

He seemed a bit affronted. "Of course I'm not going to follow it."

"I just—I'm just trying to keep you safe," she stammered.

150

"Taisin," Con said, seeing the distress on her face, "have you felt something, too?"

"Yes," she said reluctantly. Whatever it was had been increasing in strength the deeper they traveled into the Wood. At first it had been merely a whisper, as if a feather were lightly brushing against her, but now it came more insistently, like a child pulling at her hand.

"What is it?" Tali asked.

Taisin hesitated. She hadn't known what to make of it in the beginning, for the Wood was full of energies she had never encountered before. It was difficult to separate out this presence from the others, but she was increasingly convinced that this spirit—if that is what it was—had a goal. It reminded her of something she had felt once, but the memory eluded her, like an itch in the middle of her back that she couldn't quite reach. It was irritating and frightening all at once, for she sensed that this presence was not benevolent.

She said carefully, "It is intelligent. There is a purpose to this creature—or this presence. I don't know what it is. But it seems…it wants something. It seems malicious."

"Is it the Xi?" Pol asked.

Taisin thought back to what Sister Ailan had told her and what she had read. It was so bizarre to apply those dry teachings to the eerie reality of this Wood. "Sister Ailan— my teacher—she always described the Xi to me as possessing a presence of great purity. Powerful, of course, but pure. Not hot or cold; not emotional; simply *there*. Pure. This presence that I feel is not pure. I don't think it is the Xi."

Tali asked, "What do you think it wants?"

"I don't know."

"How can we protect ourselves, then?" Con asked.

Taisin turned to Tali, expecting him to answer, but the guard was looking at her with a reluctant expression on his lined face. "Taisin, you know the most about this of any of us."

Taisin realized he was relying on her now, and she felt paralyzed. She hadn't even been marked yet. She might be the most gifted in her class, but she was still a student. All at once the gaps in her knowledge seemed too great, and a cloud of panic engulfed her. How could her teachers think she was ready for this? She was only a frightened schoolgirl. She felt faint, and pressed her fingers between her eyes. She took a deep breath, and another. She could not crumple into a puddle of fear—that was not why her teachers had believed in her.

"We must stay together," she said, her voice wavering at first. "If you hear anything speaking to you—in the wind, in your ear, whatever—just ignore it. And tell someone. Don't leave the camp alone." She looked over her shoulder at the dark. It was alive with energies she hadn't yet teased apart, but one of them was waiting and listening. Taisin turned back to the others. Her mouth was dry as she said, "Promise me. Don't leave the camp alone."

They all agreed, and their nodding shadows rippled across the trees.

❧

Wrapped in her bedroll that night, the chilly air seeping through the thin canvas walls of the tent, Kaede longed for the dry heat that used to bake the streets of Cathair in the summer. She dreamed of sunlight spreading like honey over her skin; she dreamed of sweat sliding down between her shoulder blades as she ran down sweltering alleyways behind the palace. She dreamed of Taisin, standing in the shade of a stone building at the end of a maze of narrow streets, a bouquet of flowers in her hands like the prize at the end of a race. But no matter how fast Kaede ran, she couldn't quite reach her. The muscles in her legs groaned with the effort; her lungs heaved; she woke with a jerk, gasping.

Beside her Shae shifted, turning her back to Kaede. It was the middle of the night. Kaede's heart was pounding, her skin flushed as if she had truly been running. She flung off her blanket, feeling overheated. What had awakened her? She wanted to go back into that dream world. She wanted to reach Taisin, take the flowers out of her hands, touch her. A wave of longing rushed through Kaede's body.

She turned over, looking past Shae toward Taisin. She could barely make out her silhouette in the dark, but she could hear her breathing. It was uneven. Was Taisin awake, too? The thought made Kaede's skin prickle all over with excitement. It seemed impossible that Taisin could sleep through this—every nerve in Kaede's body was screaming for her to notice—but there was no answering sound or movement from Taisin.

Kaede lay awake for some time. She was tense from her dream. She counted her breaths, attempting to make them regular. She lost count. She listened to the sound of wind in the trees, remembering Taisin's warnings, but she heard nothing out of the ordinary. She did not realize she had fallen asleep again until she was awakened by shouting outside. Someone was calling for Tali.

Shae scrambled up first, pushing aside the tent flap and stumbling into the dim morning, pulling on her boots as she went. "What is it?" Shae asked, and outside Con and Pol were standing, dazed, near the ashes of the fire.

"Tali is missing," Con said, panic thick in his voice. "When we woke up this morning, he was gone."

Chapter XVIII

It was Shae who found him. He was lying in a clearing barely fifty feet from their camp on the other side of the trail. Dried leaves encircled his body as if blown by a great whirlwind. He lay on his back, arms and legs spread-eagled, his face expressionless. A strange gray dust was trapped in his salt-and-pepper beard, and a thin white film had crawled over his open brown eyes. He was cold to the touch, and there was not a mark on him.

Con knelt on the ground next to Tali's body and lifted the older man's hand. His fingers were stiff. Con was stunned; he couldn't believe that Tali was dead. He had survived so many military campaigns; how could he have been taken so easily, so silently, by—Con didn't even know what had taken him. "Who—what did this?" he demanded.

All the color had drained from Taisin's face. She knelt beside Tali's head, stretching her hand out over his eyes. She felt nothing. There was no life energy left within him;

his body was only a shell now. And she did not know whether his soul had safely traveled to the other side. The thought chilled her to the bone, and she muttered to herself, "I should have done it."

Con looked at her. "You should have done what?"

Guilt washed over Taisin, hot and sour. "I could have—I should have done a protection ritual. Around the camp."

Con's mouth opened, but he couldn't speak. A torrent of emotion battered at him: disbelief, grief, anger. Was Taisin saying she could have prevented this? He felt like he had been punched in the gut, and he had trouble breathing.

Shae squatted down beside him and squeezed his shoulder. She asked in a carefully measured voice, "Why didn't you?"

Taisin gulped, her heart pounding. She said in a rush: "My teacher told me that I shouldn't use that ritual except as a last resort. I didn't know this could happen. I thought we would be safe enough if—if we didn't leave the camp." Tears pricked at the corners of her eyes, and she blinked them back fiercely.

"Can you do that ritual now?" Pol asked. He stood at Tali's feet, his arms crossed.

"I can do it tonight when we set up camp. I can't protect us as we are moving."

"Wait," Shae said, frowning. "Taisin, why did your teacher warn you about the protection ritual?"

Taisin drew in a trembling breath. "Because it—it might draw attention to us."

"What do you mean?" Pol asked.

"Weaving a protection ritual around our camp would...rearrange the natural meridians. Those who are sensitive to the lines of energy would—if they are near enough or powerful enough, they would notice."

"The creatures we've seen," Con interjected, struggling to make sense of what she was saying. "Can they sense these things?"

"I don't know. I suppose...it's possible."

Kaede understood, suddenly, the reason for the hesitation in Taisin's voice. "You think that by doing the protection ritual, you'll draw them to us."

Taisin met her eyes somberly. "It has occurred to me."

"But what's the alternative?" Con asked. "Tali was—" His voice broke, and Shae slid her arm around his shoulders. Con wiped away the tears that burned down his face. "Tali was stronger, I thought, than all of us. For this to happen to him...We can't let it happen again." He looked across Tali's still form at Taisin, and he noticed how young and vulnerable she looked today, with purple shadows beneath her eyes and her narrow shoulders slumping. He realized that he had been on the verge of blaming her for Tali's death, but he couldn't. She was only seventeen. She had done the best she could. He felt a yawning ache inside him as he said to her, "You have to do it tonight, Taisin. Whatever protection ritual you can. We'll deal with the consequences when they come."

Taisin's lips trembled, but she squared her shoulders. "All right. I will do it tonight. But first, we must leave this place. And we must bury Tali."

"Here?" Con said.

"No. This place is—it isn't right. We must take him with us, but we have to bury him before nightfall."

None of them disagreed. It was the worst kind of luck to leave a dead body in the open overnight—especially when the person died of unnatural causes. And though there were no signs of struggle on Tali's body, there was no doubt in any of their minds that his death had been far from natural.

❧

When they broke camp, they strapped Tali's body, shrouded in his woolen blanket, onto his horse. Tali had always ridden in the lead before, but today Shae took his position and his map case. Con followed her, leading Tali's horse, and Taisin and Kaede came after him. Pol went last as usual, keeping one hand on his sword.

As they rode, Taisin stared at Tali's body, hanging face-down over his horse's flanks. Part of her still couldn't quite grasp it. How could *Tali*, of all people, have been lured away so easily? He was so solid, so dependable. Why had the Wood—or whatever was in the Wood—chosen to take him? And if it could take him, what would it do to the rest of them? The questions made her increasingly nervous, and the queasiness in her stomach rose until she abruptly pulled her horse to a halt and dismounted, running off the trail to bend over, retching. Nothing came up, but she felt like she was turning inside out, and her throat burned.

A moment later she felt a hand on her back, and Kaede was leaning over her. "Are you all right?"

"I'm fine," she gasped.

"Here," Kaede said, handing her a water skin. Taisin tried to breathe more slowly. She was panicking. She knew she had to calm down. She heard Kaede saying to the others: "Just give us a minute."

Taisin straightened up, feeling woozy. Her face was flushed, and her hands shook as she raised the water skin to her lips. The liquid trickled into her mouth, and she swallowed carefully. "I'm sorry," she muttered.

Kaede shook her head. "There's nothing to be sorry about."

"Yes, there is. If I had done the protection ritual, Tali would still be here." Taisin spoke without thinking, and now that the words were out, she was both ashamed and relieved.

"You don't know that," Kaede objected.

Taisin turned to face her. The dull gray daylight carved deep shadows beneath Kaede's eyes and darkened the hollows in her cheeks. She didn't look like the same girl who had argued with the King's Chancellor in the Council room, demanding that she be given a choice. She looked bruised. She looked sad. "What are we going to do, Kaede?" Taisin whispered. "This wasn't supposed to happen. What if Maire Morighan was wrong? What if I can't do whatever it is I'm supposed to do? What if I don't know enough?"

Kaede heard defeat hovering at the edge of Taisin's words, and it tore at her. "You know enough," Kaede insisted. "The oracle stones would not have chosen you if you didn't know enough. And what's 'enough,' anyway? You don't know everything, but nobody can." She heard herself repeating what Fin had told her on the beach at the Academy: "All you can do is make your decisions based on what you know now."

"What I know now," Taisin repeated. What she knew now was that this journey was much more dangerous than she had anticipated. Perhaps she had not wanted to acknowledge that before. In Ento, she had called that creature out of the baby's body, but it was Kaede who had faced the consequences. Now Tali's death had driven home the fact that there was a malignant force out there, and she knew she had to open her eyes and look it in the face. It frightened her, but she had never fled from something because she was afraid. Going to the Academy alone when she was eleven, leaving her family behind, had terrified her. The vision of Kaede on the beach still scared her. But she knew what to do with fear: She fought it.

"You're right," Taisin said to Kaede. "Thank you."

Before she could doubt herself again, Taisin headed back to the trail, ignoring the panic that still churned in her stomach.

❧

Just before noon, they found a roughly rectangular clearing a few feet off the path, with soil that looked like it could be broken with their makeshift tools. Taisin fitted one of their few remaining candles into a lantern and lit it, setting it on the ground where the head of the grave would be. The light was meant to guide Tali's soul to the land of the dead. Usually sages did not perform funerary rites; that responsibility typically fell to village greenwitches or, in the cities, to specialists. But there were no specialists here. Everyone did their part.

Taisin helped Shae and Kaede dig the grave while Con and Pol wrestled with Tali's body, dressing him in his cleanest clothes. The mysterious nature of his death was unlucky enough, but it would be even worse for him to be buried in the clothes he was wearing when he died. They lugged water from the river and washed his hands, but they could not remove the dirt from beneath his nails. They sponged off his face and neck, closing his eyes and covering them with a blindfold torn from Tali's cloak. And then Taisin found a stone on the riverbank that had a particularly peaceful energy, and she handed it to Con.

"His death was not…natural," she said awkwardly. "It would be best to place this in his mouth."

He looked sick to his stomach, but he nodded. Tali's body had stiffened by now, and it was difficult to pry his jaw open. Con feared for one awful moment that he might have to break it, but then, at last, Tali's mouth opened just enough, and Con slid the stone between his cold lips.

Afterward, Con had to sit still, holding his head in his hands, trying not to throw up.

It was late afternoon by the time the pit was deep enough, and the light was becoming dim. Dirt smudged all of their faces where they had wiped away sweat that had risen while they dug. Tali's body had been wrapped into his blanket again—the closest they could come to a shroud—and Con and Pol rolled it as gently as they could into the grave. The candle flickered within the lantern as if a breath had blown against it.

Con sat back on his heels and looked at the rest of them. "It's time."

They each scraped up a handful of dirt and, beginning with Con, sprinkled it into the grave. The sound of dirt pattering onto Tali's body reminded Con of rain on the roofs of Cathair: hard and cold. A wave of loss threatened to engulf him; he curled his fingers into fists, feeling his nails pressing into his palms. The others began to push the loose soil back into the grave. In the background, he heard Taisin murmuring. The words were familiar; he had heard them before, at funerals. As she repeated them, Kaede echoed her, and then Pol and Shae. Their voices, low and sorrowful, lifted the words of the lament into the heavy stillness of dusk in the Great Wood.

This fleeting world:
Life passes as quickly as the morning star,
As a rumble of thunder,
A gust of wind over the grasslands.
This fleeting life:
Brief as a spark,
Ephemeral as a dream.
Soon enough we are ghosts upon the cloud.

Chapter XIX

hey left the lantern burning at Tali's grave while they set up camp. Taisin walked in a circle around the perimeter, marking it with stones or branches. "Bring everything we'll need into this circle," she told them, "because after I set it up, no one will be able to leave without breaking the boundary."

"What about Tali?" Con said. "I want to sit vigil with him tonight."

Taisin had taken out her small brassbound trunk and opened it, but now she paused with her hand on a glass vial. "It's not safe, Con."

"Tali was like a father to me," he said. "I owe him that respect."

Taisin saw the sadness that dragged at his shoulders; his ashen face, drawn with grief. She knew that he would do it whether or not she agreed with him, so she said, "Then I will sit with you."

"Will you extend the circle of protection to the grave?" Con asked.

"I can't. The space around it must be open, so that Tali's soul can travel freely." She didn't tell him that she suspected that Tali's soul had departed long before any of their burial rituals.

Con eyed her closely, as if he guessed that she was holding something back, but he didn't question her further. "All right. We'll sit vigil together. Let me know when you're ready." He went to help Pol set up their tent, leaving Taisin kneeling on the ground.

Her fingers shook slightly as she took out the herbs that she would need for the ritual. Sister Ailan had given her these supplies for this very reason, but Taisin had never actually believed she would need them. Milk-vetch root, dried and ground up in yellowish-brown crystals, for strength. Fox nut, pounded into a pale powder, for life energy. The barest sprinkle of dragon bone scrapings, like minuscule white petals, for power. Taisin combined them all in an iron bowl, stirring them together with her index finger. The powders seemed to glitter a bit, just as Sister Ailan had told her they would. The mixture was ready.

She asked Con to stand just outside the perimeter, and she placed Shae, Pol, and Kaede at three places along the interior of the circle. It would have been better if there were a fourth person, so she could create a full compass, but they would just have to make do with three points tonight. Holding the iron bowl in her hand, Taisin walked to the northernmost edge of the circle and closed her eyes, standing still. She had performed smaller protection rituals before, but never one this major, or as important. Sister Ailan had explained it to her and assured her that she could do it, but this was no Academy examination, where she might be forgiven for making a mistake or two. Taisin's heart raced as her nerves nearly got the better of her, making her hands clammy. She took a deep breath and tried to calm herself.

First, she had to find the way in. That was how her teachers always described it: being sensitive to all the currents of energy around her until she discovered the one that called to her—the one that was her own special path into the unseen world. Meridians of energy ran through every human being and animal and plant; they lay in limitless lines in the earth and the air like a vast web. Every living thing had its place in this field of energies. The protection ritual would reshape portions of that field, reweaving the net into a barrier around their camp.

If only she could do it. Every time she thought she had found the way in, it slid away from her. She was like a fisherman trying to reel in his catch, but it leapt away from him time and time again, splashing back into the sea.

And the wind that had whispered in Tali's ear was everywhere, distracting her. It slipped beneath her collar, tickled her earlobes, caressed her skin in cool, lingering breaths. It took every effort to ignore it, to focus instead on the elusive thread of energy that had come so easily to her when she had seen that purple flower. The thought of the flower helped, and she envisioned it in her mind's eye; she could feel the life of it, pulsing. And then she had it. She felt the humming threads of life all around her, and they were different here, deep in the Wood. There was still something not quite right about them, but they were a thousand times more vibrant than they had been in Jilin. She plucked one strand out—easy as tucking a lock of hair behind her ear—and began to weave it around their camp as she walked, eyes closed, for she didn't need to see the ordinary world when she could see, instead, the extraordinary one.

At the north, south, east, and west points of the circle, she sprinkled some of the powder on the ground. She said, "Peace within, darkness without." The powder burned into the ground like fox fire. Taisin walked around the perimeter of the camp three times, and each time she felt the web of protection tightening. It was exhilarating. She felt all of the energies she controlled at her fingertips: such incredible power. She was connected to the heartbeats of every living creature in the Great Wood; everything wanted so fiercely to live, even the trees that seemed half dead.

On her third circle, Taisin stopped before each person. She opened her eyes, looking directly at them, touching her fingers to their hearts, murmuring, "Peace within, darkness without." Pol's heartbeat was strong within him. Shae was worried; her breathing was quick and anxious. Kaede was tense as well, and when Taisin reached out to touch her, she felt a jolt pass between them. Taisin was so startled she almost faltered in the ritual.

To her surprise, Kaede reached up and covered Taisin's hand with hers. Taisin pressed her palm against Kaede's heart. She felt it speeding up until it matched the pace of her own. She was breathless. Kaede's eyes were light brown; Taisin saw her pupils dilating as they looked at each other, dusk spinning out around them, cloaking them in shadow. She wished she could stay there forever, the space between them freighted with possibility.

But she had to complete the ritual. She whispered, "Peace within, darkness without."

And then, reluctantly, she closed her eyes again. She saw Kaede, Pol, and Shae bound within a circle of energies like creatures caught in a spider's web. She pulled herself away from Kaede, feeling the link between them stretching like a gossamer thread. She made her way back to the place where she had begun, and she set down the iron bowl, pressing it into the ground.

When she straightened, she folded her hands before her lips and bowed first to the circle, then to the dark Wood beyond. It was done.

～

At the head of the grave mound, the candle still burned. Taisin sat on one side of it with her hands folded in her lap, and Con sat across from her. She had never kept overnight vigil at a grave before, and she knew she was not in the best condition for it. She was drained from the protection ritual and from the day itself. The hard, cold ground pressed sharply into her shins, and the dreadful wind was worrying at her hair.

Con shifted in the dark, uncrossing his legs and trying to find a more comfortable position. As time passed, he began to nod, weariness overcoming him. "Con," Taisin whispered, and he jerked himself awake.

"I'm sorry," he said. His tongue felt heavy and thick; his senses dulled.

"It's all right," Taisin whispered. "Just—don't fall asleep." She spoke as much for her own benefit as for his, for the air here was ripe with magic. Some of it was residue from the circle of protection she had woven, but some of it was darker, more malevolent. She was not certain, but she thought she recognized a thread or two of this other magic. It had a very distinct, unusual scent: like winter. It was the smell of that fortress of ice.

The visions had come more often since she entered the Wood, and sometimes they came at particularly inopportune moments. When she was riding, sometimes she would suddenly glimpse dark brown skin, mottled like lichen. Or when she was gathering firewood, she would catch sight of that winged creature again, flying high against icicles hanging like teeth from a cavernous ceiling. It would only be the briefest glimpse, and then she would snap back into reality, knocked slightly off balance, and Pol or Kaede or Tali would ask her if she was all right. Her heart sank at that memory. Tali would never speak again.

She looked across the grave at Con; his body was rigid, and his wide-open eyes reflected the flicker of the candlelight. He no longer seemed in danger of falling asleep. He shivered as if someone had run a finger down his back, and for a moment, he cocked his head to the right, listening. "Con," Taisin said, her voice a whip crack in the stillness.

He jerked. "What?" he said hoarsely.

"Look at me." Taisin was almost certain that something was trying to lure him away, just as it had done to Tali. "Are you hearing something?"

"I don't know." He felt a caress on his cheek; he wanted to turn his face into it. It was as seductive as the sleep that had dragged at him earlier. But he struggled against it, trying to fix his eyes on Taisin. The tiny light of the candle only served to make the Wood beyond seem blacker, a spill of ink on black paper. How could it possibly be enough light to guide Tali's soul to the other side?

Taisin could sense the energy around Con; it was charged with frustrated desire. She felt it gathering in strength, like massing thunderclouds, and then it turned its attention, abruptly, to her.

She was nearly knocked over by the power of it: a gale-force wind, ice-cold, biting into her face and pulling at her clothes. Long, wordless screams buffeted at her, and she clapped her hands over her ears to protect herself from the sounds. She stared in horror across the grave, trying to anchor herself to Con, who was gaping at her. He said something, but she could not hear him. She wanted to run, but she did not dare leave the light of the candle, and she would not leave Con.

She remembered, suddenly, what had been so familiar about the wind that had come teasing at her hair earlier. Now she had only a younger sister, but there had been a time when she also had a younger brother named Sota. He was Suri's twin, and when Taisin was ten years old, Suri and Sota fell sick. Suri recovered, but Sota did not, and died. After his death, her father and mother sat vigil beside his still little body all night. Four-year-old Suri hadn't understood what was going on, and Taisin had been charged with taking care of her. She crawled into bed with her, listening while Suri mumbled the name of her brother in her sleep: *Sota, Sota, Sota*. The word was a hypnotic rhythm. It lulled Taisin into an uneasy sleep of her own, cuddled next to her little sister.

She woke later that night to hear voices—despairing, yearning voices. She felt fingers running along her arm, touching her. If the wind could form itself into hands, that was what it felt like. She went rigid with fear, goose bumps rising all over her body. Suri was still asleep, but sweat dampened her brow as if she had broken into a fever. Suri's hair was being lifted as though someone were running their fingers through it, smoothing it back from her face. Taisin was terrified. She muttered her sister's name; she gripped Suri's shoulder and shook it.

Suri opened her eyes, and the wind ceased. Warmth flooded into the room, and Taisin realized that it had been freezing before—how could Suri be sweating?

"Sota?" Suri whispered.

Taisin put her arms around her sister, trying to rock her back to sleep. "Shh," she murmured.

"Ghosts," Suri said. "Ghosts."

Those ghosts, frightening though they were, were nothing compared to what circled Taisin now. These were different. These were much more powerful. They had been wronged.

But now that she understood what they were, she felt calmer. She knew what to do.

She removed her hands from her ears. They shrieked at her, their voices pounding into her head. "Stop it!" she cried.

"Taisin!" Con was calling her name. He was trying to stand up, but he could not move. Something was pinning him down.

"It's all right," Taisin said. "It's all right." And then she said to the circling ghosts: "I will listen to you."

Instantly, the Wood disappeared; she plunged into a world of vivid color. Everything was richly green: the color of newly budded leaves, of luminescent moss, of every possible shade of pine needle. And then she was in the middle of the ocean, carried by warm currents, the water changing from sea green to midnight blue as she sank from the surface into the depths. She had fins; she was as slick as a porpoise. She broke into the air; she was on top of the tallest tree; she was the tree itself.

The images were confusing at first, until she finally understood that she was experiencing the lives of each of the ghosts speaking to her. These were not the lives of humans, and she knew with absolute certainty that they were not the lives of animals, either. These were fay, creatures who inhabited the trees and the rivers, the seas and the hills. They had lived lives that were full of wonder, and now their lives were over.

She was thrust into darkness. When she could see again, she was cold all over. She saw golden bars. She heard the

171

dragging shuffle of someone pacing in a tiny cage. She had never wanted to be free so badly. She wanted to strike at the bars with her bare hands, but the metal cut her skin. Black blood dripped from the wounds in her side. Something had been torn out of her. She bent over, falling onto her knees, feeling the icy floor beneath her.

They had been wronged.

❧

Taisin's eyes flew open. She was still standing beside Tali's grave. The night was not over. She gasped for air as if she had been underwater.

Con had moved; he was now standing directly in front of her. His hands gripped her shoulders.

"Taisin," he said. "Taisin."

"I'm here," she whispered, dazed.

He loosened his grip on her just slightly. "Are you all right?"

She shuddered. "Yes."

"Did you see something?"

She realized he had no idea what she had just experienced. "They're ghosts," she said.

A shiver ran down Con's spine. He looked beyond Taisin, but there was nothing but darkness.

Taisin reached up and pulled his hands from her shoulders, holding them in hers. "It's all right," she said. She felt the energy of the ghosts dissipating. She had satisfied them for now, but ghosts always returned until their wrongs had been righted. She only hoped they would not return tonight.

"Is it safe here?" Con asked.

She almost laughed. "Safe? No. But we must stay. We must stay with Tali until dawn." He began to pull away from her, but she did not let him go. "Sit here, right here, with me."

And so they sat together until the dawn light came, pallid and gray, and they saw that the soil of Tali's grave was newly rimed with frost.

Chapter XX

hen Taisin and Con returned to camp, Shae had brewed strong black tea for them, and Kaede and Pol had already disassembled the tents. While they waited for the rice porridge to cook, Taisin told them what had happened the night before.

"Ghosts," Pol muttered. "Just what we need."

"There are many of them," Taisin said. Her legs ached from sitting all night in the cold. "It's still not safe for us out there. We have to stay together at all times."

"Is that what took Tali?" Pol asked.

"I don't know," Taisin said. "Maybe. They were not happy spirits."

Before they departed, Taisin had to release the space where they were camped back to the Wood. She retraced her steps around the perimeter of the camp three times, grinding the remaining powders into the forest floor. She felt the meridians of energy springing back like strings snapping into position; it made her skin feel red, chapped, as though she had been scoured by a dry wind.

The days that followed were gray and heavy, as if Tali's death was a dark cloud surrounding them. They decided to set one of the packhorses free; Shae believed he would find his way back home to Jilin. They transferred the supplies to the wagon horse that Pol had been riding, and Pol rode Tali's horse instead. On the mornings that Kaede found time for target practice, Pol pushed her harder than he had before. She understood why: The bow was a weapon, and without Tali, they were one guard less.

For Kaede, the one bright moment in each day came at the end, when Taisin wove the circle of protection around their camp. Every time Taisin put her hand on Kaede's heart, warmth bloomed between them, pushing back the dark night just enough to give them room to breathe together. Kaede found herself waiting for Taisin's touch all day, turning the memory of it over and over again in her mind as they rode through the wild Wood. Every night, she felt the link between them thickening, ripening: at first a slender shoot, and then a vine that curled around them, strengthening each day. She began to wonder if Taisin might feel it, too, but Taisin never said a word about what happened between them during the ritual.

Taisin was afraid to acknowledge it. From the very first time she performed the ritual, she had known that the connection between the two of them was different than what she felt with the others. As the days passed, she became gradually aware that Kaede knew it, too. The realization thrilled her, but it also raised the specter of her vision. It shook her to know that this ritual that should protect them all was also doing the one thing she wanted to avoid. And yet, part of her—a growing part of her—wanted only to nurture the delicate bloom between them.

Sometimes that desire would subside, and Taisin thought she might succeed in preventing her vision from happening, but then her feelings returned at the most unexpected moments. When Kaede brewed tea for everyone, she took care to hand a cup directly to Taisin. Their fingers brushed together against the hot metal, and the thread between them drew tight. Taisin turned away with studied casualness, trying to hide the rising color on her cheeks. She tried to remember that she did not want to fall in love with Kaede, but more and more, she forgot. She forgot to avoid lingering near Kaede when they paused to rest during the day. She forgot to put space between them when they sat by the campfire at night.

One morning Kaede awoke to discover—her head still full of the mustiness of sleep—that Taisin had curled up beside her in the tent they shared with Shae. The warmth of her body was comforting, for the dawn air was cool and slightly damp. As she turned onto her back, Taisin moved, too, burrowing her head into Kaede's shoulder, and Kaede blinked her eyes open, feeling suddenly, acutely aware of Taisin breathing so close to her. And then Taisin shifted, stretching as she awoke, and her entire body slid against Kaede's side. At first, still half asleep, Taisin levered herself up on one elbow and looked at her, and at that moment

Kaede could have reached up and pulled her back down again—but then Taisin woke completely, and she blushed so deeply that the tips of her ears went pink.

She scooted away as quickly as she could, mumbling something apologetic, and almost tripped over Shae as she stumbled out of the tent.

Shae, who was just waking up, rubbed her face and muttered, "What's going on?"

"Nothing," Kaede whispered, closing her eyes. Maybe if she didn't get up right away, she could slide back into those delicious moments before Taisin awoke. Her whole body was tingling. What would she have done if Taisin hadn't left so abruptly? She would have kissed her. Even with Shae right there beside them, she would have done it. The thought made her feel like fire had erupted over her skin.

She threw off the blankets. She needed to get out into the cold morning. She crawled out of the tent, ignoring Shae's protests as she climbed over her.

Outside, her breath misted into the air; the whole camp was surrounded by fog. There was no sign of Taisin.

Con was stirring the fire. He looked up at Kaede's abrupt arrival. "Good morning." His brows drew together. "Are you all right?"

"What? I'm fine." She shoved her feet into boots, bending over to lace them as she asked, "Where did Pol and Taisin go?"

"To get more water."

"Oh."

Con grinned at her. "She'll be back soon enough. Would you like a cup of tea?"

Kaede turned red. But she accepted the battered metal cup with as much dignity as she could.

∽

Pol and Taisin took much longer than expected, and by the time they returned, Con, Shae, and Kaede were standing nervously beside the fire, staring down toward the river and thinking uneasy thoughts. "We were beginning to worry," Con said, unable to hide his anxiety. Taisin set down the heavy water skin she was carrying, and her eyes flickered immediately to Kaede, who looked relieved to see her.

"I apologize," Pol said, kneeling to pour water into the kettle. "I saw something, and I had to find out what it was. Taisin wouldn't let me go alone."

"What did you see?" Con asked.

"Something is following us," Pol said.

"Something?" Shae repeated, eyeing the trees warily.

"Yes. I don't know what it is. But it's not human."

Chapter XXI

On the third night after Pol's announcement, their followers finally showed themselves.

It had been drizzling all afternoon, and lighting the fire was an ordeal that put everyone in a bitter mood. They ate their supper in silence, huddled beneath oilskins as the rain dripped down, hissing, into the fire. They slumped over their food, tired and vulnerable. Even Pol, who had been so vigilant, did not notice that they were slowly being surrounded. It was Kaede who looked up after finishing her meal and saw the eyes in the dark. She stiffened just like a deer noticing he was being hunted.

"Pol," Kaede said in a harsh whisper.

He looked around sharply. Several pairs of yellow eyes glowed in the dark, reflecting the light of the fire. Shae and Pol reached for their weapons at the same time, standing up to face the dark.

"What are they?" Taisin asked in a small voice.

"Wolves," Pol said. "Will the circle of protection keep them away?"

"I don't know," Taisin said. "The circle is meant to keep out harmful magic, not—not wolves."

"But it's also meant to protect us," Pol said. "Isn't it?"

"Yes. We should stay within it while they're out there."

They sat up all night, looking out at the eyes looking in at them. Their initial fright turned inevitably to weariness, for the wolves did not seem to be interested in advancing. Kaede had the eerie suspicion that they were merely there to watch them, to assess their strengths and weaknesses. Sometimes one of them looked directly at her, and she was startled by how intelligent the gaze was.

As morning approached, the wolves began to melt away, and when dawn finally broke and there was light enough to see beyond their campfire, there was no sign of them. But all around the circle of protection that Taisin had woven were long paw prints in the rain-dampened ground, where the wolves had paced.

They had barely been in the saddle for an hour that morning when Kaede caught sight of the wolves running through the trees about fifty feet away, roughly paralleling the path. They stayed downwind of the horses, who had not yet noticed them. Pol, who was bringing up the rear, sped up briefly to ride alongside her. "Take this," he said, handing her his bow and quiver.

"What about you?" Kaede said, slinging the quiver onto her back.

He drew out his sword. "I'll need more mobility. You stay with Taisin."

Kaede nodded, trying to ignore the fear that bubbled in her stomach as Pol dropped back again. The trail was so narrow that they were riding single file. Shae was first, followed by Con, who was leading one of the packhorses. Next came Taisin, also leading a packhorse, and then Kaede; Pol rode last, his sword resting on his thighs.

As the morning wore on, Kaede began to suspect that these wolves were not entirely ordinary. They were practically flaunting themselves now; every once in a while one of them would break away from the pack and come closer to the path, either to get a better look at them or to demonstrate how bold they were. Kaede counted at least a dozen wolves, though she could not be sure, for they blended into the mottled brown of the Wood as if their coats had been made for this purpose.

Being constantly on guard after a sleepless night was a good way to render one's muscles stiff and clumsy, and that was the way Kaede felt when the wolves finally moved in. She wasn't sure what she had expected, but she knew she had not thought they would go after Pol first. He was clearly their strongest member, and he was riding Tali's horse, a great black stallion trained for battle. When she heard his horse cry out, she was so startled that she almost dropped the bow. By the time she fumbled an arrow out of the quiver and twisted in Pol's direction, he was already slashing his sword down at the wolves that had surrounded him in a ferocious, snarling wave, isolating him from Kaede and the others. One wolf sank his teeth into the horse's neck, and another bit into Pol's thigh, releasing a thick stream of red blood. He screamed, but he kept fighting, clinging to the back of his horse.

Kaede's fingers trembled on the fletching of an arrow. The wolves' brindled backs were a sea of matted fur and muscle between her and Pol. She knew that all those mornings in empty stable yards came down to this instant: the instinctual motion of hand to arrow to string—and release— and the arrow plowed into a wolf's chest, knocking him down. Kaede's blood pounded in her ears. There was no time to think; the wolves did not stop coming. She nocked another arrow, and another. Her nostrils filled with the beasts' stench.

Out of the corner of her eye she saw the packhorse tied to Con's saddle tear free from his lead rope, fleeing into the trees. Two wolves sprinted after him, and he never had a chance. They brought him down as easily as they might bring down a much smaller deer, and they howled their victory.

Con's stomach reeled as he watched the wolves tear into the packhorse; they had split into two mobs, one surrounding the horse, the other surrounding Pol. Kaede was trying to pick off the wolves around Pol, but she couldn't shoot too close to him. Con's fingers were sweaty on the hilt of his sword. Pol needed help.

"Stay with Taisin!" Con shouted at Shae, and doubled back through the trees parallel to the trail, heading toward Pol. As he approached the melee, a wolf charged him. Yellow teeth bared, she launched herself at Con's horse, who reared and struck at her with his iron-shod hooves. Con's own blade whistled in the air. He held on to his horse with his knees and slammed his sword into the wolf's shoulder. The beast's snarl turned into a whimper; Con ripped his weapon out and struck again, drops of hot blood stinging his hands. The creature collapsed, her rank scent filling the air. When Con looked up to find his next target, he saw two wolves yanking Pol from his horse onto the ground, and the guard's body disappeared beneath the pack.

"Pol!" he screamed.

Taisin heard him, and she twisted in her saddle to see Con trying to fight his way closer to the fallen guard. Terror engulfed her. Kaede was shouting at her; she was raising the bow, and an arrow flew frighteningly close to Taisin, making her flinch. It lodged in the flank of a gray wolf scarcely twenty feet away. That was when she noticed more of the beasts emerging from the trees and loping almost casually in her direction.

She could feel them: They were all hunger and vicious need. They were meant for this—to hunt and to kill—and there was a frightening beauty in their sharp golden eyes and powerful jaws. It was the beauty of a creature fulfilling her exact purpose in the world, being the precise thing she had trained her whole life to be.

The moment the first wolf leapt at her, Taisin acted entirely out of instinct, driven by panic. She had never used her knowledge of magic as a weapon before, and she knew there were proscriptions against it. None of that mattered when faced with a slavering wolf.

She forced her way into the fields of energy around her, tearing out fistfuls of the power that lived in every plant and animal, and she flung it at the wolves, knocking them down like paper dolls.

It was as easy as plucking ripe fruit from a tree. She felt like she had been born to do this. Her entire body thrilled with the power running through her. All the meridians of energy that ran across the Great Wood buckled beneath her touch. And the wolves began to run from her, yelping in fear.

Kaede stared at Taisin in amazement as she slid down from her horse, striding off the path toward the wolves. She raised her arms, flinging something at them that Kaede could not see. Whatever it was, it struck them like great punches, and Kaede saw one wolf's rib cage collapse, while another's snout was smashed, blood arcing through the air.

Taisin's eyes were shining, her hair coming loose. White light pulled at the ends until they swirled around her head in a black cloud. She looked like she was possessed by something as ferocious as the wolves themselves, and Kaede was chilled by the expression on her face. Taisin looked inhuman—powerful and frightening and hard as ice.

The wolves outside the radius of Taisin's power lifted their heads, looking in her direction. They backed away with deep-throated growls. It was as if a lightning storm had settled over her, and they wanted no part of it.

As the wolves retreated, Shae left the path to ride back toward Con and Pol, her blade dark with blood from the wolves that had left the fallen packhorse to find new prey. She did not see the ones who ran silently out of the trees east of the trail, and within an eyeblink, dragged her off her horse.

186

Shae screamed as the wolf bit down on her ankle; she tried to kick at him. Her horse reared, but it only loosened her from her saddle. She slid awkwardly, one foot caught in the stirrup, one hand tangled in her reins, and she tried to drive her sword into the wolf who had bitten her. It glanced off his shoulder, and then she was on the ground, her free hand scrabbling in the slightly damp earth, her cheek scraping against the soil. The wolves, their saliva dripping from hungry jowls, came for her.

Shae was fifteen feet away from Kaede when she was attacked. The space between them was a straight shot, and as one of the wolves raised his head to look at Kaede, she sent an arrow directly into his yellow eye.

He collapsed, but his pack mate turned in Kaede's direction and growled. She shot again, and the arrow lodged itself in the wolf's shoulder. He yelped and abandoned Shae, bounding toward Kaede instead. She loosed another arrow, but it only glanced off his flank. Then he was less than ten feet away from her, and before she could think she pulled out the iron dagger and hurled it squarely into his throat.

Finally he fell, his jaws nearly touching Maila's hooves when he slumped onto the forest floor. Hot relief flooded through Kaede's body. Her lungs heaved.

Through the buzzing of blood in her ears, she heard the wolves howling. When she looked up from the dead wolf, she saw his pack mates fleeing. The path toward Pol was clear at last, and Kaede saw that the guard's neck was bent at an unnatural angle, and his left thigh had been torn into a mass of bloody flesh.

But Shae was still alive, and as the wolves' howls faded into the distance, her gasps of pain filled the air. Con slid from his horse, dropped his bloody sword on the ground, and ran to her. Kneeling beside her, his face turned gray at the sight of her wound. Shae looked up at him, reaching out for his hand, muttering something that he could not understand.

"You're not leaving us, Shae," he said fiercely. "You're not leaving us."

Chapter XXII

K aede ran toward Taisin, who had collapsed on the ground surrounded by dead wolves. Her lips were faintly blue, and she was breathing shallowly, her forehead glistening with sweat. Kaede was afraid Taisin had been injured, but she couldn't detect any physical wounds. She knew that Taisin might have sustained other, less visible, injuries, but she had no idea how to treat them. In all the years she had studied at the Academy, she had never heard of anyone doing what Taisin had just done, and she was fairly certain that it was forbidden.

But she would not let herself think about what that meant. All she wanted right now was to make sure that Taisin was not hurt. She knelt on the ground and lifted Taisin's hand. Her pulse raced within her wrist. Kaede leaned forward, pushing back damp strands of hair from Taisin's forehead. Her eyes suddenly opened, her pupils so huge they made her brown eyes seem black. She began to shake violently, and Kaede gathered her into her arms to quell the tremors, concerned that she would harm herself. At last the shaking subsided and Taisin asked in a hoarse voice, "Are the wolves all gone?"

"Yes." Kaede was relieved; Taisin sounded mostly normal. "Are you all right?"

Taisin squinted up at her. "I don't know." Her whole body felt bruised, and the pain was excruciating. But she also remembered the way she had held all of that energy in her hands: as muscular as a snake, as powerful as a fistful of iron.

Her stomach heaved with the memory, and she scrambled away from Kaede, doubled over on her hands and knees as she threw up. She might have been invincible against those wolves, but now she was weak as a newborn, shuddering her way into a strange new world.

When she had breath to speak she asked, "How are the others?"

"Shae is wounded. Pol—I don't know—"

Her voice broke off, and Taisin looked at Kaede and saw the fear on her face. Taisin took a deep, uneven breath. She pushed herself up onto her feet, wobbling like a colt taking his first steps. She surveyed the scene: the wolves' bodies splayed in a circle around them; the mauled packhorse, with their gear strewn across the forest floor; their four skittish mounts huddled together; Con bent over Shae on the ground. Down the trail she saw Pol's body; his horse had been dragged off by the wolves.

"We should go to them," Taisin said. She had to keep moving, or the gravity of what she had just done would overwhelm her. "We have no time to lose."

Shae was seriously injured. Her leg was in horrible shape, and she had sustained some ragged slashes on her side. They bandaged her wound, but there was nothing else they could do until they set up camp, and none of them wished to remain here, surrounded by the stinking corpses of dead wolves. Kaede retrieved her dagger and most of the arrows she had shot, but she didn't have the stomach to pull out the one lodged in the wolf's eye.

There was no saving Pol. They wrapped his broken body in his blanket and slung him as gently as they could over the back of the remaining packhorse, redistributing their supplies across all the horses. Con helped Shae climb back onto her own mare; she stubbornly refused to faint and instead had to grit her teeth over every bump in the road. They managed to put an hour's slow walk between themselves and what remained of their attackers before Con insisted they stop to tend Shae's wound. The bone in Shae's shin was exposed where the wolves had torn out her flesh, and Con had to hold her down while Taisin and Kaede wrapped her leg with a clean cloth. The cuts on her side where a wolf's claws had dragged across her body were jagged, and although they cleaned them as thoroughly as possible, Taisin had a bad feeling that the wounds would become inflamed. She brewed a bitter tea that would send Shae to sleep for the time being, which was the best she could do for the pain, and then they measured out just enough space for another grave.

Con broke up the ground with his sword while Kaede and Taisin dug with their battered metal bowls. Every time his blade bit into the ground, he remembered the way it had cleaved into the wolf's shoulder. He had killed that one, but he had been too late to save Pol. He had been too late to prevent Shae from being attacked. Seeing her on the ground, bleeding, had ripped him open, too. It made him realize that he had so much to say to her. Sweat broke out on his skin despite the cool air. He did not want to even consider the possibility that Shae wouldn't survive her wounds. He rammed his sword into the earth, making Taisin and Kaede jump out of the way.

"I'm sorry," he said. They kept digging.

Night fell before the grave was deep enough. The candle they had lit for Pol's soul did nothing to push back the dark. Taisin suggested they light a fire so that Shae would not get chilled. "You two will have to gather firewood," Taisin said. "I should stay here with Shae and Pol."

"Alone?" Kaede said. She straightened, standing in the grave itself. "Con should stay with you; I'll go alone."

"No." Taisin rubbed her eyes wearily with the back of her hand. "I'll be fine here. I can protect myself, but it's not safe for either of you to be alone in the Wood."

"Come on," Con said, offering his hand to Kaede. "Let's get it over with. We should have done it earlier."

Kaede frowned, but she took Con's hand and scrambled out. The lip of the grave crumbled beneath her foot as she climbed, sending clods of dirt tumbling into the pit. Taisin began to climb in.

"You shouldn't do that," Kaede said, her skin prickling. "Wait till we return."

"There's not time," Taisin said, picking up her bowl to dig. "We have to bury Pol as soon as possible."

Con and Kaede did not stray far from the path as they foraged for fallen branches. The Wood seemed particularly malignant that night. Kaede could have sworn she saw the eyes of wolves peering out at her from the cover of darkness. And it was so cold. She had been warmer when she was digging, but now she felt the wind on her face, and it smelled sharply of snow.

When they returned to their camp, they could hear Taisin chanting to herself as she dug. She didn't stop when they returned. Kaede built the small fire as quickly as she could, and Con pulled Shae's sleeping form toward it, pillowing her head on a rolled-up blanket.

As soon as the grave was deep enough, they rolled Pol's body into it. There had been no time to wash him or to change him out of the clothes he had died in. Taisin knew it was bad form, but she didn't know what else to do—it was already too late at night for proper burial rites—and she was so exhausted that she could barely say the words of the funeral lament. But Kaede and Con helped her, and together they laid Pol to rest.

✺

In the morning, Shae awoke feverish and in pain. Taisin had learned some rudimentary healing practices at the Academy, but she was not trained as a healer, and Kaede had never reached that far in her studies. Con refused to give up; his stomach churned at the thought of losing Shae. "We'll just keep going," he said. "We'll find the Xi in time. They'll help." He heard the desperation in his voice, and he turned away so that he didn't have to see the awful sympathy in Kaede's face.

They were nearly packed and ready to go when the dog came trotting down the trail toward them. At first Kaede thought it was another wolf, and her dagger was in her hand before she realized it was not a wild animal. Though he was tall as a wolf, he moved differently, and his brown eyes lacked the feral sharpness she had seen in those beasts. He barked at them, and Taisin and Con jumped at the sound. When they were all staring at him, the dog began to wag his tail.

Behind him, coming down the trail, was a white-haired woman. She walked with a slight limp, leaning on a horned staff, and as she approached she called out, "Good morning, travelers! That's my dog, Cavin; he's harmless enough." When she was standing at the edge of their camp she paused and smiled. "On a little journey, are we?" she said lightly.

The three of them were silent. Con did not know what to make of the strange old woman. She looked innocuous, but he knew that a helpless old woman could never survive on her own in the Great Wood. Tali would not trust her. Con could almost hear him warning them: *Don't be fooled by the appearance of weakness.*

Con stepped forward, putting himself between her and the others. "Who are you?" he asked.

The woman cocked her head at him, hearing his defensiveness. "I am only here to help. I saw the wolves yesterday, running past my cottage. I thought that someone might be in need of my assistance."

"What kind of assistance?" Con asked.

"One of your party is injured, I see. Perhaps I can help."

Despite his doubts, hope flared inside him. "How?"

"Let me see her, and I will tell you what I can do."

Chapter XXIII

er name, she told them, was Mona. She was blind in her left eye, but she seemed to have no trouble examining Shae's injuries. Con watched her carefully, noting the practiced way she handled the bandages, her touch light and quick. When Mona suggested they bring Shae back to her cottage where she could treat her, he agreed.

Taisin, who had said nothing during the exam, now asked, "Are you a healer?" A note of skepticism could be heard in her voice.

Mona looked at her out of her one good eye—it was startlingly blue compared to the filmy white covering the other—and said, "I am a greenwitch."

Taisin was surprised. "And you live here in the Wood, alone?"

The old woman smiled crookedly. "Solitude, young one, teaches many things not found within the walls of your Academy."

Taisin stared at her, startled, for she had not mentioned the Academy of Sages. But it was obvious that Mona had guessed Taisin was a student there. Before she could ask how Mona had known, the woman got up. "We'd better go," she said. "Your friend must not wait any longer."

Mona's cottage was about an hour's walk into the Wood, away from the river Nir. It was a roughly built log cabin with mud plastered into the cracks, and there was one door and one square window covered with greased paper. But the interior was unexpectedly cheerful, with a colorful quilt thrown over the bed in the corner and dried herbs hanging from the ceiling. On one wall was a fireplace in which the remains of a fire glowed; on the other wall was an iron-bound trunk surrounded by stacks of leather-bound books. The sight of them astonished Taisin. A cottage like this one was the last place she would have expected to find so many books. They were costly items and difficult to obtain.

Mona told them to put Shae on the bed, and then asked them to build up the fire. "There's wood out back, behind the lean-to," she said. "And I would much appreciate it if one of you could bring me some water. You'll see the well by the woodpile. And you"—she motioned to Taisin—"I could use your help."

Shae was shivering. Mona had built up the fire until it roared, but though the heat of it sent sweat trickling between Taisin's shoulder blades, it seemed to have no effect on the guard, who was lying on the bed beneath several heavy quilts. Mona had given Shae something to make her sleep before she treated her wounds, but even asleep she was restless and agitated. Her face was white, her lips almost blue, and she breathed shallowly.

"Will she recover?" Taisin asked, watching the old woman touching Shae's forehead and cheeks with the back of her hand.

"She has a fever. There is poison inside her."

"From the wounds?"

"From the wolves. They're dirty beasts."

"Can you save her?" Taisin was afraid to know the answer, but she had to ask.

"I don't know yet." Mona left the bedside and went to the stack of books piled near the trunk. She pulled out a thick volume bound in black leather and propped it open on the mantle above the fireplace, holding it in place with a heavy pewter candlestick. Taisin came closer to look; on the page was a recipe listing at least two dozen ingredients. She recognized a few of them—milk vetch, aralia root, sage. But she didn't know many of the others: goldthread, blue aralia, skullcap.

"What is this for?" Taisin asked.

"Your friend is very weak. She has suffered a great shock." Mona opened the trunk, and inside there were dozens of little boxes and vials stacked one upon the other. "Her energies have been severely depleted. She has bled quite a bit. Her body could overcome the injury to her leg on its own if she were strong and healthy, but the wolf's bite has drained her." Mona began to pull out a number of boxes and handed them to Taisin. "Put them on the table by the clay pot."

"Are you making a tonic?" Taisin had learned about healing tonics at the Academy, but her knowledge of them was limited to the relatively harmless brew she had made for Shae the night before. It had not kept the pain away for long.

"It is a kind of tonic," Mona said, pushing herself up from the trunk to set down two more vials on the table.

"What will it do?"

"If it works, it will restore her vigor and strengthen her blood, and drive out the infection." Mona opened one of the boxes and pulled out dried flowers, rusty brown in color, and dropped them into the clay pot. She added little round seeds and the scrapings of a gnarled, flesh-colored root; furry, blue-gray leaves and pale orange blossoms. When all of the ingredients had been combined and crushed into a fine powder, she drew a small knife from her pocket and bent down to hold it in the hottest part of the flames.

"What is that for?" Taisin asked.

"There is another ingredient," Mona said, and a moment later she straightened, waving the knife in the air to let the blade cool off.

Something in Mona's voice made Taisin recoil. "What is it?"

"Your blood."

Taisin stepped back, her foot banging into the trunk. "What?"

Mona did not move; she held the blade lightly. It was only a paring knife. "Your blood," she said again. The woman's blind white eye moved as if it could see. "The tonic will not work without it."

198

"No tonics require human blood," Taisin objected, her skin prickling.

"Do you know every tonic?" Mona asked mildly. "What a scholar you are."

Taisin flushed. "No, I—" She clenched her fingers into fists. "I'm not saying I know everything. But I have never heard of blood as an element in healing rituals."

"Blood is the water of life. Your friend has been drained of too much of hers." Mona took a step closer to her, and Taisin had the impression that the old woman could see right into her mind. It was unnerving. "You are young, and I know that the energies run strong within you," Mona continued. "I felt it yesterday, when you defended yourself from those wolves. I felt the way you pulled and stretched the meridians to do your bidding. That is not something the Academy teaches its pupils, is it? And yet you knew how to do it."

Taisin stared at her, shocked. "You—you felt that?"

Mona gave her a shrewd look. "You should know better, Taisin. You know that when you do something like that, others can sense it."

"The wolves would have killed me—"

"And your friend will die if you don't give her your blood."

Taisin's heart pounded. She glanced at Shae, at her white face and heaving chest. When she turned back to Mona, the woman was watching her with a patient expression. "How much do you need?"

"Not so much. You are strong enough that a little will go a long way."

Taisin took a deep breath. "All right."

"Come here, then, and give me your arm."

Taisin went to her, knees shaking, and rolled up her left sleeve. Mona held her arm steady over the bowl of herbs, their bitter scent wafting up to her nostrils. Mona placed the knife against Taisin's skin, and with a short, quick move, sliced into her forearm. Taisin gasped; it stung. She watched as blood welled up in the cut, and let out a short moan when Mona wrapped her fingers above it, squeezing. The blood dripped, hot and red, onto the herbs.

Mona was saying something, but Taisin couldn't understand her. The words were in another language—something brutal and dark, like a knuckle scraping against stone. She felt light-headed as her blood drained from her, making a slight hissing sound when it struck the mixture in the clay pot. She couldn't look at the cut anymore; it was a mouth on her arm; it screamed at her.

She turned her eyes away, feeling sick. She stared at the fire, at the hearthstones, at the candlestick holding the black leather book open, the words crawling like worms across the page.

And then Mona was smearing an ointment over the cut, and she pressed a cloth against it. "Hold it there," Mona ordered, and began to crush the herbs into the blood. She poured in water from a black bottle; she knelt before the hearth and shoved the pot into the coals. She made a sign in the air—a circle—and she folded her hands together and touched them to her forehead, her mouth, her heart. A log fell with a crash, sending up sparks.

After several moments Mona stood again, and Taisin asked nervously, "Is it ready?"

"No, not for at least another hour. The herbs must absorb the blood fully." Mona looked tired, and she sat down in the rocking chair. "Let me see your arm."

Taisin had almost forgotten about it, but now she peeled back the rag. The ointment had left an oily residue on the cloth, which was now stained red, but the cut itself had stopped bleeding. She didn't resist when Mona wrapped a strip of linen around it, tucking the ends into place firmly. Her arm throbbed a little, and Mona said, "You should sit down. You've lost blood now, too."

Dazed, Taisin sank down to the floor. As Mona rocked nearby, Taisin stared at the iron pot in the fire, wondering if she had been right to let the greenwitch take her blood.

Chapter XXIV

on paced back and forth in the clearing outside the cottage, his shoulders taut with worry. Earlier, they had heard Shae crying out in pain, but hours had now passed with no sounds from within. Taisin was still inside with Mona, who had shooed Con and Kaede away once they delivered the firewood and water. "You'll just be in the way," the old woman had said. "You'd best wait outside."

So they tended to their horses. They built a small fire in the stone-lined pit in the middle of the clearing, and they boiled water for tea. They cooked a cup of rice to eat, but neither Con nor Kaede had much experience with cooking, and the rice began to burn. They added more water, and then it became too wet. They ate it anyway, feeling gloomy and tired.

Afterward, Kaede pulled out her bedroll. She was so worn out she was sure she could sleep in broad daylight, but Con was too wound up, and he began to pace. His agitation was contagious, and she was about to give up on sleeping when he sat down on one of the logs beside the fire pit, demanding in frustration, "Why haven't they come outside yet? This woman must not know what she's doing. I was too eager to believe in her."

Kaede rolled over, pillowing her head on her bent arm to look at him. "She said she's a greenwitch."

He put his head in his hands. "But what do we really know about her?" he asked, his voice muffled. "Mona, is that her name? Who would want to live out here alone?"

"She has a dog," Kaede pointed out drily. Cavin was lying just outside the cottage door, apparently asleep.

Con let out his breath in an exasperated sigh. "You're making jokes, Kaede?"

She groaned, lying back again and blinking up at the gray sky. It seemed unusually bright today. "I'm sorry, Con. You know I'm worried about Shae, too."

He nodded briefly. "She seems unusual, though. This greenwitch."

"Do you know many?" Kaede rubbed her hand across her eyes. Yes, she was positive: The cloud cover was thinner today.

"A few. I met a few when I went up north last year. Aren't they women who never passed the tests required to become sages?"

"Some of them are. But I've heard of others, in recent years, who have rejected the sagehood and chosen to call themselves greenwitches instead."

"Why?"

She glanced over at the cottage. The door was still closed.

"There are some greenwitches who claim that the Academy—and the Council—are too distant from the people of this kingdom," Kaede explained. "They believe that sages should be among the people, not removed from them."

He was surprised. "I haven't heard anything about this."

"I don't think the Council wants it to be widely known."

He quickly understood. "It would stir up trouble if people knew that some are resisting the Council's orders."

"And there are fewer sages made every year," Kaede pointed out. "They don't want to lose anyone."

"What about you? Aren't you due to join their ranks?"

"I will never be a sage," she said, and she realized that the idea of it no longer made her feel inadequate. It felt, instead, perfectly ordinary.

"But you've been a student there for six years."

"I've read the classics, but I'm not meant to be a sage. I don't have the skill."

"Why didn't you leave the Academy earlier, then?"

She turned back onto her side, propping her head on her hand, and gave him a tiny smile. "I have a powerful father, Con. He—and my mother, who would have been a sage if she hadn't married him—wanted me to be there. I'm sure they hoped I'd develop the abilities, but…I don't think it's something you can learn."

"What are you going to do, then? When we return."

The question startled her. They had been on the road for almost five weeks now, but it felt like years. Her life before—the Academy, her family, her obligations—was a different world, one she could barely believe she had ever lived in.

The real world was here and now: this clearing, where the clouds overhead were thin enough to remind her what a blue sky might look like. The dirt under her nails, the healing scars on her hands, the ache in her shoulders and back from digging Pol's grave. Returning to her previous life seemed impossible. What would she do?

"I don't know," she said at last. "My father wants me to marry someone."

"Who?"

"I haven't met him." She grimaced. "Someone named Lord Win."

His eyebrows rose. "Really? I've met him. He's—"

"Don't tell me," she interrupted, sitting up. "I don't want to know anything about him. I don't intend to marry him."

Con's lips twitched as though he were amused, but he only said mildly, "I didn't expect you would."

Kaede sighed. "Tell that to my father."

"All right, I will."

She gave him a skeptical look. "What do you mean?"

"When we return, I'll talk to your father."

"My father won't listen to you."

"Why not?" He waggled his eyebrows at her. "You don't believe in my powers of persuasion?"

She rolled her eyes. "My father is the most stubborn man alive. He usually gets what he wants."

"Have a little faith in me." He grinned at her. "I am your future King."

She smiled faintly. She knew he was joking with her, but the thought of the future was sobering. Tali and Pol, both dead, and now Shae hovering on the edge. She said quietly, "I hope Shae will be all right."

Con stiffened; his grin vanished. "Shae is going to be fine," he insisted. He picked up a stick and began to poke at the fire.

"Of course she is," Kaede agreed. Con's brows were knitted with worry again, and she was sorry she had brought it up. If she had doubted his feelings for Shae before, she no longer did.

She watched Con run a hand through his hair; it had grown at least an inch since they had left Cathair, and now it stuck out everywhere, as if he were a porcupine. Kaede noticed he had grown a beard, too, and she wondered when he had stopped shaving. It had been some time, she guessed. Wearing dirty, bloodstained clothes, he looked more like a highway bandit than a prince. But when they returned— *when*, she told herself, not *if*—he would also return to his obligations, and they did not include falling in love with a guard.

Kaede asked, "Has your father spoken to you about marriage?"

"No." Sparks flew up as Con broke apart one of the burning pieces of wood. "He has been busy with his new bride," he said bitterly. "And by the time we return, I suspect I'll have a new half brother or half sister." He stared at the fire with a dour expression. "I'm guessing it'll be at least another year before my father realizes he could use me that way."

At that moment, the cottage door opened, and Taisin came outside. "We're finished," she said. She looked exhausted, with purple smudges beneath her eyes and yellow and red stains on the front of her tunic.

Con stood up and asked immediately, "How is she?"

Taisin sat down on the log, rubbing at her tired eyes. "She is as well as she can be, given the circumstances."

"Is she in pain?" Con asked.

"She is sleeping. Now all we can do is wait."

࿊

They slept away the afternoon, curled up around the fire pit, and even Con dozed a little. When Taisin awoke, evening was falling in lush, soft shadows around them, and Mona was pulling an iron teapot out of the fire.

Taisin pushed herself up, blinking in the firelight. "How is Shae?" she asked, her voice thick with sleep.

"She's resting," Mona answered.

Con was holding a small iron cup of tea. "She looks a little better," he said. He had gone inside the cottage as soon as Mona came out, and he had been relieved to see some improvement. Shae's fever had cooled somewhat, although she was still hot to the touch.

Mona poured another cup and handed it to Taisin. "Be careful. It's hot."

Taisin took it gingerly, holding it by the rim. The fragrance of summer flowers wafted up at her. "Where's Kaede?" she asked.

"She'll be back soon. Ah! There she is now."

Kaede came from the lean-to behind the cottage carrying an earthenware jar. "Is this what you were looking for?" she asked, handing it to Mona.

"Oh, yes," the woman said. Her smile spread wrinkles across her whole face. With a deft twist, she opened the jar. "I haven't had visitors in so long." She sounded both eager and a bit uncertain. "The occasion deserves something special, doesn't it?" She handed the jar back to Kaede, who sniffed it: honey. Her mouth watered instantly; it had been so long since she had tasted something sweet that she wanted to upend the entire jar into her mouth. Mona laughed at her. "Use this, my dear," she said, and handed her a wooden spoon and a steaming cup of tea. Then she turned to Con and added, "Although I'm afraid I can't offer you anything to compete with the King's table."

He paused, teacup half-raised to his mouth. He hadn't told her who he was. "How did—do you know who I am?"

"I have seen your face before, Your Highness," she said.

"Where?"

She shook her head, clucking her tongue. "I cannot reveal my secrets. I know you and your companions are embarked on a very important journey, and I am so pleased that I have been able to do my part in it."

"Did you know to expect us?" Kaede asked.

"Expect?" Mona repeated. "I don't think that is the right word, exactly. Although I have been seeing pieces of you all for years, you know."

Kaede considered the old woman's impish expression. "Do you have the Sight?"

"It is not what you would call the Sight," Mona said, clucking her tongue again. "No, not what you would know. Young Taisin here may have an idea…she has visions I would never dream of having." Mona gave Taisin a smile that was almost proud, and Taisin looked nervous. "Do not be afraid of your visions," Mona said to Taisin, speaking as if she were addressing a small child. "You must be open to them—open to everything under the sun and the moon, though these are both obscured to us now...sadly."

Con set his teacup gently on the ground and said, "Madam, you are undoubtedly a wise woman. May I ask how many years you have lived here in the Great Wood?"

She turned her head toward him almost coquettishly. "I am not averse to some flattery, indeed I am not, young prince. I have lived beneath these trees for longer than you have been alive, certainly."

He smiled at her. "Then you must surely know much about this Wood that I—that we do not. Will you look at our maps and share your knowledge about the land here?"

"Oh, maps," Mona said, her voice lilting. "What have maps to do with anything? They do not show the true path." She sighed. "But of course I will look at them, though I assure you they are useless."

Puzzled, Con went and retrieved the maps from their long carrying case. He spread them out on the ground near Mona, taking care to avoid the fire. The light flickered over the paper as the old woman crouched down and stared at the lines demarcating the Great Wood, the river Nir, the Kell. Con pointed at a spot south of the intersection of the two rivers and said, "Is this where we are?"

Mona squinted down at the map and said, "That may be. Yes, that may be." She gestured broadly at the northern portion of the map, which was largely unmarked forest. "All of that is wrong. All wrong."

"Have you been north of the Kell?" Con asked.

"No, not I," Mona objected, as if affronted. "I stay to my side of the boundary."

"So there is still an agreed-upon boundary?" Con said.

"Well, I have agreed to my own boundary." Mona laughed as if she had told a joke. Then her face grew serious, and she pointed at the line of the Kell. "This," she said. "This is the boundary I have agreed upon. I stay on my side, and they don't bother me."

"Who?" Con asked.

"The fay, of course," Mona said.

"You mean the Xi?" Kaede said.

"The Xi are only one of many races of fay peoples," Mona said. She added with an arch smile, "Perhaps the most arrogant ones. The Fairy Queen, of course, purports to rule them all."

Kaede asked curiously, "What other fay races are there?"

Mona shook her head. "It is not so simple, young one. Many of them have died out. There were wars between many races; few survived." But then she seemed truly delighted as she added, "And yet life moves in its cycles, doesn't it? I believe some fairies survived after all. I saw the loveliest little sprite the other day—moving just like a hummingbird. Do you know those? So pretty."

A thrill ran through Taisin as she heard Mona describe the sprite. Was that the name of the creature she saw in her visions? She burned with questions, but Mona picked up her staff and levered herself to her feet. "Nonetheless, it makes no difference to you," she said. "You won't see anything that doesn't want to be seen."

Con said, "Madam, we must travel north of the Kell. We'll surely encounter the Xi, won't we?"

She gave him a measuring look and answered, "It is unwise of you to cross the river."

"We have an invitation from the Fairy Queen," Con said.

"An invitation?" Mona said, her white eyebrows rising. "A true invitation?"

"Yes," Con said.

Mona shrugged. "Then perhaps all will be well."

"Do you know where we should cross the river?" he asked. "Is there a bridge?"

"I have been to the river, but never forded it. You will be safe enough on this side if you keep quiet about your destination—the Wood listens, you know. But on the other side, it is not a place for humans." She paused for a moment as if considering whether or not to tell them something. At last she said, "When I visited the Kell some years ago, I saw the Xi. They guard the border, I think. A great phalanx of them, hunters all. With bows and swords and grand horses. They kindly allowed me to leave without an arrow in my back."

And then Mona looked up at the darkening sky and seemed to remember something. "Oh, my, it is growing late! Taisin, you had better come with me; I'll need your assistance sitting up with our invalid tonight."

Chapter XXV

y now, Taisin recognized parts of the fortress—the long, sloping corridor; the cavernous ceiling hung with icicles sharp as swords; the endless ranks of golden cages. And then there were the creatures she had seen, each one equally strange and beautiful. Some had scales like fish, and they slipped beneath still pools. Others, with fingers as gnarled as tree roots, nevertheless moved with the grace of leaves in a summer breeze. But the only creature she had seen whole was the winged fairy, who repeatedly flew down that corridor as if she were doomed to traverse the same small space for eternity.

It wasn't until late at night in Mona's cottage, when Shae was finally resting peacefully, that Taisin saw the other woman. Mona was asleep in her chair by the fire, and perhaps it was the greenwitch's presence that made it possible for Taisin to finally see her. One moment Taisin was lying on the pallet she had made on the floor next to the bed, and the next she was moving swiftly down the same corridor she had floated through countless times before—but this time, she was walking.

She could feel the contours of her body—this woman's body—and she wore a gown of some kind of heavy fabric. A cloak of ermine was draped around her shoulders. The floor was cold beneath the thin soles of her shoes, but she was used to the cold; it no longer bothered her. Taisin felt a fierce protectiveness for the ice, and it surprised her. This woman was in love with the mountain she had raised, block by block, from the frozen northern sea. She was no one to be toyed with, for she could shape icebergs into towers so high they scratched the sky. Taisin felt the power in the woman's veins, and she was awed by the strength of it. The way Taisin herself had felt when she had ripped into the fabric of the world to kill those wolves—that was only the beginning of what this woman could do.

She walked briskly to the end of the corridor, and Taisin saw her hand pushing open a door. The sight that greeted her made the woman swell with pride and determination. It was a nursery. On a dais, as if it were a throne, was a cradle made of crystal. Small hands reached up from within, and the woman went to the cradle and lifted out a baby. It was a perfect child in many ways. It had soft, sweet skin, and tiny fingers and dimpled knuckles. Verdant green eyes looked up at her from beneath long black lashes. Then the child opened its mouth and turned its head, and sank a row of pearly little fangs into the woman's arm.

Taisin felt the pain herself; it was as though she had been stabbed by a half-dozen little needles, each one poison-tipped. She jerked on the floor of Mona's cottage, and in the fortress the woman snarled at the baby and threw it, hard, against the edge of the cradle.

Blood smeared against the crystal, and Taisin was stunned by the strength of the woman's rage. It boiled out of her: pain and anger and choking, bitter disappointment.

And then, in a jarring, disorienting lurch, Taisin felt Mona's hand on her, shaking her, calling her name, and she awoke on the floor of the cottage.

The old woman was standing over her, that one milky eye fixed on her as though it could see into her mind. "Where did you go?" Mona muttered, prodding at her with the end of her staff. "No use in flying off to unsafe places. Keep your wits about you."

Taisin pushed her hair away from her eyes; her hand came away damp with sweat. "I will," she said. "I do."

Mona gave her a skeptical look. "You are walking a fine line."

Taisin was confused. The vision of the ice fortress still clung to her, making this world seem hazy, unreal. "What do you mean?"

Mona shook her head as if Taisin were a rebellious child. "What you did yesterday to those wolves—I haven't felt anything like that since...well, not since I was a very young girl. You had better keep an eye on yourself. These things have a way of turning."

Taisin went cold all over. Mona's blue eye was icy as she gazed at her, unblinking, and Taisin felt utterly exposed, as though Mona were peeling back layer upon layer of her defenses and examining each one. Taisin remembered how it felt to bend the meridians of energy to her will: like she was invincible. She realized—half ashamed, half defiant—that she yearned to feel that way again. To hold the webbing of the world in her hands, and to use it.

Mona bent down and clutched Taisin's chin in her bony hand and nearly spit in her face as she said, "You listen to me, young Taisin. You have a strong heart, but even the strongest heart can be tempted."

Taisin tried to pull back, but Mona's iron grip was bruising in its strength. It seemed to reach through her—within her—and smothered the flame of that desire until all that remained was a hard, hot little ember.

Mona let go, and Taisin fell back, gasping and weak. The old woman gestured toward Shae, pushing up her sleeves. "She's ready for her next infusion. Will you bring the herbs?"

Taisin was transfixed by the sight of Mona's bare forearm: There was a mark there, but though it was roughly the same size and shape as a sage's mark, it was a solid black circle, not the symbols that Taisin had seen before. It was as though Mona had once been marked, but had since chosen to efface the symbol—or to erase it. Mona saw her eyeing the mark, and she said shortly, "We don't all make the right choices when we're young."

"What do you mean? Are you a marked sage?"

"No."

"But what is that—"

"I might have once been marked, but I am no longer."

Taisin was incredulous. "How could you reject your station like that? It is an honor to be marked." Another possibility came to her, and the idea that the Council might

216

have stripped Mona of her marking made her look at the greenwitch uneasily. It could only be a horrible thing that would cause the Council to revoke a sage's status.

Mona's eyes narrowed and she leaned down so that she was peering directly into Taisin's eyes with her single good one. "Not everything they teach you is true. I have chosen my own path. So must you." She backed away and returned to Shae's bedside. "Now will you bring me those herbs?"

༄

Later that night, Mona slept again in her rocking chair, gently snoring. But Taisin couldn't sleep anymore; her thoughts circled endlessly around Mona's strange words, the awful vision, and the black mark.

Shivering, she wrapped her blanket tighter around herself and crawled over to the hearth to stir the coals. The flaring light illuminated the books stacked around the trunk nearby, and as the shadows leapt over the bindings, she began to wonder what was in them. She glanced at Mona, who was still asleep, and then reached for the closest volume, pulling it down as quietly as possible and opening it in her lap. It was a journal of some sort containing long lists of what looked like herbs or plants. The last quarter of the pages were blank, and she realized they must be Mona's own records. She closed the book and pulled out another, and another, motivated by a rising compulsion she did not understand. She felt as if she were searching for something. But book after book disappointed her—they all seemed to be journals of plant life, notations about tonics or medicines. In every one, the handwriting was the same: tiny, precise, taking up no more room than was necessary. Taisin assumed it was Mona's work, and it made sense, for she had known precisely what to do for Shae's injuries. Mona had spent her whole life, apparently, studying the medicinal properties of herbs.

The last book on the stack nearest to Taisin was the largest yet, and Taisin opened it expecting more of the same. But this time, there were illustrations, too, and they were not illustrations of plants. The drawings—sometimes crude, but always lifelike—depicted creatures like the ones she saw in her visions. Holding her breath in excitement, she stopped at a picture of a being with wings just like a hummingbird's. There were notes there, too, in Mona's handwriting. *Sprite*, Taisin read. She turned the page. A slender woman with hair like sea kelp: *asrai. Found in the icy waters of the north.* A dwarflike being with legs as thick as tree trunks: *knocker.* And another creature that looked as if it had been sprung from the limbs of an oak tree: *wood nymph.* Taisin stared at it, her mouth open, remembering the body they had buried outside of Jilin.

"Find something interesting?" Mona said.

Taisin started, looking up at the greenwitch. "Are these creatures...are these all fairies?" Taisin asked, her heart racing.

Mona cocked her head, reminding Taisin of a bird with a very sharp beak. For a moment Mona's shadow seemed to arch overhead malevolently, but then Mona settled back into her chair, and she was just an old woman again. "What a silly question," Mona finally said, though there was no sting in her voice. "What else could they be?"

Taisin looked back at the drawing of the wood nymph.

Notes were scrawled around the picture. "Is this your handwriting?"

"Some of it is. Some of that book was wrong. I had to correct it."

"You mean this book was..." Taisin trailed off, thinking. "Where did this book come from?"

"I rescued it from the Academy," Mona said, and she sounded almost cheerful about it.

"You *rescued* it?"

Mona leaned down, the birdlike look back in her eye. "You trust your teachers, do you?"

"Yes," Taisin said, feeling defensive. "Why shouldn't I?"

"Did they teach you about these fairies?"

Taisin hesitated. "No, but—"

"But what, my dear? They have sent you on this journey through the Great Wood without even telling you about the creatures you might encounter?" Mona put her bony hand on her chest, a look of sorrow sweeping over her face. "I wouldn't trust anyone who did that to me. Why should you?"

Taisin was disconcerted. Was Mona right? She thought of Sister Ailan, who had always seemed to be so honorable and honest. She thought of Maire Morighan and the other teachers, who had all been generous and kind to her, and answered every question she posed, no matter what it was. Had she been asking the wrong questions?

Mona seemed to see the confusion in her face, for the old woman said, "You read that book tonight. And when you return to the Academy, perhaps *you* will have something to teach your teachers."

Chapter XXVI

hey spent two nights at Mona's cottage. Taisin showed Con and Kaede the book of fairies, and they pored over its yellowed pages for hours. By the second night, Shae's fever was gone, but she was still too weak to travel. When Mona offered to shelter Shae until she was recovered enough to return to Jilin, they knew they had to move on. Midsummer—and their appointment with the Fairy Queen—was less than a fortnight away, and they had no idea if they would arrive in time.

Con lingered by Shae's bedside on the morning of their departure. She drifted in and out of a drugged sleep, and all he could do was hold her hand. "We're coming back," he whispered, as much for himself as for her. His eyes were hot with suppressed tears. "I promise you."

They left Shae's horse behind, along with her gear and a tent, but they took all the remaining food supplies. There wasn't much, and Kaede began to wonder if she would have to attempt to hunt on her own. She felt extremely vulnerable now, traveling only with Taisin and Con. The two days at Mona's cottage had been a reprieve from cold reality, but now, as they made their way down an overgrown trail that surely hadn't seen human traffic in generations, that reality returned. They had lost their leader in Tali. They had lost Pol and Shae, who knew how to survive in the wilderness. Now they were only three, and Kaede was terrified that the Wood might demand another sacrifice. They took care to stay within sight of each other at all times, and Kaede carried Pol's bow across her lap.

She watched Taisin's back as they rode, wondering what she was thinking. She had been a little distant since the wolf attack, and it made Kaede anxious. What if the things that Taisin had done to those wolves had changed her? There were warnings, rules against using the energies to harm any living being. But had she done anything worse than what Kaede had also done, using Pol's bow?

When the time came for Taisin to perform the protection ritual around their camp, Kaede was tense, wondering if there would be something different in Taisin tonight. And when Taisin's fingers pressed firmly against Kaede's chest, something *had* changed. But it was not what Kaede expected. There was a new strength to her; there were no hesitations in her movements. And the connection that had grown between them was still there. It had slackened a bit in last few days, but now it tightened again. Perhaps because of Taisin's new confidence, today the connection opened up, and for the first time, each could see a tiny part of the other.

In the breathless moment before Taisin realized what she

had done, Kaede saw some of the truth that Taisin was hiding from her. Taisin was falling in love with her—the emotions were as clear and hot as a summer sky. But beneath them was the bitter tang of fear.

When Taisin broke the connection, Kaede staggered. She was overjoyed, but she was also confused. She reached out for Taisin's hand, but she had already turned away to finish the ritual. When it was done, her face was a carefully controlled mask; she would not meet Kaede's eyes.

Con saw the tension between them, and he came to Kaede as Taisin put away her supplies and asked, "What happened?"

Kaede looked up at him, dazed. She couldn't tell him. She wasn't even sure what it meant. And had Taisin seen her own feelings as well? She reddened to think of it.

"Kaede?"

"It's nothing," she said. But her heart hammered in her chest, and she trembled as she went to light the campfire.

In the middle of the night, Taisin woke Kaede to take over the watch, shaking her shoulder gently. Kaede pushed herself up, and Taisin pulled back. Con was asleep in his bedroll on the other side of the low-burning fire, and the trees arched above in a rib cage of bare branches.

Kaede fumbled for words. Her mouth was clumsy, fogged with uneasy sleep. "What did—tell me—"

She half expected Taisin to flee from her, but when Taisin remained where she was, her face pale and tense, Kaede tried again.

"Why—why are you afraid of your feelings?" she whispered.

Taisin bit her lip. She looked away from Kaede; she looked down at her hands; they twisted together as if she were trying to weave a rope around her wrists. She said something so softly that Kaede could not hear it.

Kaede pushed aside her blankets, leaning toward Taisin. "You can tell me."

Taisin touched Kaede's cheek very gently. Her fingers were cold. Kaede reached for her, but Taisin drew back, flushing. Kaede waited. Taisin's eyes, reflecting the firelight, looked like tiny burning stars. Finally she said in a low voice, "I'm going to be a sage."

"I know that."

"I can't—I can't be with anyone." Her words were full of regret. "I'm sorry. I'm so sorry."

The misery in her voice made Kaede ache. She wanted to ease Taisin's pain, but she had no idea how.

Taisin turned away, wrapping her blankets around herself, and then lay down with her back to Kaede. The distance between them, though it was only a few feet, had never seemed so great.

෨

The third day after leaving Shae behind, they came to the river Kell. It was a grand sight to behold. The Nir and the Kell branched off from a wide, tumbling rush of water coming from the north, the Nir continuing south and the Kell running east. Both rivers were swollen with rainfall and thick with boulders that created dozens of small, swift waterfalls. The rains that had doused the travelers repeatedly on their journey had fed into the rivers, making them particularly treacherous to cross.

They agreed to travel east to search for a better place to ford the Kell, and when they came to a shallow beach in the early afternoon, Con stopped. "Perhaps we should just cross here. There are fewer boulders in the river, and who knows how far we'd have to go to find a calmer spot."

Taisin looked out at the river. He seemed to be right— the way was mostly clear. On the far side, the trees looked just like they did on this side. There was no sign of the Xi. "It will be cold," Taisin said.

"We'd better cross soon, then," Kaede said, "or wait until morning. It'll be difficult to dry off after night falls."

Con squinted up at the hard, bright gray sky. "We have time. I don't think we should wait."

They unwound the longest coil of rope they had, tying each horse to it. They secured their bedrolls and supplies as well as they could.

"Hold on to your horse if you lose your footing," Con advised, trying to remember what Tali had taught him. "They will swim." As soon as he was ready, before he could second-guess himself, he led his horse into the river. The packhorse went next, followed by Taisin and her horse, and finally Kaede stepped into the water, leading Maila.

At first, it was just cold. Kaede shivered when the water rose above her boots and began to seep through the fabric of her trousers, but she was not prepared for the icy wash of it when she was chest-deep in the river. They were barely twenty feet from the bank at that point, and there was more than three quarters of the way to go. She began to wonder if this had been a wise choice, but Con was already too far ahead to turn back. She gritted her teeth and plunged deeper into the Kell.

She quickly realized that though the river had appeared to be unobstructed here, the boulders were merely underwater, and the river itself was deeper than it seemed. The closer she swam toward the center of the Kell, the colder it became and the swifter it flowed. Her knee smashed into a submerged boulder and she cried out at the impact. River water gushed into her mouth, nearly choking her. She felt like she was struggling in the embrace of a slippery, suffocating beast, and for a moment it pulled her down below. When she fought her way back to the surface, her eyes stung and everything was askew. She saw the trees on the far bank at a strange angle; she saw the gray sky lurching above; she saw Maila battling against the current. Kaede lunged toward her horse, grabbing onto the stirrups beneath the water and kicking back with her legs.

This was not like swimming in the ocean by Seatown. The water there would rise up and buoy her before the waves crested over her head. She knew how to float on those waves, how to close her eyes and pinch her nose shut when the wave came toward her. She knew that those waves would push her inexorably toward the beach, and she and her brothers used to laughingly skim along their crests until they were spit out on the sand. But here the river was pulling her downstream, and she was trying desperately to elude its powerful grip. Ahead of her she saw Con approaching the opposite bank, and Taisin was almost through the wide, fast center. Kaede kept her eyes on them, and she had just crossed the halfway point when Taisin's head went underneath and did not come up again.

It happened so swiftly—as if she had simply been swallowed. Kaede felt as though she had been punched in the gut.

"Taisin!" she screamed, and freezing water went down her throat. She spit out, coughing, floundering, the entire world heaving with the rush of the river.

Kaede sucked in as much air as she could and dived down after her. The water was clear, but there was very little light beneath the surface; all she could see of Taisin was a murky fluttering ahead of her, as if someone were spinning, struggling to escape a trap. She kicked forward, her lungs beginning to burn, and miraculously, she found Taisin's hand. She gripped her fingers as firmly as she could and lunged up toward the light. When she broke through she gasped, desperate for air, and yanked again at Taisin.

She bobbed up to the surface, limp, her body still pulled downstream, her face pale and her eyes closed.

Con had already climbed out of the river, and two of the horses stood shivering on the bank, but now he saw Kaede and Taisin struggling. He pulled out another rope, tying one end to his horse's saddle and then wrapping it around his waist before he began wading back into the water. Kaede tried to sling Taisin's arm around her, but the river was too strong. All she could do was drag her while keeping Taisin's head above water. When Con was waist-deep in the river he threw the rope in Kaede's direction. At first it missed them entirely, and Kaede just stubbornly pushed on toward the bank. She no longer felt the cold; it was as if all the blood in her body had turned to ice. Now there was only one thing to do: overcome the river, and she had no intention of giving up.

The second time Con threw the rope Kaede caught it, rough and wet, in her right hand. She struggled to wrap it around Taisin's waist, and several desperate minutes later, after they had been dragged another twenty feet downstream, she succeeded, and Con began to pull them onto the bank. When her feet touched the riverbed again, Kaede put her arms around Taisin's motionless body and picked her up, the weight of her partially supported by the water, and carried her until Con met her and helped lay Taisin down on the riverbank. They pushed at Taisin's chest, hard, until water bubbled out of her mouth and her eyes opened. She coughed, rolling over, and Kaede helped her up onto her hands and knees, her body convulsing as she spit the water out of her lungs. Taisin began to shake with cold, and Kaede said to Con, "We need to build a fire."

He pulled a mostly dry bedroll out from within the gear packed onto his horse and tossed it to Kaede. "I'll find firewood," he said. "You need to get her out of those wet clothes." He had stripped off his own shirt and was pulling on another, drier one, but he did not bother to change out of his wet trousers before heading off into the trees.

Kaede began to unbutton Taisin's tunic, pulling the heavy, wet cloth away from her chilled skin. Goose bumps rose on Taisin's shoulders when she felt the air, and she shivered more violently. Kaede pulled the blanket toward them and draped it over Taisin, who attempted to unlace her boots with numb fingers. "Just sit there," Kaede ordered, throwing the wet tunic aside. "I'll do that." She listened to Taisin's chattering teeth as she worked the wet laces, wanting to curse at the knots Taisin had tied. But at last she had them undone and pulled the soaked leather off, and as she reached for the clasps that fastened Taisin's trousers, Taisin put her hands on Kaede's to stop her.

"Thank you," Taisin said. Her lips were bluish-purple, her fingers like icicles.

All of a sudden, Kaede realized she was she was staring at Taisin, stripped to the waist, the medallion like a black eye hanging around her neck. Her face was white as snow but for rough red spots burning on her cheeks, and Kaede felt herself flush in response.

They heard Con returning, his footsteps seeming inordinately loud. Taisin pulled the blanket around her bare shoulders, covering herself, and Kaede backed away, sitting on her heels. "You don't have to thank me," she said awkwardly. She looked away; she looked at the river that had almost taken Taisin away from them. From her.

It was deceptively beautiful, for being such a monstrous thing.

They staked out the horses close to the fire, where Taisin sat huddled in the blanket. Kaede hung the kettle over the flames, and before night fell she had brewed tea for them all to sip, crouching close to the blaze.

"Everything's going to be wet for days unless we stay here tomorrow," Con said. "We'll have to lay everything out on the riverbank and hope they dry."

"Is it safe to stay here?" Kaede asked. "What was it like in the Wood?" She glanced at the trees nearby; the low light turned all colors into shadows upon shadows.

"It looked no different than the Wood south of the river. It might be a good idea to stay here and scout around a bit—see if there is a trail. We can leave our things here to dry while we explore this bank."

"Tonight, at least, all we have to do is eat and sleep," Kaede said. "That was not an easy crossing." She put down her cup and went to retrieve supplies for supper. But just at the edge of the camp she saw something that made her halt. There was a horse and rider, nearly obscured by the twilight. And then she saw another beside him. "Taisin," Kaede said in a low voice. "Con. Look."

Taisin and Con scrambled to their feet. Con's sword rang as he pulled it out of its scabbard.

More riders emerged out of the dusk, ghostlike, until they had surrounded the camp. As they came closer they seemed to take on something of a glow. They were tall and pale, with white clothing and eerie, sparkling eyes. Some of them wore swords on their belts; others had quivers of arrows strapped to their backs. There were men and women both, but they all shared the same otherworldly beauty: hard and cold and perfect.

One of the riders pushed his horse a few steps closer to the three humans. He asked in a peculiar accent: "Who are you, and why have you crossed over into our lands?"

PART IV

Some seek to act upon the world,
But success will not follow.
The world is inviolable:
It has no beginning and no end.
Those who seek to change it will be changed;
Those who grasp onto stones will find water.

—Book of Changes

Chapter XXVII

aede couldn't tear her eyes away from the riders. They were the most foreign-looking people she had ever seen, and she didn't feel fear so much as curiosity and a rising excitement. Were these the Xi at last?

In answer to their question, Con stepped forward, squaring his shoulders. "I am Con Isae Tan, prince of the Kingdom. Are you representatives of the Xi?"

The rider who had spoken inclined his head. "We are. Why are you here?"

"I have come at the invitation of your queen. Will you allow me to show you the invitation?"

"Show us, then."

Con went to his saddlebags to retrieve the invitation, still ensconced in its intricately carved box. He handed it to the rider, who opened it and unrolled the scroll. "This is an invitation for King Cai, not you."

"I am his only son," Con said. "He has sent me in his stead."

The rider gazed at him, expressionless, and Con felt perspiration rising on his forehead. The man's blue eyes were so penetrating that Con had difficulty maintaining his composure. Finally the rider said, "Come closer, princeling."

Con moved toward him, and to his surprise, the rider dismounted. Con halted, unsure of what to do, and the rider walked slowly around him, examining him as if he were a new dog, acquired for a particular purpose. Con had the disconcerting feeling that the man might pry open his mouth and examine his teeth, but then the rider only asked, "Who are your companions?"

Con let out his breath in relief. He had apparently passed some kind of test. "They are representatives from the Council of Sages."

"The Council of Sages," he said. "I have not heard of them in...many of your generations."

All the riders' eyes flickered to Taisin and Kaede, and Kaede felt as though she had just been buffeted by a strong wind. She stepped back, startled by the force of their gaze. Their leader came to look at her, circling her as he had done to Con. His eyes narrowed on her as if he saw something odd, and for a long moment they locked on hers. She stared back, fascinated—she had never seen eyes of such deep blue—and just as she began to wonder why he was so interested in her, he turned away and moved on to Taisin.

Taisin had watched with growing anxiety as he examined Con and Kaede as if they were fantastical creatures. When he approached her, she felt his curiosity ripple through the meridians between them, and then it sharpened, his eyes focusing on her. He came closer and extended a hand until his fingertips nearly touched her chest. She felt the medallion, hidden beneath her tunic, suddenly burning against her skin. "What do you have there?" he asked.

Wordlessly, her skin buzzing where the medallion radiated heat, she pulled the chain over her head and held it out to him. In his hand, the stone took on a dull light as if it were awakening at his touch. He gazed at it, and she saw him clench his jaw just slightly. "This is not yours to keep," he said. "But you shall wear it until our queen tells you otherwise." He placed it over her head so quickly she barely had time to notice how close he was—a glimpse of the paleness of his throat—and then he moved away and the chain was warm around her neck again.

Behind him several of the riders dismounted and moved toward their belongings as if to take them. "What are you doing?" Con asked, startled.

The man turned toward him and said, "You and your companions will come with us."

"Where?" Con demanded.

"We will take you to your meeting with our queen."

"Right now? It is nearly full night."

The man gave him a tiny smile. "Your meeting is scheduled for Midsummer, and that is scarcely one week from now. We've no time to waste."

"Wait," Taisin said.

The leader turned. "Yes?"

"Who are you?"

He did not answer at first, and even looked back at the

other riders as though they were sharing a secret. At last he said, "We are the Fairy Hunt. You may call me the Huntsman."

They set off as soon as the horses were saddled, with the Huntsman riding in the lead. Though the Wood was pitch-black all around them, the riders of the Fairy Hunt stood out against the dark. Kaede thought that it wasn't exactly as if they glowed, but rather there was a lightness about them. Their skin was almost translucent, and she could swear she saw the texture of their muscles moving beneath it. She wondered if their blood was red like hers, or if it was some other queer color. Did it flow as thickly as mercury, or was it thin as water? She had never felt so different from someone in her life.

The Xi stopped only to allow their human charges to relieve themselves, and they would have continued without further pause until Con insisted that they be allowed to rest their horses and to eat. Dawn was breaking by then, and the Wood was slowly coming into light. Kaede was exhausted and her stomach growled, and she felt almost too tired and light-headed to find her way from her horse to their supplies. The Hunt had dismounted, too, and the riders were ranged around the three of them in a loose ring, as if to prevent them from running away. Kaede did her best to ignore them as she pulled out their food. They were down to eating biscuits, now, dried hard and nearly tasteless. She took one and handed the tin to Con and Taisin, who looked as tired as she felt. "Tea," Kaede muttered to them. "I'll start the fire."

The Xi watched her curiously as she began to gather wood, but as she approached the edge of their ring, one of them stopped her and asked, "Where are you going?"

"I need to find more wood to build a fire," she said, raising her eyes to the slender man's blue ones. She shivered.

The rider looked behind her and said something to one of the others in a language she did not understand, then turned back to Kaede. "Fire is all you need?" he said, his eyebrows raised as if he were amused. He opened his hand and there, in his palm, a flame danced for her.

She backed away. "I—I want to boil water."

He cocked his head at her. He was younger than the one who led them, she noticed. His face was smooth as a baby's; his hair like white silk capped over his shapely head. His full, pale pink lips curved upward in a smile, and she felt distinctly uncomfortable. He extended his arm, holding out the burning golden flame, and went toward the small pile of wood she had left on the forest floor, and set the pile alight.

Swallowing, Kaede set up the iron tripod and hung the kettle over the fire. It was as hot as any natural fire, but it did not eat away at the wood; instead, it licked at the fallen branches, almost caressing them. But it still caused the water to boil—perhaps more quickly, even— and the tea tasted no different than it had the day before. Con, Taisin, and Kaede squatted on the ground around the fire, for it was good to feel its warmth, and Kaede tried to soften her biscuit in the tea before she ate the rest of it.

Some of the Xi came a bit closer to observe them, but most seemed to rapidly lose interest in their activities and began to pace back and forth, eager to move on. The young one who had started the fire came close enough to lean over Kaede's shoulder and look at the biscuit in her hand. He asked, "What is that called?"

There was a disconcerting gleam in his eye, as if he wanted to have a bite of her rather than the biscuit. Before she could answer, the Huntsman called to him in a sharp tone of voice, and the young one looked briefly petulant before he withdrew, going back to the edge of the circle of riders.

When they finished eating, they packed their cups and kettle back into their saddlebags, and the Huntsman snuffed out the fire. He passed his hands over the flames once, and then the woodpile was bare and cold, not burned at all. Kaede wondered if it would even be warm if she touched it. "It is time to leave," he said, and though his voice was barely louder than a whisper, all of the Hunt turned in unison to their horses, prepared to go.

They rode steadily that day, stopping only when Con or Kaede or Taisin requested it. The Xi did not seem to eat; nor did their horses seem to need any rest. Kaede felt Maila tire as the day progressed, but she continued on as if compelled. The trees around them began to change as they left the river behind. Oak trees gradually gave way to evergreens. The evergreens grew taller and taller. By late afternoon, they were riding through a forest of trees with trunks wider than the length of the wagon they had left behind in Jilin. The branches drooped down at them, heavy with soft, dark green needles. The colors here were richer than they had been south of the river, where half the trees had turned brown from lack of sunlight. The sky was still gray here, but there was something different about the quality of the air. It was warmer, for one thing, almost as warm as it should be at midsummer. But there was something else, too, and it visibly affected the members of the Fairy Hunt. The farther they rode from the Kell, the more the Xi seemed to shine. They were coming home.

At nightfall, worn to the bone and feeling as though she might fall asleep in the saddle, Kaede was relieved when the Huntsman stopped and told them they could set up camp. He had chosen a clearing near a brook that ran over a rocky streambed, and when Kaede knelt by its side to refill her water skin, the liquid was shockingly cold on her hands. The icy taste of it made her throat momentarily numb. She came fully awake and saw Con and Taisin, too, reeling from the water's chill.

"We should drink *that* in the morning," Con said, and Kaede laughed. Even Taisin, who was so tired she felt like her body had been dragged across that rocky streambed, couldn't help but smile. The three of them looked at one another, and for a moment they felt entirely human again. Weary, hungry, and cold, but human. Kaede felt her muscles begin to relax. For all the strangeness of their escort, she had Con and Taisin with her, and they would do all right.

They slept soundly that night, curled up in their blankets near the Xi's magical fire, the ghostly riders spread around them, again, in a ring. When she woke the next morning, Kaede lay there in silence for a while, blinking her eyes at the early light. Some of the riders were gone. Those who remained did not look like they had slept at all, but nor did they look tired. One of them saw that Kaede had awoken, and he nodded to her almost pleasantly—as if this were an entirely normal thing, for him to be guarding a group of sleeping, worn-out humans in the middle of the Great Wood. And she realized that yes, that was what they were doing—these Xi were *guarding* them. She and Taisin and Con were not prisoners. They were being protected.

The idea startled her. She rolled over onto her back, looking up at the sky cupped by the circle of trees around their camp. She thought there was something wrong with her eyes at first, and she blinked several times, but it was still there: On the edges of the bowl of sky, there was the faintest trace of blue.

Chapter XXVIII

They traveled for a week in the company of the Fairy Hunt. Kaede often watched the riders surreptitiously, marveling at the grace of their movements. They were like dancers, sinuous and light on their feet, yet there was always something about them that marked them as plainly inhuman. There was a curious play of light and shadow in their faces that made it difficult to understand their expressions. And when one of them looked at her, Kaede found it almost impossible to look away. It was disturbing.

One evening the Huntsman came and sat with them, and at first Taisin, Con, and Kaede simply stared at him, for none of the riders ever joined them at the fire. Finally Kaede, who had just finished eating her tasteless biscuit, blurted out, "Do you ever eat?" Immediately she colored, and Con and Taisin tensed.

But the Huntsman only raised his eyebrows, and Kaede thought she recognized his expression. He was amused. "We eat," he said. "But not while we are on duty."

"Duty?" she repeated, her mouth dry.

"We eat when you sleep," he explained.

"Oh."

They all sat in silence for several more minutes, and then the Huntsman stood and walked away. Con, Taisin, and Kaede looked at one another in confusion.

"Why did you say that?" Con whispered.

"I don't know," Kaede whispered back. "Aren't you curious?"

He gave her an exasperated look, and then Taisin reached out and put a hand on Kaede's arm. Her skin tingled at Taisin's touch. The Huntsman was returning, and he had something in his hand.

He held it out to them with something of a flourish. "Would you like to try some of our food?" he asked. Lying on an unfolded cloth was a square of something that was yellowish-white in color. To Kaede, it looked like a white bean cake, but there was something different about its texture.

"What is it?" Kaede asked. Taisin's hand fell away, leaving a palpable sense of absence behind.

"Cheese," he answered. With a bone-handled knife, he sliced off a small piece and offered it to her.

It tasted nothing like what she expected. It was savory rather than bland; it was chewy rather than soft. The sharp flavor lingered on her tongue after she swallowed it. She wasn't sure if she liked it or not, but she tried to smile at the Huntsman and said, "Thank you."

The corners of his mouth twitched.

As they traveled north, the trees became taller, greener, stronger. And the quality of the light changed. It was as though all those layers of cloud were gradually being peeled away until, at last, on the sixth day they rode with the Xi, they saw the sun.

It had been so long since Kaede had felt its warmth that its first touch brought tears to her eyes; she wanted to strip off all her clothes and stand naked in the light. Taisin had forgotten the way it infused every leaf with vibrant color, causing the veins to stand out in sharp relief against the tender green. And Con could not remember if he had ever seen a sky so blue: robin's egg blue, smooth as glossy porcelain, untouched by clouds.

That same day, they came to a long row of trees planted on either side of the path. In the morning, the path had been only dirt covered in fallen pine needles, but by midmorning, the pine needles were swept away, and by noon the horses stepped onto pavement. It was not like the pavement used in any human city; this was white stone, perfectly cut in long rectangles. At intervals, diamonds of black stone were inlaid in the road, polished until they sparkled in the sunlight. The road became as broad as the largest square in Cathair, with elegant, gold-leafed trees marching down the center. In the distance the Xi city, Taninli, glimmered.

When at last they saw the crystal gates ahead of them, the Huntsman pulled his horse to a halt and turned back to look at his human charges. "We will ride directly to the palace," he told them. "Some of our people may turn out to look at you, but do not be alarmed."

Kaede glanced at Taisin, who seemed slightly ill. As the Huntsman rode ahead, Kaede pushed her horse toward Taisin's and asked, "Are you all right?"

"I'm fine," she said, but she sounded hesitant. Taisin had felt the city coming as early as two days ago; it was an unmistakable knot of energies coalescing together all at once. The closer they came, the more light-headed she felt, and she only hoped that she would be able to adjust to it quickly. So far, though, it was making her feel queasy.

Kaede wasn't affected the same way that Taisin was, but she, too, felt a bit out of sorts as they rode through the gates. The world seemed askew somehow; the shadows fell in the wrong places here, or perhaps her eyes simply weren't accustomed to the angles in the buildings and streets. And the buildings themselves were so strange and exotic. The stone was too smooth to be carved from a mountain, the glass too clear to come from an ordinary forge. The walls were perfectly straight or miraculously curved. Giant windows, cut into facets that held the light like prisms, climbed up the tallest towers. And every structure seemed to fit into the one beside it like a puzzle piece; the only spaces must have been deliberately left open.

In those spaces, the Xi waited and watched. They peered out from balconies, or from beneath archways between houses, or from meticulously landscaped parks that opened onto the white stone boulevard. At first Kaede gazed back at them. In the sunlight, their skin was no longer deathly pale; it was like new-fallen snow, bright and pristine. Their hair, she realized, was a thousand different shades between white and silver; their eyes were sharp, glowing jewels. The pressure of so many eyes on her made her a bit breathless, and after several minutes, she had to look down at her hands, fingers tightly gripping her reins, so that she no longer saw them.

That was when she realized that all the sounds she normally associated with a city—the noise of wagon wheels and beggars and merchants hawking their wares—were absent here. There was only the rise and fall of whispering in the language of the Xi, a kind of hypnotic music. The more she listened to it, the more it made her feel disconnected from her body. But gradually the boulevard climbed out of the heart of the city, and as they left the crowds behind, the whispering faded. At last Kaede allowed herself to look up again, and she saw that they were nearing the glittering crest of Taninli, and before them was the palace of the Fairy Queen.

When they reached the palace gates, the sun hung straight overhead, beaming down hot on their heads. They rode into a grand, circular courtyard, over paving stones set with a mosaic of gold and green in a pattern of swirls. Their horses, lulled into a half doze by the very air around them, were led away by silent-footed Xi clad in tunics the color of fallen autumn leaves. The Huntsman led them inside the palace through doors as tall as a three-story building, and inside it was cool and comfortable beneath ceilings so high Kaede was sure she saw birds flying above her. The Huntsman took them down wide, empty halls filled with light, and Kaede wondered where everyone was. Was the

Huntsman taking care to avoid the inhabitants of the palace, or were the inhabitants avoiding them? A bead of sweat trickled down her forehead. It was warm as midsummer, and she realized with a jolt that it *was* midsummer. Tonight was Midsummer's Eve, and tomorrow would be her eighteenth birthday.

They arrived at a set of smaller doors made of a fine-grained white wood, and the Huntsman turned the round crystal handles and said, "You will be very comfortable here."

Inside there was an apartment of many rooms furnished with chairs carved out of polished tree trunks, with cushions of rose and gold and green silk. The floor was covered in soft carpets, and at the far end of the room tall glass doors opened onto a broad balcony. Sunlight streamed through the windows, filling the room with a lovely midday glow. Con turned to the Huntsman and asked, "When will we see the Fairy Queen?"

"Tomorrow. Tonight is Midsummer's Eve, and we have other matters to attend to." He paused in the doorway and added, "It would be best if you remain here tonight."

"Why?" Con asked.

"It is a night of great celebration for my people. It would be unfortunate if anything were to befall you on the night before your audience with my queen." He looked at each of them to make his point clear. "I ask you to stay here." And then he left them alone, closing the door behind him. Though he had phrased his words as a request, Kaede had a feeling that they would not be able to open that door until he let them out.

Chapter XXIX

aede chose a round room with walls lined with windows. The vista of the city below was astounding—hill upon hill of buildings formed out of the same white stone that built this palace, every window sparkling. Far below she saw the Wood, a sea of trees all around Taninli. Though it was bright as midday inside, she lay down on the round bed in the middle of the round room, and as soon as her head fell upon the silken pillow, she was asleep.

Con took a square room with a balcony running along two entire walls. He opened the doors, letting the filmy white curtains flutter out into the afternoon. The breezes smelled of jasmine. He stood outside for some time, gazing down at the city, and his eyes were dazzled. The longer he looked, the more his mind became filled with a delicious fog. All the pain of the journey could be erased if he just gave in to this extraordinary place. But he felt a persistent, nagging worry in the back of his mind, and as he leaned forward into the sunlight, he closed his eyes. He saw his red-veined eyelids, the colors of countless ordinary human campfires that had warmed his hands night after night. He remembered Tali, and Pol, and Shae, who had looked at him out of pain-filled brown eyes in Mona's cottage. He had promised her he would come back for her. The worry turned to impatient determination; his hands clenched into fists. He turned his back on the glamour of the city and went back inside, where he began to pace.

Taisin's room was filled with trees; they seemed to grow out of the very floor, with smooth, polished bark the color of rust. Glossy leaves, amber on one side and bright green on the other, shaded her bed from the sun that poured in through windows in the ceiling. Tall glass doors opened onto a little round balcony, and when she stepped outside she looked out over a lush, wild garden. In the midst of all the sculptured buildings, the sight of trees and stones and running water was surprising, but as she looked closer, she could see that even this garden had been cultivated with the utmost care. She yawned, and raising a hand to her mouth she went back into the room, stretching. The bed was inviting. After weeks of sleeping on the ground, the feather bed beneath her back was like clouds. She sank into it and slept so soundly that for the first time in weeks, she did not dream of the fortress.

❧

Kaede awoke after dark, and when she opened her eyes there were lights dancing on the ceiling, reflected from the city below. She pushed herself up, feeling groggy, and went to the closest window. Down below, Taninli was ablaze with fairy lights: thousands upon thousands of them, winking like fireflies in a summer evening.

She left her room, walking down the short, curved corridor that led to the sitting room, and found Con at a table that had been laid with enough food for twenty. He looked up at her with glazed eyes. "Welcome," he said in a thick voice, "to our banquet."

She sat down across from him, gaping at the spread before her. She could not identify most of what she saw. There was a silver tureen of some kind of fragrant soup; plates piled high with colorful fruits; breads that were round and baked with golden-brown crusts. "What is this?" she asked, picking up an oblong fruit, its bright pink skin shading into orange.

"I don't know, but I recommend it," Con said, and handed her a wooden-handled knife with a blade made of thin, strong stone.

She tested the edge with her finger; it was sharp. When she peeled the skin of the fruit she held in her hand, the flesh that emerged was soft, juicy, and golden. She bit into it and the sweetness startled her; it was like liquid sugar with a tart, lingering tang. She discovered that there were several different kinds of cheese, and she especially liked the soft white one that crumbled in her fingers. She ate until her stomach was full, and then Con poured something from a decanter shaped like a bird into the crystal goblet at her elbow. "I have never tasted anything like this," he said.

She looked at him dubiously. "What is it?"

"I think it's wine."

It smelled like newly budding roses. The fragrance itself was intoxicating enough, and she put it down and looked at Con. "Is there water?" she asked.

He laughed at her, and she realized that he had drunk the wine—perhaps he had drunk too much of it. He had shaved off the beard he had grown during their journey, and it made him look younger and more vulnerable. "There," he said, pointing to a crystal pitcher down the table. "I think that is water."

She stood up to fetch it as Taisin came in from the balcony. The sound of celebration followed her through the open doors—music and voices, all mingled together in a joyous crescendo. "It's midnight," Taisin said, joining them at the table. She picked up a chunk of bread, but like Kaede, she avoided the wine.

Kaede poured water into two goblets, handing one to Taisin. "How do you know?"

"The celebration," Taisin said, gesturing toward the balcony. "It's turned a corner. It must be Midsummer Day now."

Kaede took her goblet of water out to the balcony. Below, among the winking fairy lights, she thought she could see the Xi themselves flooding through the streets. She rubbed her eyes, not sure if they were playing tricks on her. Everything here—Taninli, the palace, the food they ate—seemed obscured by a thin but persistent fog. It was as though some of her senses had been dulled, but others had been sharpened. She was more conscious than ever of the rhythm of the blood in her veins, but she felt oddly disengaged from her breath. Every now and then snatches of music floated up to her, played on instruments she had never heard before. It was so beautiful that it made Kaede's heart ache. She longed to be a part of it, to dance among the Xi, and she realized she was gripping the balustrade with white fingers, her goblet tipping precariously until water splashed down on the white stone. She righted it, stepping back, and blinked, pressing her fingers to her temples.

The door behind her opened with a scrape. It was an unexpectedly ordinary sound for Taninli. She looked over her shoulder and saw Taisin coming to join her. "Happy birthday," Taisin said.

"Thank you." Kaede had not expected Taisin to remember, and she felt inordinately pleased about it.

Taisin stood beside her, looking down at the sea of celebrants. The lights glowed on her skin, making her seem gilded. Kaede could not stop staring at her, and she wondered if even the water in those pitchers was somehow thickened with magic, for nothing seemed usual tonight. The Huntsman might have warned them to stay in these rooms, but he could not prevent the air from carrying the scent of their celebrations up to them, a potent, alluring perfume. Taisin turned to look at her, and her lips parted.

Kaede straightened, taking one step forward, and Taisin seemed to lean toward her just enough—and Kaede saw, then, that what she had hoped for could come true. If she wished it, if she reached out and touched her, Taisin would come to her easily; she only wanted a bit of suggestion. The space between them hummed. It was the most natural thing in the world to slide her finger beneath the strand of hair that fell across Taisin's eyes and tuck it behind her ear. Heat suffused Taisin's cheeks, and Kaede drew her closer, her breath a soft tickle across Taisin's lips, and kissed her.

Everything focused.

Taisin felt every place their bodies touched, and she felt every place they did not. Kaede slid her hands down Taisin's back. Taisin felt the blood singing in her veins; all of her was surging up to meet Kaede, who pressed her closer. They moved, clumsy with desire, and one of them bumped against the crystal goblet, knocking it off the balustrade to shatter, loudly, at their feet.

They broke apart, staring dazedly at the fragments of crystal. The lights below were sharp as diamonds.

Taisin recovered first. "I'll get a cloth," she said, her voice husky, and departed abruptly.

Kaede squatted down and picked up the stem, taking care to not cut herself on the jagged edge. Her breath was ragged in her throat; her limbs felt weak, as though she had just climbed a thousand steps; her hand holding the broken stem shook. A shadow fell over her, and when she looked up, it was not Taisin but Con who handed her a cloth.

"What happened? Taisin told me you needed this, and then ran off."

Below them they heard the roar of the crowd in celebration. Her heart was pounding as loudly as the crowd. "I dropped—I dropped the goblet," she muttered. She took the cloth from him and began to sweep up the broken shards. They glinted in the light spilling out from the sitting room.

"Be careful. You'll cut yourself."

"I'll be fine," she said, but she felt the beginnings of panic whirling in her stomach—*why had Taisin left?*—and she swept up a piece of glass that nicked her thumb. A small drop of blood welled up through her skin. She pressed the white cloth to it, the red blooming like a rose, and her finger smarted from the cut.

~

Taisin shut herself in her room and sat on the edge of her bed, and all she could think of was how much she wanted to go back to Kaede. Her whole body quivered from wanting it.

Nothing had prepared her for this. None of her books, none of her teachers had said a single thing about what to do with this wild energy pouring through her. She had no idea how to deal with it. She took a deep, trembling breath, trying to moderate the pulsing of her blood. She could still taste Kaede's lips. She pressed her hands to her eyes, but all she could see was Kaede's face.

She curled up on the bed, clutching a pillow to her chest, and gradually the beating of her heart slowed. She counted her breaths, hoping that it would calm her down. One, ten, one hundred breaths. Again and again, until she could push away the lingering sensation of Kaede's hands on her back.

But what if she couldn't fight this anymore? Had she been a fool to even try?

She stubbornly tried to recall every detail of that first vision she had when she was still at the Academy. The beach, the boat, Kaede's face when she pushed away from

255

the shore. The feeling that the most precious thing in her world was leaving her, and it might never return.

Sister Ailan had told her that her vision was a vision of the truth. But what was the truth? Was it that Kaede would leave her behind? Or was it that she loved her?

She heard the whistle of the wind in her ear, singing across the ice. She could no longer feel the softness of the bed beneath her. Cold seeped through her clothing, into her skin, until she felt the icy floor of the fortress beneath her feet.

Now that she had seen the way that glass could be manipulated in Taninli, she knew that the ice was only a cold imitation. She stood in the ice fortress, her fingers curled into fists, and gazed out the window—yes, this was real glass, hard and unyielding—at the landscape before her. The walls of the fortress descended like a mountainside to the ice fields below. In the distance the ocean was azure blue beneath the ice floes, reflecting the great arc of the sky above. Behind her there was motion: the fluttering of wings, the darting shape of another creature. The sprite. It had a message for her, and when she had heard it she reached out and plucked the fairy from the air, pinning its wings back. She watched the sprite's face stretch out in fear, and she whispered to it, soothing it, stroking its hair. An imperfect thing, this one.

But it would be a pity to blame the messenger.

She let it go, feeling its wings brush against her fingers before it bobbed away. She felt its fear, and it both saddened and exhilarated her. She turned back to the frozen vistas outside the window. Soon, she thought, and it sent a thrill through her. Soon her visitors would arrive.

Taisin sensed the woman's anticipation with a clarity she had never experienced before. Beneath that, she felt the heady rush of the woman's power, as if her veins ran with fire. It filled her body, lying on that soft bed in the Fairy Queen's palace, the same way Kaede had filled all of her senses when they kissed.

Chapter XXX

aede did not know what to do. She went to Taisin's room and stood outside the door, but she could not bring herself to knock. She could barely believe what had just happened—it was all so surreal, this place with its impossibly smooth walls and intoxicating lights. Perhaps they hadn't really kissed at all; perhaps it was all just an illusion. But she could still feel Taisin's mouth against hers, the bones of her spine beneath her fingers. Kaede's entire body burned at the memory. But Taisin had fled from her. Kaede remembered their whispered conversation in the middle of the night after leaving Mona's cottage. Taisin was promised elsewhere. What had made Kaede think Taisin had changed her mind? Kaede's heart sank. She turned away from the closed door and went back to her own room.

She spent a restless night in bed, dreaming of walking down the corridor between her room and Taisin's. Each time she knocked on the door, and each time she woke up just before it opened, every muscle tense.

When dawn came, she dressed and went into the sitting room. No one was there, but the table was already laden with fresh fruit and warm bread. There was even a strange object that she eventually recognized as a teapot, and when she lifted the hinged lid, a rich aroma was released. She poured a small amount into one of the delicate porcelain cups and sipped it cautiously. It had an unusual, roasted flavor that she immediately liked.

She finished two cups of it before Taisin appeared. Though she made no sound, Kaede noticed her immediately, standing hesitantly in the doorway. When their eyes met, Taisin blushed, and the sight of her flaming cheeks gave Kaede some courage. She would have gone to her at once, but then Con brushed past Taisin, entering the room with a yawn.

"Are you sure we're not all dreaming?" Con said in a voice still laced with sleep. He picked up an orange fruit and began to peel it, revealing a light pink interior. He pulled off a segment and sighed with pleasure. "This is much better than camping."

Kaede choked on a laugh, and he smiled at her. She wondered if he had said that on purpose, for she felt the tension in the room dissipate—at least a little.

Taisin sat down and took a piece of bread, stealing a glance at Kaede as she said, "I have to agree with you." Kaede caught the end of her look, and all of her came alive with awareness. She thought: Maybe she has changed her mind after all.

❧

That morning, they each made use of the bathing chamber adjacent to the sitting room; they each dressed in the cleanest of their clothes; and then there was nothing to do but pace the stone floor and wait for the Huntsman to arrive.

After so many weeks on the road, the last hour was the hardest to bear. Kaede surreptitiously watched Taisin, who had braided her wet hair and fixed it with a black comb on her head. Her neck was exposed, scrubbed clean and pink, and every time Kaede glanced at her, the pink crept a little farther up until Taisin turned away and went, trembling, to stand by the window, her back to the room. Kaede sat in a chair and looked down at her hands; she could still feel the small of Taisin's back beneath them. Her heart fluttered in her throat. She didn't know how long she could stand this queer pretense that nothing had happened between them. But when she thought of what she might say to Taisin, the words would not come. Her mouth was dry; her palms were clammy. It was like an illness, she thought, or an enchantment: these feelings that cloaked everything in a fog of desire. Here she was in the Fairy Queen's palace at last, after a journey that had killed two men who did not deserve to die; after her hands had been bloodied more than once; and she could barely even remember why she was here. All she wanted was to kiss Taisin again.

Con, who normally would have been sensitive to the strained silence that gripped Kaede and Taisin, was consumed by his own anxieties. Before leaving Cathair, he had discussed the Kingdom's position on the Borderlands Treaty with his father and Lord Raiden, but now that he was here in Taninli, he realized that all the advice they had given him was worthless. King Cai and Lord Raiden knew every detail of the political machinations that were about to erupt in civil war in the southern provinces, but they had no idea what was going on in the Wood. He wondered if they even truly believed that the Fairy Queen existed. She was a figure lost to the mists of history, and though the Council of Sages took her invitation seriously, Con knew that his father only submitted to the Council because of tradition. His father was a man of action; he did his best to ignore the unseen world that the sages worked in. If the Council ever made a demand on him that challenged his power, Con was sure that his father would deny it.

King Cai had told him to play the diplomat; to flatter the Queen yet promise nothing. Con knew that he would not be able to do this. He had seen too much on the way to Taninli to doubt the significance of the Queen's invitation. This was no mere social call, and he was almost sick from nerves. He had visited governors of distant provinces before; he had attended state banquets and done his best to charm those his father asked him to charm. But he was certain that those experiences had been nothing compared to this. He suspected that the Queen had more in mind than a simple renewal of that ancient treaty, and he did not know if he had the power to give it to her—or the judgment to decide if he could.

When the Huntsman came to the door at last, Con sprang up, agitation vying with relief on his face. "Finally," he said. "It's been a long morning."

The Huntsman gave him a sympathetic look. "Shall we go?"

He led them down long corridors of gray-veined marble, past banks of sunny windows, and through a rotunda in which a statue of a unicorn lifted its head toward the arched ceiling. At its feet a stone phoenix spread its wings. They passed Xi dressed in every shade between white and pale blue, who seemed to melt out of sight as soon as Kaede noticed them. The effect was disquieting; it made her wonder if the whole palace was just an extraordinary illusion.

The throne room was reached by climbing one last wide flight of stairs that culminated in grand redwood doors. They reminded Kaede of the doors to the Council chambers; they even had similar handles set in the very center. They opened into a long, broad hall; windows along one wall overlooked a garden sculpted into a perfect wilderness. At the far end of the room, a low dais supported a crystal throne cushioned in green silk. Seated there was the Fairy Queen. When she saw them enter, she leaned forward slightly, laying her right hand on the armrest.

It was a long walk to the dais, and their footsteps echoed in the high-ceilinged room. The Huntsman reached the Queen first and bowed deeply before introducing the humans. He spoke in his own language, but Con recognized their names, and when the Queen's eyes flicked over him, he shivered. The Queen's face was glowing, ageless; her eyes were the color of gold. She was beautiful, but it was a fearsome kind of beauty, like the mirrored edge of a finely crafted blade.

Con swallowed; his mouth was so dry. He stepped forward and bowed to the Queen. "Your Majesty," he said formally, "I come as a representative of my father, King Cai Simin Tan. He regrets that he is personally unable to respond to your invitation."

The Queen spoke in his language: "Why have you come in his place?"

"Our kingdom is suffering through a difficult time, and my father could not be spared."

"Tell me about this difficulty," the Queen said. She studied him intently, and Con had to look away to avoid her eyes. He realized that there was no furniture in the entire room except for her throne; all visitors had to either stand or kneel before her. It was an old trick; his father employed the same strategy. The thought galvanized him. But he allowed himself to look slightly past the Queen as he spoke, so that he would not have to withstand the full force of her gaze.

"For the last several years, Your Majesty, our winters have been…extremely hard. Many of our provinces have experienced storms that have been extraordinarily fierce. Livestock have died; food stores have been destroyed unexpectedly. We have survived these winters, but each summer the harvests have been increasingly poor. This year, summer has not come. My people are starving. Several of the provinces are on the verge of insurrection. This is why my father could not be here." He paused, taking a deep breath. "And there have been other things. There have been sightings of strange creatures near the border of the Wood. Creatures that are not human. We have encountered them ourselves on our journey here."

"What have you seen?"

He told her about the reports his father had received about creatures, possibly fay, entering the Kingdom in the north. He told her about the creature in Ento, and the body that had been found outside of Jilin. The Queen's face remained impassive as he spoke, and when he finished she asked, "Is that all?"

Con bristled. She sounded as if she thought what he had told her was of no consequence. "No, that is not all, Your Majesty. We came here at your invitation, but along the way we lost two of our party. One—Tali, who was a guard to me since I was a boy—he was killed by whatever tortured spirits are haunting the Great Wood that separates your land from mine. And another guard, Pol, was mauled to death by wolves who attacked our entire party. A third, Shae—" Here his voice almost broke, but he continued on with a fresh burst of anger. "Shae was nearly killed as well, and we were forced to leave her behind to make sure we arrived here as you asked, because my people have heard nothing from your kind in generations, and to receive such an invitation during a time of catastrophe—it—" He broke off, trying to compose himself. He looked straight at the Queen. "It could not be a coincidence. We are here, Your Majesty. Why have you asked us to come?"

The Queen swept her eyes over him from head to toe; he felt the hairs on the back of his neck rise. Finally she said, "I am sorry to hear about your companions. And you are correct. My invitation to your king was not a coincidence. But the answer to your question is somewhat…involved." She settled back in her throne and turned her eyes to the long windows.

"Our ties with your people have been mostly severed,

but once, it was different. Once, our lands were more closely entwined. Once, our people mingled with each other. But it was not an entirely peaceful commingling. We live so many generations longer than your people do. Some things that we remember, you forget. We could not coexist without misunderstanding each other.

"So, in time, there was war. A long, bloody war. It destroyed countless numbers of my people as well as yours. At the end of it, the survivors on both sides drew up a treaty to prevent such destruction from ever happening again. Afterward, the remaining fay scattered. The Xi remained here in Taninli, but the lesser fay retreated to their own hollows and mountains and forests. And gradually, your people forgot about us. We both kept to our sides of the bargain. Even if there has been isolation, there has also been peace.

"All this happened before I was born. Few of my people were alive when the treaty was signed. And in the intervening years, some of my people have become curious about your kind. You live such short lives compared to ours; we wonder what makes them worth living."

The Queen looked at Con with a trace of regret on her face, and for the first time that day, the glamour she wore cracked. She did not look old in a human sense, but there were centuries in her, and there had been pain.

She continued: "One Xi woman lived near the border between our land and yours. She encountered a human man one summer, and she took him as a lover. She became pregnant. She was terrified, for she knew her halfling child might not be welcome in either of our lands. She came to

Taninli and begged for my mercy. I gave her shelter here while she labored, but she did not survive childbirth. The halfling did survive. It was a girl. I raised her as my own daughter."

The Queen's face hardened, and once again she gazed out the windows. "She was given everything, this girl—every delicacy, every bauble, every privilege I could give her—but she always wanted more. She was stubborn. She would never acknowledge that she was not truly Xi. She demanded to be named my heir, but it was impossible. The time has not yet come for me to name an heir, and when it does, I will not choose a halfling."

The words were spoken coldly, but it seemed as if the Queen were holding her emotions tightly in check. A blue vein in her right temple throbbed. Taisin began to tense up; she had a dreadful fear that she knew what the Queen was about to say.

"When she realized I would not change my mind—that she would never rule the fay as she desired—she left Taninli. It has been a dozen years since she walked out of this city's gates. In that time, I have sensed her power growing. I believe she is drinking up the energies of the fay and discarding them when they become too weak to benefit her. The ones who survive have come to me seeking help, but I can do nothing for them. She takes their lives; she becomes stronger with each fairy who dies."

Taisin felt sick. All the cages she had seen in her visions; the glimpses of the fay trapped within them—she knew now that they had been imprisoned there by this woman.

The Queen said, "I believe she has built a fortress for herself in the north."

Taisin's skin prickled. She could see that fortress of ice in her mind's eye as clearly as if she stood before it in the snow.

"The meridians of the world are tangled up there, forced into some kind of knot that she has created. She has gathered winter all around her; I can feel the cold from here. Her actions have altered the seasons elsewhere. I have tried to bring the seasons into alignment here in Taninli, but the chaos you describe in your kingdom—it can only be a symptom of what she has done."

The Queen leaned forward and looked at each of them in turn. "I have called you here because she must be stopped before she does more harm to this world. She has been playing with terrible powers, and soon she will destroy more than can be saved."

Con asked: "How can she be stopped?"

"She must die," the Queen said. "That is the only way the energies she has taken can be returned to the world." A tiny, grim smile twisted her lips. "And only a human can kill her."

The Queen's words rang in Con's ears, and he felt a chill spreading over his skin. "But if she is so powerful, how could any human succeed?" he asked. "Surely this is a task meant for one of your own."

"My people are peaceful," the Queen said curtly. "We cannot take the life of our own kind."

"But she is only half Xi—"

"She is one of us, even if she could never be Queen. That is the truth she has always refused to see. Our blood, just as much as yours, runs in her veins. And there is only one weapon that can kill one of the Xi."

"What weapon?" Con asked. "Why would we have such a weapon?"

"One of you already has this weapon. It is a simple one. You have brought it with you." The Fairy Queen turned her golden eyes to Kaede, who felt a shock run through herself. She remembered Fin handing the iron dagger to her, hilt first. *The Xi don't like iron*, Fin had told her.

A heavy certainty settled over her, and Kaede said to the Fairy Queen, "You would have us be murderers."

Taisin stepped forward. "I will do it," she said, her heart pounding. She refused to send Kaede to face this woman.

"No," Con objected. "Taisin—"

"You are the Council's girl, aren't you?" the Queen said, looking at Taisin.

She flushed. "How did you know?"

"Everything they know, and many things they have forgotten, I know." The Queen examined Taisin's determined face intently. "But you have seen things even I haven't seen."

"I have seen the fortress of ice," Taisin admitted. Kaede and Con swiveled to stare at her.

"You never said anything about that," Kaede said, stunned.

Taisin's face paled, and she couldn't meet Kaede's eyes. The things she had seen—the cages, the ice, the sea—should she have told Kaede and the others about them? The visions had been so strange; she hadn't understood them.

The Queen asked, "Have you seen *her*?"

Taisin twisted her hands together. She felt guilty and frightened. "Yes. I've seen her."

The Queen's eyes narrowed. "Do not let her deceive you."

"She is so strong," Taisin said.

"I will give you her name," the Queen said, "so that you may see her for who she truly is."

"Her name?" Taisin was confused. "But how—"

"I named her when she was born. Her name is Elowen."

As she said the name, Taisin felt something inside her shift—as if a bolt had been thrown back from a door, and now all she had to do was nudge it open.

"There is power in naming," the Queen said. "And now you have an advantage, however small, against her."

Con asked: "If we do not kill her—if Elowen remains alive—what will happen?"

"She is like a rising storm. She must be stopped soon." The Queen turned to Kaede again. "You have the weapon. You must do this."

Kaede's fingers curled into fists. All of her balked at the Queen's demand. "I am no assassin."

The Queen gave her a measuring look. "I am not seeking an assassin. I am seeking a hunter."

❧

In their sitting room, Con paced back and forth in front of the balcony doors. The Fairy Queen had asked for their decision by end of the day, and Con felt trapped. If what she said was true—and Taisin seemed to believe her—then how could they refuse? Yet Con believed the Queen was asking them to undertake a suicide mission, though Kaede argued that he couldn't predict the outcome. As the hours passed, they talked in circles until Kaede abruptly asked Taisin, "Why haven't you told us about your visions?"

Startled, Taisin responded, "I didn't know what they meant. What use would it have been for me to tell you?"

Kaede looked hurt. "We might have helped you figure them out."

Taisin reddened, feeling chagrined. "I'm sorry. I just— Sister Ailan—" She sat down in one of the armchairs, a miserable expression on her face.

Con stopped pacing and turned to her. "What have you seen?" he asked gently.

She closed her eyes and pinched the bridge of her nose as if her head ached. "I see the fortress, repeatedly. It is made of ice, like a mountain floating on the sea. I see the fay in cages. They can't stand being imprisoned; I think some of them are dying from it. I see her—Elowen. She has a nursery. There was a baby there, like the one we saw in Ento. I don't know what she's trying to do, but it's—" A wave of revulsion swept through Taisin as she recalled the sight of the infant monster smashed against the floor. "She is cruel. She is more powerful than anyone I have ever encountered, except for the Fairy Queen herself."

"Is the fortress guarded?" Con asked.

"I don't think so."

"Then we might have the advantage of surprise," Con suggested.

Taisin frowned. "The fortress is surrounded by open sea. I think we would be visible from quite a far distance."

"Then she could kill us before we even step foot in her fortress," Kaede said. She leaned against the table, her arms crossed.

"True, but..." Taisin trailed off, biting her lip.

"What is it?" Kaede asked. "What are you not saying?"

"I think...I think she will allow us to come." Taisin seemed hopeful and frightened all at once.

"Why?"

"Because she will not think we are a threat. We are three humans with a tiny little dagger."

Con rubbed at his chin, considering Taisin's words. He wondered what Tali would do, and a pang went through him. He looked at Taisin, pale-faced and stiff in her chair carved out of a tree trunk, and then at Kaede, who had dark shadows beneath her eyes. He had known Kaede since they were children; he could remember her in pigtails, chasing him and her brother across the broad palace courtyards. He remembered that her eighteenth birthday was today; she was of age now. But he could not shake the feeling that all of this had come too soon for her, and Taisin was just as young. Tali would never let them take the risk of going after Elowen. Tali would have done it himself.

"Elowen has to be stopped," Con said, "but I will do it."

"What do you mean?" Kaede asked. "The Queen said—"

"I don't care what the Queen said. You've been carrying that dagger, but I can't let you kill her, Kaede. I'll do it."

"Con—"

"You're not going to do it," Taisin protested. "You can't face her. She is very powerful. She'll destroy you."

"If she's so powerful, she can destroy you, too," Con argued.

"I've felt her," Taisin objected. "I'm the only one who has a chance against her. You can't do it." She clenched her hands in her lap stubbornly, but inside, doubt swirled. Elowen was so strong; Taisin had no idea if she could actually defeat her. She only knew that Con—or Kaede—would be defenseless against her.

Kaede was watching Taisin closely. She pulled a chair out from the table and set it in front of Taisin. She sat down, her elbows resting on her knees, and leaned toward Taisin as she looked her in the eye. "You seem to want to do this yourself," Kaede said, "but I don't think that's a good idea." There were only a couple of feet separating them now, and Kaede felt as if that space was pulsing with the beat of her heart. Taisin's cheeks turned pink, but she did not look away. Kaede almost forgot what she was going to say. She took a shallow breath. "If we go, we go together. You and me and Con. We've made it this far; we have to stay together." She looked up at Con. "Do you agree?"

He crossed his arms. "Only if you both promise that neither of you will attempt to face her alone."

"I promise," Kaede said. "Taisin, do you?"

Taisin's stomach quivered. She closed her eyes, rubbing her hand over her face as she remembered the vision of Kaede leaving the shore. Con had stayed on the beach with her. She hoped they would be able to change that future. "Yes," she said at last, reluctantly. "I promise."

"Then we'll go to this fortress," Con said, "and we'll do this together."

When the Huntsman came to their door later, he did not seem surprised by their decision. "I will put things in order," he told them. "We will leave in the morning."

Chapter XXXI

T had not taken long for Taisin to pack up her belongings. Her knapsack waited by the door, and she lay in bed unable to sleep. Supper had been subdued, and Taisin had fled to her room afterward to avoid Kaede. But now, lying here in the dark, Kaede's face was all she could see.

If she had to describe it to someone else, she would dutifully relate the obvious details: light brown eyes, a pleasant nose and chin, and a mouth that smiled easily. But such a description omitted all of what made Kaede's face so extraordinary to Taisin. The mischievous gleam in Kaede's eyes when she saw something funny; the way her eyebrows arched in exaggerated reaction to Con's jokes; the shape of her lips, and the warm, firm texture of them.

Taisin approached the memory of their kiss gingerly, as though it were a wild beast that might knock her down, and yet part of her hoped it would do just that. If she was to be a sage, she would have to turn away from that beast forever.

She would never be able to marry; she would not even be allowed to take a lover. And though she had only had the briefest taste of what she would have to give up, she understood now why sages made that vow. The desire that had awakened within her was like a fog descending on a mountain valley, filling every hollow, slipping between tree limbs, tickling every leaf with its seductive breath. It left no room for the calm contemplation necessary to do a sage's work. And though Taisin had only ever wanted to be a sage, now she wondered how she could possibly deny this feeling inside her.

She splayed her fingers across her heart; she felt the rhythmic beat there, the rise and fall of her lungs beneath. Her body was like a new thing to her; she had never known this ache before. It made her skin flush and her eyes dilate, and some part of her marveled at the focus of the energy that ran through her. All it wanted was one thing: to consume her entirely. To drive her up out of bed in the dark of midnight, to slip barefoot into the corridor between their rooms, and to deliver her, trembling, to Kaede.

❧

Kaede was asleep, dreaming of a hunter running lightly through the Wood, a quiver on her back. She would sight her quarry and draw the arrow as smoothly as if her body were made of quicksilver. The arrowhead was cold as iron. It was Fin's dagger, protruding from the graceful wooden shaft like an eyesore—and then the shaft turned into her hand.

There was a sound that Kaede later recognized as a door closing, and she awoke to find Taisin standing beside her bed.

Confused, her body tingling into awareness, Kaede whispered, "Is something wrong?"

"No," Taisin said, her voice barely audible.

Kaede pushed herself up, heat coursing through her. "Do you need something?" Kaede asked, flustered.

Taisin's hands flew up to cover her mouth, whether to hide embarrassment or laughter Kaede wasn't sure, but a sort of half-choked sound emerged from her, and Kaede said, "Is it about…last night?" It wasn't until the words were out that she realized what they were, and perhaps if she had been awake when Taisin arrived instead of deep in a dream, she might have never had the courage to continue. But now, still shaking off the musty fog of sleep, she said all in a rush, "I didn't mean to upset you, Taisin. I know you'll be a sage, and I'm sorry I kissed you—if I could take it back—"

"Oh, no," Taisin said quickly, firmly. "No." She came to the bed and sat down on the edge of it, and Kaede felt everything sink toward her. "Don't ever say that," Taisin whispered, a catch in her throat, and now Kaede was more awake than she could ever remember. She heard Taisin's breath quickening, and as they leaned toward each other she could smell the scent of her skin. She wanted to put her nose against Taisin's throat and inhale all of it, all of her. She bent her head toward the shadow of Taisin's neck; her mouth brushed over the fluttering of her pulse.

Taisin was wearing an old tunic, the cloth soft with use. Some of the buttons were coming loose, and when she unbuttoned the first one, it hung down on a single thread. She took Kaede's hand in hers and put it on her skin, and gooseflesh rose at the touch of her fingers. Kaede moved her hand, tracing the shape of Taisin's collarbone. She pushed the tunic back, and Taisin's long black hair brushed over her bare shoulders. And then Kaede leaned toward her and they kissed again. Her mouth opened; she breathed her in.

Taisin remembered the way it had felt when she pulled life into that tiny purple blossom, the torrent of energy through her body. She remembered the way that power rippled through Elowen like molten ore, hot and precious. This was even more exquisitely immediate; there was nothing between her and dizzying sensation. Here was the touch of Kaede's fingers on her skin, and there the soft insistence of her mouth. Taisin felt as though there were a thousand purple flowers blooming inside her, a sea of them, each opening her black eye to the sun, trembling to see the wide-open sky.

೧

Taisin slid into sleep so easily; her body was at ease, vulnerable.

The ice fortress swam into focus almost immediately—she was there again, standing at the window overlooking the beach. This time she felt as though she were merging into the body of the woman who stood there. *Elowen.* She formed the name on her lips, asleep in the tower room with Kaede beside her, and she felt the woman in the fortress come alive. Elowen turned her head just slightly, as though she sensed a presence nearby. She left the window and walked toward white velvet curtains hanging against the icy wall. There was a silver cord dangling from the ceiling, and as she pulled it, the curtains parted and revealed a mirror. It was made of glass like all mirrors, but there was something different about this one, though Taisin could not at first discern the difference. All she knew was that she was gazing at the reflection through Elowen's eyes, and she saw a beautiful woman there.

She was tall, willowy, with long, golden-white hair that swept to her waist. She had yellow-brown eyes and sharp cheekbones, and her lips were the color of a bruised pink rose. Her skin was milky white and smooth as a newborn's. She wore a gown of white silk belted with a gold chain, and her fingers were covered with jeweled rings. When she moved her hands, they flashed in the brilliant sunlight: diamonds, rubies, sapphires.

She smiled at herself in the mirror, and Taisin felt her own lips turning up at the corners. Elowen said to her: "You know my name, but I do not know yours." Taisin heard the words as though she were standing in that frozen palace with Elowen; she heard them as though she had spoken them herself. Fear flooded through her as she realized that Elowen could see her, too. As Elowen sensed her agitation, she threw back her head and laughed. The sound echoed.

Taisin did not at first realize that Elowen had begun to push into her consciousness. They were already so close. They were breathing the same breath; their veins ran with the same blood. Taisin felt disoriented; she felt doubled. She couldn't tell where Elowen ended and she began. But in that round tower room in Taninli, her shoulder bumped against

Kaede, and Taisin drew a breath all on her own, and she remembered who she was. She nearly awoke, but Elowen reached through that mirror and held her there, transfixed, half asleep, half aware, as she demanded, *Who are you?*

Taisin pushed back. It was like running in quicksand, trying to extricate herself from Elowen's power. It was like struggling against a cold, fierce current, and she was afraid she would drown. But she fought her way up, remembering the grip of the freezing river Kell, and when she came to the surface, just as before, Kaede had her arms around her.

She gasped, drawing breath after greedy breath in the dark of Kaede's tower room.

Kaede was whispering to her, stroking her hair back from her damp forehead.

Her blood was roaring, her heart pounding.

Kaede gathered her close and held her until her lungs felt like they were her own again.

"It was her," Taisin whispered.

"Who?" Kaede asked.

"The Fairy Queen's daughter." She would not say her name.

"What do you mean?"

"I saw her," Taisin said, and she knew that Elowen was angry.

Dawn was breaking, spreading soft pink light across the eastern sky above the city. Kaede propped her head up on her hand, looking down at Taisin's pale and tired face. She ran a finger over the line of Taisin's mouth.

"She knows who I am," Taisin said.

Kaede's hand stilled. "What does that mean?"

"I don't know," Taisin whispered, but fear filled her. She felt tears pricking at the corners of her eyes. She reached up and pulled Kaede down, pressing her face into her neck. She could not forget the way that Elowen had engulfed her, all power and might, and she had no idea how they could possibly kill her.

Chapter XXXII

hey breakfasted together, sitting at one corner of the table with their knees touching. Despite the shadow of Taisin's vision, they felt enveloped in an enchantment: one in which even the drinking of tea was as magical as any fairy glamour.

When Con came out to join them, Taisin and Kaede hastily scooted apart, but the expressions on their faces were so plain that he laughed out loud. "I see that things have changed," he observed, and Kaede flushed so deeply she couldn't look at him.

The Huntsman came to collect them shortly after breakfast. He told them that the Fairy Hunt would accompany them to the northern edge of the Wood, and then they would have to continue on without their Xi escort. "We will not travel through the lands that she has taken for her own," he explained as he led them through the palace to the outer courtyard.

"But how will we find her?" Taisin asked, hurrying to catch up with his long strides.

"You have a token of hers," he said.

"I do?" Apprehension quivered in her as she tried to think of what she could be carrying that had been Elowen's, and then her stomach dropped. "The medallion," she said, and the alarm in her voice caused the Huntsman to stop and turn back to her. "Is that how—why I have seen so much of her fortress?" she demanded.

The Huntsman regarded her pale cheeks and wide, dark eyes, and said as kindly as he could, "If you were already sensitive, then yes, her medallion may have enabled you to see more of her."

Taisin felt for the chain around her neck and pulled the medallion out. It was black and opaque, as usual, but she felt newly aware of it, and now she wondered how she had ever not known that it once belonged to Elowen. "How did she lose it?" she asked.

Sadness washed over the Huntsman's face. "She left it behind when she left Taninli. It was a gift from the Fairy Queen."

He came toward her and touched the black stone with a gentle finger. A tiny glow burned in the stone for a moment. "It wants to be reunited with her. It will show you the way."

Taisin closed her hand around the medallion, intending to take it off; she wouldn't wear Elowen's chain around her neck. But at the last minute, struggling against an equally powerful desire to keep it, she slid it back beneath her tunic. When she felt the stone pressing coldly against her skin, she was disconcerted by the sense of relief that flooded through her. The Huntsman nodded at her as if she had made the right decision. "The longer you wear it," he said, "the more it also becomes yours."

⁓

In the courtyard, half a dozen riders of the Fairy Hunt awaited them, along with riding horses and packhorses loaded with canvas-covered gear. Con did not see their own, ordinary steeds, and he asked, "Where are our horses?"

"They are resting for your return journey back to your kingdom," said the Huntsman. "You shall ride our horses as far as you can. The dogs will take your supplies the rest of the way."

Eight dogs, each with thick gray coats shading into white bellies and paws, had been led into the courtyard by a thin, spry Xi woman. She spoke to the Huntsman in their language, and her green eyes glanced quickly over the humans. She said nothing to them before she left, but she bent down to her dogs and each met her nose to nose in a solemn farewell.

They left Taninli by the same route they had taken through the city when they arrived. At first the few Xi they saw were simply going about their business as usual, but as they descended into the streets, more and more Xi emerged from their homes to watch them ride past. Once again, Kaede had to look down to avoid their eyes. She couldn't bear to see the doubt in their faces—or, even worse, the hope.

Outside the city gates they turned north, leaving the

boulevard almost immediately and riding straight into the Wood. The manicured trees quickly turned wild, and within an hour of leaving Taninli and its pocket of summer behind, the air began to carry the bite of cold. The horses and dogs moved swiftly—more swiftly than horses or dogs should move, Kaede thought. When she looked ahead of them the trees were a bit blurry, and the dogs blended into the landscape, running silently over fallen leaves. She felt increasingly detached from her body as the day progressed, and it would have disturbed her if her senses had been more alert, but instead, she felt a kind of haze that prevented her from doing anything but staying in the saddle.

At night they stopped beside a bubbling stream to water the animals, and the Xi set up small, strange tents in the spaces between trees. They were round, like bubbles made of canvas, stretched tight over ingeniously bent poles. Kaede crawled into the one the Huntsman told her was hers, and she slept as soon as she lay down on the fur-covered pallet.

The next morning she emerged from her solitary tent, and one of the riders gave her a horn cup full of a hot, bitter drink. It was shocking on her tongue, and when she looked up she saw a barren landscape around her. Tree branches that should have been heavy with green needles were stripped clean, as if a giant had come and swept them bare with his fingers.

A dog butted against her leg, and she bent down to stroke him. His brown eyes regarded her with gentle curiosity, and then she saw Taisin come out from a nearby tent, and soon Con emerged from another. There was no time to do more than wish one another a good morning, for the

Fairy Hunt was readying to go, and they thrust cups of the hot drink into Con's and Taisin's hands and told them to hurry.

They rode again.

⁓

Midmorning on the third day after leaving Taninli, the trees abruptly ended. Kaede twisted back in her saddle and stared at the bare trees behind her, trunks the color of ash. Her breath made clouds in the air. The Huntsman was dismounting from his horse, and his boots touched down in snow. She looked north, away from the Wood, and the land was a broad expanse of white stretching toward a faraway horizon. The blue sky arched there in the distance, but above her head the sun was blocked by clouds.

The Huntsman and the other riders were taking bundles down from their horses, and Kaede watched them in confusion, for it was too early in the day to set up camp. They were unpacking long, slim pieces of wood that folded and unfolded in strange ways, and when they put them together, they formed a strong sledge. Stacks of firewood were then lashed onto the sledge, and most of the provisions that had been carried by the packhorses were transferred there as well. The dogs submitted to being harnessed to it, and before she knew what was happening—there was still something wrong with her sense of time—the Huntsman was asking her to dismount from her horse.

"What's going on?" she asked, trying to inhale the chilly air to wake herself up. Con and Taisin seemed as muddled as she was.

"We must leave you here," the Huntsman said. "Your way lies over the ice field."

Kaede shook her head; it felt woolly.

Taisin said, "We are close."

"Yes," the Huntsman said. "I would suggest you put on your warmer clothing."

One of the Xi came to take Kaede's horse away, and she felt the lick of winter against her skin as she looked out over the glacier.

"We have given you everything we can," the Huntsman was saying. He explained how to use the round oil lamps; how to strap the broad snowshoes onto their feet; how to command the dogs.

Kaede blinked again. The light was so odd here. She turned to the Huntsman, willing herself to focus on him. He seemed just slightly worried. "Tell your queen," she said, "that we will do the best we can."

He looked at her gravely and, for the first time, came to her and squeezed her shoulder in the way her father had done once, when she was a little girl and had been knocked down in a fight with her brother Tanis. She had not cried, even though her nose was bleeding, and her father had crouched down to her eye level, his large, warm hand engulfing her shoulder and upper arm, and said somberly, "My little hellion." But she had known that he was proud of her in that moment, and the memory of him suddenly made a lump rise in her throat, and she had to turn away from the Huntsman to stare at the ice.

Chapter XXXIII

aisin and Kaede walked ahead of the sledge, leading the dogs north, while Con followed behind in their tracks to make sure the load remained stable. Every step across the snow sloughed off a bit of the fog that had clung to them as they traveled with the Hunt, and by midafternoon the vista ahead shone with a clarity that was startling to eyes recently glamoured by Xi magic. The sun was bright overhead; the ice field was broad and unbroken; the air stung their skin with its briskness.

Taisin and Kaede did not speak, for they were wrapped from head to foot in furs, and it was hard going. But more than once they glanced at each other, and each was surprised by the pool of happiness that spread through herself even as she trudged through the falling temperatures and growing dusk.

Their first night on the ice field, they built a small, hot fire in the lee of the sledge, and boiled water for their first hot drinks since morning. The wind had risen and was whipping up the snow in frozen imitations of dust devils, but the night sky was clear and black, with thousands of stars spread in unfamiliar constellations overhead. They crouched as close to the fire as they could, eating a supper of dried fruit and hard, round crackers that tasted, ingeniously, of cheese.

Afterward, as Kaede fed the dogs, Con and Taisin pitched the two tents and unpacked their sleeping furs. Con took five of the dogs into his tent, and Taisin and Kaede took the other three. With the dogs curled up around them, their nest was cozy enough. Kaede slid her arm across Taisin's stomach and nestled her nose into the crook of her neck, and sleep overcame her moments after she lay down. Taisin was awake for only a few minutes more, long enough to wonder if Elowen would come to her tonight, but she was so tired that she couldn't even be properly anxious about it.

Sometime in the hours before dawn, Kaede awoke to hear Taisin speaking. They had shifted apart; Taisin was turned away from her, one arm flung out over the furs. One of the dogs let out a low growl, and Taisin's voice changed, deepening. Kaede could not understand what she was saying, for the words made no sense. The dog beside her tensed up. When she reached out to calm him, she felt his fur rising stiffly down his back.

Kaede shook Taisin's shoulder. "Taisin," she whispered. One of the dogs barked.

Taisin jerked awake, letting out a half-strangled moan. "What? Who is there?"

"It's me," Kaede said.

Taisin pushed herself up. It was too dark to see, but she

felt the dogs creeping back to her, their hackles lowered now, and one rubbed his head against her arm.

"Why did you wake me?" Taisin asked, her voice rough. It didn't sound quite like her own.

"You were talking in your sleep."

"What did I say?"

Kaede thought she sounded nervous. "I couldn't understand you. It wasn't...it was not our language." A beat later, Taisin lay down again, and Kaede asked, "Did you see *her* again?"

"I can't remember," Taisin answered. It was unsettling; her mind was so fuzzy. She lay awake for some time, trying to sort through the hazy memories that kept slipping away from her. But it was no use, and now she could not sleep, and the wind was buffeting the walls of their tent, keening like an army of ghosts.

"Kaede," she whispered, wondering if she had fallen asleep.

She had not. "Yes?" Kaede murmured, and she shifted closer. She heard Taisin's breath grow short; she felt her own skin suffused all over with heat.

Taisin turned to her. How strange and wonderful, she thought, that in the middle of this bizarre journey, there should be this: Kaede, who kissed her.

After a few moments, the dogs slunk off to the foot of the tent, affronted. Kaede stifled a laugh, her hands sliding around Taisin's waist, and later, they slept again.

In the morning, Taisin drew out the medallion and cupped it in her hands. She thought of the fortress of ice; she could imagine the walls of it so clearly, the windows bright in the sunlight, the sea all around it deep sapphire blue. The stone became warm; it pulsed like a tiny heart. Taisin felt it tugging at her until she faced northeast. On the horizon, the blue sky faded into the field of ice, making the land seem endless. "We go there," Taisin said, her voice small, swallowed up by the world of the glacier.

The dogs barked as if in affirmation.

Kaede woke again on the second night to the sound of Taisin's voice. This time she lay still and listened. It might have been the language of the Xi, but Kaede could not make out the different words. They flowed into one another in a singsong pattern that reminded her of chanting, but she had never heard any chanting like this. And then Taisin arched her back and laughed out loud, and the voice that came out of her body sounded nothing like her. The dogs, who had already been stirring awake, backed away and began to growl low in their throats.

"Taisin!" Kaede called, reaching out to touch Taisin's arm.

Suddenly Taisin's body went limp, her eyes blinking open in the darkness of the tent. She let out a weak sigh. "Am I dreaming?" she whispered.

One of the dogs whined and went to lick her face with his rough, wet tongue.

"Am I dreaming?" she asked again, more loudly.

"I don't know," Kaede said, disturbed by the confusion in Taisin's voice.

"I don't want to dream anymore." Taisin sounded as if she were on the verge of tears.

"What were you dreaming of?"

"Elowen," Taisin answered, and the dogs barked. She gave a panicked laugh and added, "She wants to know who you are."

Kaede felt drenched in cold. "What? Why does she want—"

"I don't know. I don't know what she's doing to me," Taisin said, her voice rising.

Kaede pulled her close, pressing her lips to Taisin's hair. "You shouldn't say her name again." She felt useless, and it frustrated her.

Taisin was groggy. She knew that Elowen had been inside her again, but things were different now that Elowen was aware of her. In the past, Taisin had seen the fortress clearly; when she awoke, she remembered. Now she had the feeling that Elowen had been erasing her memory somehow. Her mind felt rubbed clean in some places, and in others it felt like it had been scratched raw. It frightened her.

Kaede fell asleep again; the dogs stretched out, content, on either side of them; but Taisin lay awake thinking for a long time. She could not allow Elowen to take over her mind, and she began to formulate a plan to prevent it from happening.

On the third day, Taisin crumpled in midstep, and when Con and Kaede ran to help her up, she snarled at them. Elowen's voice came spitting out of her: *"Fools."*

They halted, shocked, their hands outstretched to Taisin, lying on the snow. Her face was twisted into a grimace; her

293

eyes were glazed. She began to mutter to herself in the same strange language that Kaede had heard at night. "What is wrong with her?" Con demanded.

"She has been like this before," Kaede said. "The Fairy Queen's daughter visits her when she's asleep." The fact that Elowen seemed to be visiting Taisin now while she was awake was extremely disturbing.

Taisin's eyes were half shut, and her face was so pale it was almost white. Con asked, "What can we do?"

They ended up carrying her to the sledge, making room for her among their tents and blankets. She struggled a bit at first, and Con had to pin her arms to her side while Kaede held her legs. She wondered whether they would have to tie her down, but when they settled her onto the sledge, Taisin's body relaxed. She looked up at them with dreamy eyes and said in Elowen's voice, silky and cold, "It is such a pleasure to meet you both, at last." She laughed, her whole body shaking with mirth while Kaede and Con watched her, horrified.

But as quickly as it had begun, the laughter choked off, and Taisin let out a moan as if she were in pain. She curled up, holding her head in her hands. Kaede stroked Taisin's feverish forehead and asked, "Taisin, what can we do?"

Taisin jerked away from her touch as though it hurt her, and for the first time, Kaede truly wanted to kill Elowen. The anger filled her unexpectedly; her fingers curled into fists.

Taisin, her eyes squeezed shut, said in a shaking voice, "I'll be all right. We just need to go."

So they continued on.

That afternoon they came to a cliff. When Con and Kaede walked to the edge, they saw that the ice field ended in what seemed to be a sheer wall of white. It plunged down a hundred feet to a beach. In the distance, they could see the ocean: intense, cold blue dotted with ice floes.

Con looked in either direction and pointed south. "There. It looks like the cliff is lower there."

Kaede nodded. "All right. Let's go."

After walking for two hours, they found that the ice field did slope down to the beach, but it was a steep descent. "We could continue on," Con said, "and see if there is an easier way down. But we're going farther and farther away from the direction Taisin told us to go."

"We might be able to climb down," Kaede said. "Some areas are not as steep as others. We'll have to be careful, though."

"What about the sledge?" Con asked.

"We can leave the sledge up here. We'll leave half the firewood for the return journey, and the dogs will have no problem."

"And Taisin?"

She glanced back at Taisin, who was sitting on the sledge with a dazed look on her face. The sight of her twisted Kaede's stomach into knots. The closer they drew to Elowen's fortress, the more Kaede wanted to finish this—and finish it quickly. She felt a hard determination growing in her, and though the feeling was new, it was not unwelcome. It gave her courage, and she knew she would need that soon, for she had every intention of making Elowen pay for what she was doing to Taisin.

Kaede met Con's worried gaze and said, "We'll tie her to us. We have rope, don't we?"

He considered it for a moment. "I suppose we have no other choice," he said reluctantly.

Kaede unhitched the dogs, who seemed both surprised and excited at being allowed to roam free at this time of day. Some of them ran along the edge of the cliff, but two sat down behind her as she grimly approached Taisin with the rope. She wasn't sure how Taisin would react to being tied to them; all day she had been slipping further away, and it wasn't clear if she was actually aware of what was going on. But she did not fight when Kaede came with the rope, and just as Kaede knotted it tight beneath her armpits, she gripped Kaede's hand and said fiercely, "I am still here. I am still here. Don't let her tell you otherwise."

Kaede looked into Taisin's dark brown eyes; the sun was reflected in them in bright white spots, and she knew it was Taisin speaking, not Elowen. "I won't," Kaede assured her. "You will have to climb down after Con. Can you do it? I'll stay beside you."

Taisin nodded, though her face was pallid and drawn. "I can do it."

Con descended over the edge first, his belly flat against the snow, and a few of the dogs followed him. They had already bundled their supplies together and pushed them over the cliff, where they slid down the slope until the bundles lodged against an outcropping of ice. Con began to make his way carefully toward the supplies as Kaede helped

Taisin begin her descent. From her vantage point on top of the cliff, Kaede kept an eye on Con as he shoved one of the larger packs along. She was reaching for her gloves, which she had removed to tighten the knots in the rope linking them together, when he slipped.

The rope jerked, and Taisin screamed as she was pulled down the cliff face. Kaede reached for Taisin's hand but was just a moment too late, and the rope tightened around Kaede's waist and yanked her toward the edge.

She fell to her knees and dug her fingers into the ice, but the rope dragged her painfully over the lip of the cliff until her legs were dangling over the precipice, her chest flat on the ground, her chin scraped raw against the snow.

Her heartbeat thundered in her ears; panic rushed through her body. She could not see Con or Taisin. The pack leader came and snuffed at her head. She called out, "Con!"

But he did not respond. And the rope continued to pull at her. Dead weights. Fear threatened to overwhelm her.

She let out her breath in a sob. She began to swing her right leg out, searching for footing—searching for anything. She kicked the glacier wall; small pellets of ice and snow rained down the cliffside, but there was nothing to break her fall.

Her fingers were freezing. Her hands began to slip. The ice would cut into her palms any minute now, and she would die leaving bloody handprints in the snow.

Chapter XXXIV

Her cheek was pressed against the ground. She gritted her teeth. Seen up close, the hard-packed snow became glittering ice crystals, sharp as a thousand tiny blades. Her breath steamed out of her; she watched the ice crystals melting. Her hands and arms and back screamed with the strain of clinging to the cliff's edge, but she wasn't about to give up.

And then she slipped again, sliding down a few more inches. Her stomach lurched; sweat broke out on her skin. Her boots scraped against the cliff wall until suddenly—finally—her toe found a tiny outcropping in the glacier wall, no wider than a hand span.

She could hardly believe it. She was breathless with relief. And then she began to drag herself toward the ledge.

It was brutal work. She felt as though her arms might rip themselves out of her body before she was done, and she might even welcome it.

But the ledge was just wide enough to support some of

her weight, and when at last both of her feet were dug into it, she allowed herself to rest for a count of five, her face pressed against her arm, still clinging to the top of the glacier. Then she steeled herself and turned just slightly—just enough—and looked down.

The edge of the ice sheet was particularly steep where she had fallen, but just below her, it banked at a shallower angle. Taisin's body was sprawled there, and a splash of red marked the snow near her head. The sight filled Kaede with dread, and she had to force herself to look past Taisin, where the ground plummeted down again. The slope was not as precipitous there as it was near Kaede, but it was steep enough that she couldn't see what had happened to Con, for the rope attaching them together had disappeared into a crevice.

Looking around her, she realized that Con's fall had dragged her over the edge of the glacier at a particularly bad place. He had begun his descent several feet to her left, where the incline was less hazardous. Something had made him slip, yanking him—and Taisin and Kaede in turn— down to the right, where the cliff wall was nearly vertical.

As she pondered how she was going to climb down from her precarious perch, she suddenly felt the rope around her waist slacken. She looked down; Taisin was still motionless on the snow. But the rope that had gone into the crevice was loose now. Con must have cut himself free. Relief flooded through her. She hadn't known how she could continue on with both him and Taisin weighing her down.

"Con!" she shouted.

There was a long silence. But at last she heard his ragged voice below. "I'm here," he called faintly.

"Are you all right?" she yelled.

Again, a pause. There was a scrabbling noise. His voice came again, thick with effort: "I'm climbing out."

"I'm coming down," Kaede called. She took a deep breath and flexed her fingers, for they were chilled to the bone. But there was no other way: She had to climb down, inch by inch.

It was even slower going than before. She had to search out small toeholds in the glacier wall, and then she had to find places to grip in the ice. Below her, Con still hadn't reappeared, but they called to each other regularly, and she had no time to worry about him. Her shoulders burned, and all she could do was focus on each handhold, each step.

At last she came to the place where Taisin had fallen, and the ground was less steep here, so Kaede turned over onto her backside and carefully scooted down to her. Some of her anxiety ebbed when she saw that Taisin still breathed; the snow beneath her nose was slightly melted. The blood seemed to have come from a long, shallow scrape on her chin. Kaede reached out and touched her shoulder. "Taisin," she said. When there was no response, she shook her lightly, and then said her name more loudly. She was about to consider taking more serious action—though she didn't know what that would be—when she felt Taisin stir beneath her hand. And then she let out a low moan, and her eyes fluttered open.

Kaede was elated. "Are you all right?" she asked, and Taisin pushed herself up, putting a hand to her face where the cut on her chin was bleeding. Her fingers came away wet. "It's just a cut," Kaede said, attempting to reassure her. "Is anything else hurt?"

Taisin felt her head gently. "I think…I think I hit my head." Her tongue seemed to have trouble forming words, but oddly, she felt more like herself than she had for days. Perhaps the fall had somehow dislodged Elowen's grip on her. She began to move, and before Kaede could stop her she slipped on the ice, sliding down several inches, and she gasped, scrabbling for hold on the slick surface.

"Slowly!" Kaede called. "Don't move too quickly." Below them there was a crashing sound, and a cloud of snow flew up from the beach. "Con!" Kaede crawled down a few feet, but she could not see him.

"It's just the—the supplies," his voice came back to them. "I'm all right."

Kaede looked at Taisin, who was gradually realizing the severity of the situation, and said, "We must go very carefully, on our hands and knees. Don't try to rush it."

Taisin nodded just slightly. "I'll follow you."

Kaede began to creep down the slope, the rope snaking between them like an umbilical cord.

❦

It was late in the day before they reached the bottom, and it felt as though every last inch of their bodies had been pricked by ice crystals. They were cold and stiff and hot and sweaty all at once, and Kaede would have done anything at that moment for a fire and a bath and a soft bed to collapse into. But there was only the frozen, sandy beach stretching as far as the eye could see, and Con, sitting on the ground propped up against the packs they had pushed over the edge. The bundle that had been packed with firewood had burst open when it hit the ground, and pieces of wood were scattered all over the snow. The dogs, who had climbed down on their own, waited nearby, their breath steaming out in the air.

At first Kaede couldn't understand why Con's left leg was bent at such a strange angle, but as she walked the last few feet to him, she realized that his face was white with pain. He was pressing his hand to his knee, and it was bloody.

"What happened?" she asked, halting.

"My leg," he said hoarsely. "I think it's broken."

Taisin knelt down beside him, holding her shoulder back a little, as if it had been twisted. Kaede rubbed a hand over her tired eyes, leaving streaks of blood across her face. She winced; her fingers were raw and bleeding from the ice.

Taisin bent over Con's leg, and she said hesitantly, "I can set it."

"You don't sound too sure of that," he said, and there was yet a note of grim humor in his voice.

"I saw Mona do it with Shae's leg."

"But you are not Mona."

"I'm as good as you're going to get."

Kaede looked back at the way they had come. The edge of the glacier was jagged, a series of huge steps torn from the earth. She saw that the crevice he had fallen into was a slim slash in the ground—little more than a couple of feet across. There was a smear of blood across the mouth of it. It must have taken a prodigious effort for Con to pull himself out of there. She said to Taisin, "What can I do to help?"

They broke down one of the tent poles and ripped apart the canvas, using it to bind the pole to Con's leg. Kaede had to hold him down as Taisin worked. By the end of it, he had nearly fainted, and Kaede wished she had thought to bring Shae's flask with them.

The dogs were arrayed in a half circle around them, watching attentively. The sky was darkening. Kaede said, "We'll just have to camp here tonight."

Taisin helped her stake out the remaining tent. There wasn't enough room inside for the three of them and all the dogs, but at least the glacier wall created a sort of windbreak. Kaede collected the pieces of wood and built a fire, and Taisin brewed the same tea for Con that she had made for Shae when she was injured. After they ate their cold supper, several of the dogs curled up together, huddling against their packs, and Taisin and Kaede helped Con crawl into the tent. A few of the dogs followed, whining pathetically as the tent flap closed, and Kaede said, "Oh, let them in. We'll be warmer with them inside."

Taisin had been quiet for most of the evening, but now as her two companions readied for sleep and the dogs nosed their way under the furs, she said, "I'll stay up and keep watch."

"Watch for what?" Con asked, grunting as he lay down, trying to prop his leg up at a more comfortable angle.

"I can't go to sleep, Con," Taisin said, though her face was drawn with weariness.

"But you're exhausted," Kaede said. Taisin was still favoring her shoulder, but she hadn't allowed anyone to examine it.

"Yes. But we're too close to…to her. Today—maybe because I was unconscious after that fall—she seems to have left me. At least temporarily. But if I sleep, it would be like opening the door to her again."

"Are you sure you can stay awake? Do you want me to sit up with you?" Kaede asked.

"No. I'll be fine. It's been a long time since I've had the luxury of stillness." She folded her legs beneath her and pulled the furs around her shoulders so that she wouldn't freeze, and as Con and Kaede slept, she sat, her eyes half open, watching the dark.

❧

It took the better part of the morning for them to fashion a sort of sled for Con, for he could not walk long distances, and Kaede refused to leave him behind. They lashed together the remaining canvas from the tent they had torn up to create a sling, and tied it to the dogs' harness. As long as Con held on, he could be dragged, albeit roughly, across the ground. They set off again after a quick noon meal that Taisin ate only because Kaede forced her to; she had sunk into a daze and had begun to murmur to herself. Kaede realized that she was reciting the Thirty Blessings repeatedly from memory, as though that would keep Elowen at bay.

As the day drew to a close and the stars began to shine in the dark blue sky, Taisin was determined to keep going. Kaede suggested that they stop, but Taisin refused. "Just a little farther," she insisted, and she did not wait to see if her companions followed. She knew they would. Elowen was so close to her now; it was like they were in the same room, divided only by a painted screen.

It was pitch-black before Taisin consented to stop. There was a new moon that night, and even the stars seemed to be dimmed. The small fire they lit only served to make everything outside its circle of light seem darker. After they had pitched their tent, fed the dogs, and passed around their own rations for the night, Kaede was so tired she only wanted to crawl into her furs and sleep. But as she burrowed into the warmth of her bedroll, a curious sound began to knock at the edges of her consciousness. In the distance there was a gentle ringing, like two pieces of metal rubbing against each other. She wondered irritably what was making the noise, and why it was bothering her. But the dogs were so warm against her flank and she was so tired that it didn't bother her for long, and soon she was fast asleep.

It wasn't until morning that she learned what had been the source of the ringing sound. As soon as she stepped out of the tent onto the frozen shore, she saw a small dock scarcely twenty feet from where they had set up camp. At the end of the dock was a rowboat tethered with a sparkling silver chain. The boat bobbed gently on the ocean waves curling onto the shore. And there in the distance, like a snow-covered mountain erupting from the sea, she saw the fortress of ice, its windows glinting in the light of the rising sun.

Chapter XXXV

aisin told them her plan while they ate their morning meal. Though she hadn't slept in days, she felt unnaturally aware, as if all her senses were on high alert. The air here was frigid, but peculiarly exhilarating. "Elowen knows me," she began. "She has been inside me; she has seen through my eyes. I think she expects me to come for her; she's even a little curious."

"You can't go," Kaede said, shaking her head. "You're not well."

"I agree."

Kaede's brows rose. "What?" She had not expected Taisin to give in so easily.

"If I go, I think it will be too dangerous. She could use me." All night, Taisin had agonized over this, initially not wanting to admit it to herself. But Mona's warning echoed in her head: *You have a strong heart, but even the strongest heart can be tempted.* And she had felt the temptation already. Experiencing Elowen's power in her visions had awakened a disturbing hunger to have that power herself. Part of her yearned to go to Elowen immediately; she sensed that Elowen would welcome her as a disciple. Yet everything she had learned at the Academy told her that Elowen's power was a gross perversion of natural law; and even if her teachers had kept some things from her, Taisin believed there had been a reason. She wanted to return to the iron-bound fortress and ask her teachers, directly, for the truth.

Last night, sitting awake in the dark tent, everything became crystal clear. If she went to Elowen, she would be tempted to join her and become as corrupt with power as Elowen herself. As much as Taisin wanted to believe she would be able to resist Elowen, she knew she could not take the risk. When she looked hard at herself, examined her deepmost desires, she realized that she did not entirely trust herself. The realization burned at first, but then it made the decision easy. There was one person whom she trusted completely. Someone Taisin knew would do the right thing. She looked at Kaede. "She could use me," Taisin said, "but I don't think she could use you."

"Why not?"

"You're by nature much more closed off to the energies than I am."

Kaede gave a short laugh. "This is why I've never been able to pass the Academy exams."

Taisin smiled faintly. "Yes, well, in this case, I think it will be an advantage. Because even though you are closed off, you've spent many years studying the practice, and I think it has made you quite self-contained. It's like you've built a little wall around yourself."

"Good. Then I'll go."

Con, who had been listening to the two of them silently until now, interrupted: "You can't go alone. I'm coming with you."

Kaede protested, "Con, your leg—"

"Damn my leg," he said, frustrated. "You can't go alone."

"She's not going alone," Taisin interjected. "I'm going with her."

Kaede's forehead wrinkled. "You just said—"

"Listen," Taisin said fiercely. "Elowen has been inside me. But I haven't just been helplessly letting her in. I've learned some things from her."

Con was uneasy. "What have you learned?"

"I can do it, too." She turned to Kaede. "I can be inside you, to help you fight her."

"Inside my mind?" Kaede said uncertainly.

"Yes."

Con said: "Taisin, I'm sure you're capable of a great many things, but this—this doesn't sound safe. Look at what she has done to you."

"It will be different," Taisin insisted, keeping her eyes on Kaede. Kaede grounded her. "If we are together; if you are willing; it will be different."

Kaede asked, "But if she can't use me because I'm so... self-contained, why can you do it?

Taisin's cheeks burned. "Because you have already opened yourself to me." There was an upwelling emotion in Taisin's face that reached straight into Kaede's belly and tugged at her. Her own face colored. Taisin said hurriedly, "I tried it very quickly last night, when you were asleep. I can do it."

"All right," Kaede said, feeling awkward. She took a breath. "So, let's say your theory holds: She can't use me the way she might use you."

"Then you will go to the fortress," Taisin said, "and I will stay here with Con. And when you need my help, I will be there with you."

"How will you know when I need your help?"

"She has put so much energy into this place that it's practically glowing with it. It magnifies everything that's alive. I think I'll be able to feel when you need me."

"What if you can't?"

"I know I can. I can already sense your feelings, even now." Kaede's stomach gave a little lurch, and Taisin had the grace to look embarrassed. She continued, "And when the time comes, I'll help you."

Kaede said, "You'll help me kill her."

The words hung heavily in the air.

Taisin said, "Yes."

⁓

They decided that Kaede would leave that very morning. There was no reason to wait any longer.

She decided to bring nothing but the clothes on her back and the iron dagger that Fin had given her. She unsheathed it and looked at it again. Its blade was dark, inelegant; the textured skin that covered the hilt was nearly black, as though many hands had held it over the decades. It was cold and heavy and sharp, and it had been made for killing. Though she had carried it at her side ever since she had left the Academy, it seemed oddly unfamiliar to her, as if she had never truly looked at it before. She thought she could smell the tang of iron in the air. She wanted for this to be finished.

She moved to resheathe the dagger, but Con said, "Wait." He was sitting by the fire, his broken leg covered with a blanket. "You shouldn't wear it at your waist."

"Why?"

He held out his hand. "Let me see it." She gave it to him and then squatted down nearby. Taisin watched them both curiously. Con ran his hand over the edge of the blade, turning the dagger around. "It's a solid knife," he said. "This is what the Fairy Queen was talking about? Your weapon?"

"I think so. It is made of iron."

"The Xi can't tolerate iron," Taisin said.

He was silent for a few minutes, thinking. Finally he looked at Kaede seriously and said, "I am not a guard, but I have spent my life in the company of them, and I hope you'll take my advice."

"Please," Kaede said, "tell me."

"You should conceal this dagger. If you wear it openly, she'll see it; from what Taisin has said of this woman's power, I believe she could easily disarm you. Your only advantage—besides Taisin—will be surprise. And you've seen how open the land is here. We can't surprise her with our approach—surely she knows we're here already—but you can keep this weapon a secret until you need to use it."

"Where should I conceal it?"

She was dressed in the clothing the Fairy Hunt had given them all: fur-lined boots, warm woolen leggings beneath supple leather leg guards, tunic and fur vest and cloak. Con tapped at her boots. "You can slide it in here. Give me your scabbard and I can fit it into your boot." She took it off, and while he worked out a way to tie it to her leg, he said, "Don't forget your goal. You're not there to negotiate; you're there to kill. Take every advantage you can, Kaede. I don't think it's going to be a fair fight."

After he had lashed the scabbard onto her shin, she fitted her boot over it. The dagger was like a hard splint against her leg, but the boot concealed it neatly, and she could reach in and pull it out without much effort. When she was ready to go, Taisin offered to help with the boat and began to walk toward the dock, leaving Kaede with Con as he inspected the boot and the dagger one last time.

"I wish I could go with you," he muttered.

"You have to watch over Taisin," she told him. "She does things in her sleep sometimes, when she is being visited. She'll talk, or start shaking. You have to make sure she's all right."

"I will." He smiled faintly. "You watch out for yourself. I mean to bring you back to Cathair after this, you know, and make sure you don't have to marry that Lord Win."

She surprised herself by laughing. "I can't wait to have that conversation with my father. Thanks for giving me something to live for, Con."

The corners of his mouth lifted, but his eyes were sad.

At the dock, Kaede surveyed the rowboat. It was small; it looked as though it had never been used before. Elowen had made it especially for them.

Taisin stood beside her. "Are you ready?" she asked.

"As ready as I'm going to be."

"I will be with you." Taisin bit her lip and then asked hesitantly, "Do you trust me?"

"Trust you," Kaede repeated, as if it were an odd thought. "I love you."

Taisin's face twisted with sorrow and fear. This was the moment she had seen in that vision, and she felt it anew, and it was so much worse than she had ever anticipated. Yet she was the one who was sending Kaede to do this terrible thing. Had she always known it? Had part of the dread always been because she knew, somehow, that she was the reason Kaede left?

She cupped Kaede's face in her hands and pressed a hard kiss to her mouth. She whispered: "And I love you."

Kaede wanted to put her arms around Taisin, but she forced herself to step away. It would be easier, she told herself, if she didn't linger.

Her boots scratched against the wooden dock, and she lowered herself into the boat.

Chapter XXXVI

She tried to not look back as she rowed. She didn't know if she would have the courage to keep going if she saw Taisin and Con on the beach behind her. So she lifted and lowered the oar, watching the icy water fall in clear droplets from the blade, and soon the fortress loomed large ahead of her.

When the bottom of the boat scraped onto the icy beach, she jumped out, her boots splashing into the shallow water as she dragged the boat onto the shore. There was no dock on this side, only the fortress. It was like an iceberg—if an iceberg could form in such a way that towers erupted from it. All around the island the ocean was a deep azure blue, and the colors here were so bright and crisp that Kaede had to squint. There was a causeway leading from the shore into the fortress, and at the end of it she could see doors. The island seemed deserted; the snowy ground was scrubbed clean by the wind. There was no sign of activity, human or fay. She moved toward the causeway, her feet scarring the snow for the first time.

The doors to the fortress were made of some kind of white stone, and in the center of each was a round silver ring hanging from a gleaming hinge. Kaede reached out and wrapped her fingers around one of the rings—it was as thick as her own wrist—and when she lifted it, the door swung open. Inside, sunlight spilled through windows set high in walls so tall that Kaede could barely make out the ceiling far above. The hall she stood in was bare of ornamentation but for a pattern inlaid in the floor. Giant diamonds of glass marked out an impressive star. Opposite the doors, a flight of stairs that seemed to be built of blocks of ice curved up out of sight. There was no other exit from the hall, so Kaede crossed the cold floor and began to climb the stairs. With each step she felt the dagger nestled hard against her leg, nudging the muscles of her calf, reminding her of her purpose.

The stairs ended in a long chamber lined with uncurtained windows. Everywhere she looked, the fortress had the faint blue tinge of ice; even the sunlight seemed less golden than white. She stepped into a slanting square of light coming through one of the windows, and though she felt its warmth on her face, it had no effect on the ice all around her. She went to look out the window and saw the sloping shoulder of the fortress, dusted with snow. Far below was the beach, and there was the boat she had rowed, a dark mark against the white. There was certainly no chance she had arrived unnoticed. Where was Elowen?

She heard a faint sound behind her—like the flapping of delicate wings—but when she spun around, her heartbeat quickening, there was nothing there, only a faint shadow disappearing through a doorway she had not noticed before. She forced herself to walk toward it, even though every nerve in her body was telling her to run away from this place. A cold sweat broke out on her forehead.

The corridor she entered curved upward. At first the walls were square with the floor, but as she continued on, they began to curve, too, until the corridor was more like a tunnel carved out of the interior of a mountain. There were still windows in the thick walls, but now they were irregularly cut in the ceiling or at floor level. Tunnels branched off to the sides; some of them slanted down; others had steps carved into them leading up. Once she passed a huge archway, and the sight beyond it caused her to stop and look again. There was a crystal cradle there, and a rocking chair, and on the floor a smear of what looked like blood. It was a nursery. She was drawn inside almost against her will, her curiosity vying against the desire to flee. The hairs on the back of her neck rose as she approached the cradle, but it was empty, and the blood was long dried.

Somewhat relieved—for the memory of the Ento creature had reared up fresh in her mind—she went back out into the corridor, and the shadow fluttered in the distance again. She followed it with renewed determination, but she only ever saw the shadow out of the corner of her eye. The tunnel was so interminable that she was unprepared when it abruptly ended in a vast chamber as large as a cavern. Far above, icicles hung from the rough ceiling. Round windows scattered high in the walls revealed the blue sky, and sunlight streamed in over a sight that caused Kaede to catch her breath. The cavernous room was filled with golden cages, round and square and rectangular, some stacked on top of each other, others standing alone. Inside the cages were the fay she had seen in Mona's book. Some of them looked at her, and their eyes were pinpoints of light: gold and silver and emerald green. The ones closest to her crept to the bars of their cages, and a few extended their arms, reaching for her. One, an excited creature with wings, began to throw itself against the bars, creating a ringing noise. That sound attracted the attention of its neighbors, and a whisper began to spread throughout the chamber, a moving wave of voices that Kaede realized, with a sinking feeling, she had heard before. These were the sounds that Taisin had made at night in her dreams: the eerie, half-senseless murmurings of beings trapped behind bars.

On the far side of the cavern was a door, and Kaede knew, as soon as she glimpsed it, that this was her destination. Her stomach heaved, for this meant that she had to walk through the cavern, past all the cages and all those strange creatures with their sad, brilliant eyes. She took a deep breath and stepped into the prison.

As she walked, she saw that some of the cages were empty, and some of the fay looked almost human. Some were very small—barely the size of her hand, tiny humanoid beings with butterfly-like wings in riotous shades of gold and orange. Several were hunched over in their cages, paying no attention to her as she passed. There were some who looked like human women, but had skin the color of moss and lips like bark; they moved with a lissome grace, treading circles in their cages. One of them reached out to her, and her fingers resembled roots twisting up from the ground. There were cages large enough to contain pools built into the floor, and beings with silvery scales instead of skin swam beneath the surface. Some of the imprisoned fay looked like harmless children, and these horrified her the most, for she wondered if any of them had ever been sheltered in that nursery.

By the time she reached the other side of the cavern, the whispering words had ceased. She glanced back, and the fay in her vicinity were watching her with expectant eyes. In one motion, as if pulled by a greater force, they looked behind her, and a shiver ran down her spine. She turned around slowly, half expecting a monster to rise up and consume her—but there was nothing but the door. An ordinary, human-sized door, with an ordinary, human-sized handle. She walked to it, and when she put her hand on the doorknob, a sigh ran through all the creatures in the hall. She squared her shoulders, nervous sweat dampening her skin, and opened the door.

The first thing she saw was a long expanse of shining ice—the floor was like a frozen lake in midwinter—and at the far end was a dais and a throne that looked just like the Fairy Queen's. But on this throne, Elowen waited. She had golden hair and eyes, high cheekbones, and her mouth was a red slash across white skin. She was clothed from head to toe in white fur, and at her right hand a fairy no more than a foot tall hovered in midair, her wings fluttering like a hummingbird's. A sprite, Kaede remembered.

"Welcome," Elowen said. "Please come closer; it is so rare that I have visitors." She spoke in Kaede's language with the same accent the Fairy Queen had.

Kaede was moving before she knew what she was doing. The floor was slick and cold; she could feel it seeping through the soles of her boots as she walked toward the throne. She also felt the unexpected, dizzying sensation of someone pushing into her mind. Everything suddenly tipped off-balance; the icy floor and walls and windows spun around her; she fell to her knees.

Her vision went black.

There was a deep, insistent tugging, as though someone were trying to pull the very core of her out through her mouth. She moaned, her fingernails scraping against the ice.

Just as suddenly, the pressure eased, and the blackness exploded into blinding white light. She blinked and blinked; the light became white walls and floor and windows—and a throne.

She was twenty feet away from Elowen, and the dagger was pressing against her calf. Her breath steamed out of her.

"That's a surprise," Elowen said. "You're not the one I expected. Who are you?"

"My name is Kaede," she said before she could stop herself.

"*Kaede*," Elowen said, her tongue caressing the sounds as though they were made of the sweetest honey. Kaede felt her entire body quiver, and for a moment she thought she might do anything at all for Elowen—anything. Still on her knees, she gazed up at Elowen, who seemed to glow with a radiant light.

"What brings you to my fortress?" Elowen asked.

"I have come to kill you," Kaede said, the words pouring out of her, and Elowen laughed.

"Is that so? Wonderful. I hope you will allow me to offer you some refreshment before you undertake your task." From nowhere, a chair appeared in the middle of the floor, and when Elowen said, "Sit down," Kaede obeyed her.

A little round table was drawn up nearby, and on that table stood a crystal goblet filled with golden liquid. "Drink," Elowen said. The word was freighted with such seductiveness that Kaede picked up the goblet without hesitation. She could smell the fragrance wafting up from the wine: honey, peaches, flowers in midsummer, as intoxicating as first love. Kaede's eyelids fluttered as the scent of it wrapped around her.

She raised it to her lips, and just as she was about to take a sip, Taisin flooded into her as though a dam had broken. Kaede couldn't breathe; Taisin was breathing for her. She felt oddly doubled, as if she could see everything twice as clearly. The goblet—the wine—she knew instantly that she must not drink it. With shaking hands, she set it roughly back down on the table. Some of the wine splashed over the rim, spilling onto her hand. She rubbed the sticky liquid onto the edge of her cloak. She could feel Taisin's heart beating in time with her own, and it made her light-headed. To have Taisin so close to her—inside her—and yet not physically present—it was an extraordinarily strange experience. She looked at her hands; they were her own hands, and yet it was like seeing them for the first time. The palms were torn up from the descent down the glacier wall, the skin scabbed over where the ice had cut her. She felt as though Taisin were sliding her own hands into hers, like gloves—but Kaede was the glove. She was the armor that Taisin had put on, here, to face Elowen.

Elowen looked at Kaede with narrowed eyes, unable to discern exactly what had happened, but certain that something had changed. Earlier, Kaede's mind had been a closed box; that was not unexpected for an ordinary human, but no ordinary human should be able to resist the wine. The girl should have drunk it and fallen into a delirium; that was what happened when Elowen issued a command: It was obeyed. Who was this girl? Elowen decided to change her strategy.

She said, "I see my mother has sent someone to challenge me." She twisted the word *mother* in her mouth as if it tasted bitter. She saw the shock on Kaede's face, and a smile pulled at her lips. "Does that come as a surprise to you? No wonder—my mother was always so ashamed of her own weakness for *humans*. She tried to make sure that no one knew I was her true daughter. Not even, it seems, the human she sent to kill me." The sprite floated down to alight on the armrest of the throne, and Elowen stroked her yellow hair, making her shiver. "I suppose she thinks it's some kind of poetic justice: sending a human to do the job. But I think it's more like cowardice. She didn't have the nerve to do it herself. What do you think?"

"I—I don't know," Kaede said. Taisin was fully within her; Kaede couldn't discern which of them was speaking.

Elowen pulled a disappointed face. "Oh, come now. I have so few visitors. You must indulge me with a little conversation. Tell me: What did my mother do to convince you to become a murderer?"

Kaede felt Taisin tense with fear inside her, and the fear spread into her own body as she faced Elowen's catlike golden eyes. Neither of them knew what to say.

Elowen was impatient. "I suppose she told you that I am selfish; that I hunger for power that should never be mine. Did she tell you that? She is wrong, Kaede. She knows nothing of what I want—she has never known. But she can be very convincing, it is true. I believe she has convinced you, even though she did it with lies."

Taisin rejected Elowen's words, but Kaede wanted to know: "What lies?"

"Ah," Elowen said, as though pleased to be asked. "Did she tell you that she raised me with every luxury? That I had everything a girl could wish for? She lied. A thousand baubles are nothing when you are raised to know that you were a mistake—the result of a tragic accident. She told me that my human half meant that I would never be as powerful as an ordinary Xi; that I would be doomed to live a short life and die decades before she would need to name her heir." Elowen's face filled with anger. "I was such a disappointment to her. Do you know what it is like to grow up under that shadow? To have your only parent look at you with disgust?"

Even though Kaede recoiled from the golden-eyed woman in front of her, part of her recognized that Elowen's bitterness disguised a deeper hurt, and Kaede's sympathy showed on her face.

"You understand," Elowen said, her voice turning soft and gentle. "How hard it is, to be rejected by one's own flesh and blood. I see that you have experienced this, too."

Kaede wanted to object, but she felt Taisin pulling her back. Taisin's thoughts came through as clearly as if she had spoken them out loud: *She is trying to manipulate you.* Kaede stayed silent, and Elowen went on.

"How could I endure it? I couldn't. I had to leave. I traveled to your kingdom, though I kept myself cloaked and concealed. I knew that I would never be able to find my father—my mother would never even tell me his name—but I wanted to see what sort of people he came from. I soon learned that my mother, for all her secret weakness for humans, knows nothing about them. She couldn't see, as I did, that the shortness of your life makes you work so much harder than any Xi. It's the fear of death that does it, I think. Don't you agree?"

Taisin and Kaede said together: "Yes."

Elowen smiled. "Yes. And when I learned this, I came north to this place. It called to me; the meridians seemed to speak my name. I knew what I had to do. I raised this fortress, and I called the fay here, to help me. They feed me willingly; they have made me so strong." Her face was suffused with pleasure in her own power, and she leaned forward, asking in a coquettish tone, "Can you guess what I'm doing, Kaede?"

Kaede swallowed. "No."

"I am creating a new race of beings—one that has all the relentless determination of a human and all the power of the fay." Her smile faltered a bit. "It isn't easy, but I've learned from my human side. I'm close to success. And when my people are ready, my mother will have no choice but to submit to me, for I will be so much more powerful than her. She will give up her throne to me. I will rule all the Xi and all the fay, and one day, perhaps, I will go to your kingdom and rule that, too. Who could be a better choice than me? I am both fay and human; I understand both worlds."

Elowen sat back in her throne, a serene look on her face as she folded her ringed hands in her lap. "Now," she continued pleasantly, "you said that you came here to kill me. But I am willing to forget that, Kaede, because I see that my mother has lied to you. And because I do not reject my human half the way that she does, I will extend an invitation to you. It is quite admirable that you have come all this way to me. Of course, I thought it would be someone else—your companion, perhaps?—but you are the one who took the last few steps. And to reward you, I will offer you the chance to serve me. You will live a long life, and your parents will see how wrong they were about you, just as my mother was wrong about me. They will have to bow down to you, as my representative. So, I ask you: Will you join me?"

Elowen's words had been spoken in such a calm, measured tone of voice that it seemed almost irrational to disagree with her. Taisin was frantic, fearing that Kaede would give in to Elowen. And Kaede did feel a certain amount of compassion for the Fairy Queen's daughter, but she could never say yes. She thought of her father, who had his own expectations for her. She had chafed under his demands before, but he had never treated her in the way that Elowen assumed. Kaede knew that he loved her. Perhaps the Fairy Queen loved her daughter, too, but Elowen had never been able to see it.

Kaede said: "I'm sorry. I can't join you."

Elowen's face flushed; her mouth twisted. "That was an unwise decision," she said, and she stood up. "You know that I can't allow you to leave this place alive."

She stretched her right hand toward Kaede, her fingers curling. It was as if she was drawing the air toward her;

Kaede could feel the currents in the room bending to her will. And then, to her horror, the air turned and rushed at her; it swirled around her throat like a thousand scarves, tightening until she had lost all her breath. Elowen was regarding her coolly, as if she were merely an unpleasant task to take care of, little larger than an insect she could crush beneath her shoe. Kaede reached her hands up to her throat, her eyes blinking as she began to faint. She could not breathe; her fingers scrabbled at her skin, but there was nothing there to grab onto.

Taisin, she thought dimly. But she felt no response, and everything began to shatter into spots of white upon black.

Chapter XXXVII

iny sparks danced before her eyes; they were as beautiful as fireflies in a purple twilight. And then the sparks multiplied until they were all she could see, and she wondered if she was flying up into the night sky, coming closer and closer to that giant cloud of stars she had seen above the ice field.

She was no longer in her body; she felt free. She was as small as a drop of dew quivering on a spider's web; she was a minute in an hour in a day in a million years. So much had passed to bring her to this moment: births, deaths, countless insignificant decisions that made her who she had become. All of that—all of her—could end now. She could return to the limitless state that every living creature once was in and will be again.

But she was not ready. Not yet.

And not without regret, she turned away from the pull of the starry sky, and far below her, she saw the fortress, a mountain of white snow. She saw the azure sea broken with ice floes. She saw the beach. She saw Con kneeling on the cold ground gripping Taisin's hands in his. She saw Taisin, her eyes wide open and looking directly at her. Her gaze was magnetic; it pulled her down, down, until she was plummeting toward the earth, toward Taisin and through her. Now, with a stunning clarity, she could feel every fiber of Taisin's being. She could feel her pain, her excitement, her fear. There was the clenching and release of the muscle of her heart. And there was the love between them: a revelation. A way in.

In those brief moments when she was floating free, Kaede had almost forgotten what it was like to be corporeal. Then, she was being channeled through Taisin back into her own flesh and bones again, as if she were being squeezed into clothes that were much too small. Her body was so limited, so attached to the ground. She couldn't, at first, remember how to move, but Taisin did, and she was still within her. Kaede watched her own hand fly up; it grasped the currents of air that Elowen had wrapped around her throat and tore through them. It was like ripping a great bolt of silk, and the air fell in ragged ribbons away from her.

Elowen stood in front of her throne with her arm still outstretched. She looked as shocked as Kaede felt. In that heartbeat, they were equals, and Kaede knew she had to act before Elowen regained her wits. She reached down to her boot, feeling her blood rushing into her fingertips, and drew out the dagger and threw it at her.

But there was no time to even hope it would reach its mark, for Elowen flung it aside with a fistful of energy. The dagger clattered to the floor and slid until it lodged itself in the wall beneath the windows, and then Elowen began to advance on her.

Kaede ran for the dagger, but her boots slipped. The icy floor came rushing up to slam into her hands and knees. She slid; she scrambled on all fours toward the wall. Taisin was gathering up the energy she would need for one more assault, and Kaede felt Taisin's strength rising inside her like a fever.

Elowen came after her, vowing that she would put her own hands around this human's throat. But at the last moment, Kaede's fingers found the dagger, and as she whirled around, Taisin spoke through her.

"Elowen!"

The woman stopped, startled by the sound of her name on someone else's lips.

Kaede swung her hand and slashed through Elowen's gown, cutting into her leg. Elowen let out a scream; she looked down at the blood that dripped onto the floor. A curious steam rose from the wound, and the fabric around it curled back as if it were burning away.

"What have you done?" Elowen shrieked. The skin of her face was nearly translucent; her veins were black rivers beneath her temples.

Kaede pushed herself to her feet. The handle of the dagger fitted into her palm like an old friend. She felt Taisin readying herself. "Elowen," they said together, and Kaede charged at the Fairy Queen's daughter and plunged the dagger into her heart.

Elowen's eyes widened; her mouth parted. Her blood streamed over Kaede's hand. She fell, looking as frightened as a child facing the dark.

Kaede stared at Elowen's body, stunned. The moment the blade made contact with Elowen's heart, all the power that had surged between her and Taisin drained away, and now she felt emptied, unsteady. Her hands were shaking; they were wet with blood. Without thinking, she smeared them over her thighs. When she looked back, the same scene awaited her: Elowen lay there with her eyes half-open, the dagger fixed in her chest, blood pooling down on the floor. It was indeed made of ice, and it was melting.

She forced herself to kneel down and pull the dagger out. The wound itself was burned black as if the iron had scorched Elowen's flesh, and Kaede had to swallow her nausea as she wiped the blade on the very edge of Elowen's ermine cloak.

As she resheathed the dagger in her boot and stood up, the sprite who had fluttered near Elowen's throne bobbed into sight. She was a girl, or she looked like one, except she had little wings growing from her shoulder blades. Her skin was as golden as her hair, and she looked up at Kaede with wide blue eyes that were both sad and triumphant. Then she fluttered down to Elowen's waist, where she pushed aside the folds of the fur robe to reveal a silver key ring. She picked up the ring in her little hands and struggled to fly up to Kaede's eye level, where she said something that Kaede did not understand.

Frustrated, the girl gestured to the open door at the end of the throne room. Kaede heard a rising cacophony coming from the cavern beyond. The girl was shaking the keys, causing them to clink together like bells, and Kaede realized they were the keys to the cages. The fay wanted to be set free.

"Of course," Kaede said out loud. "You should free them." When the girl gave her a puzzled look, Kaede pointed to the door, gesturing the act of turning a key in its lock. The girl understood, and a brilliant smile spread over her delicate features. She even bounced a little in the air before flying speedily down the length of the throne room toward the door.

Kaede looked back at Elowen. The weight of what she had done settled over her again. She took a ragged breath.

She could not leave the body there. It felt wrong.

She glanced around the room for something to use as a shroud, but there was nothing. Finally she settled for folding Elowen's cloak more securely around her. Her flesh was still warm, and it seemed unreal that she was truly dead. Taking a deep breath, Kaede dragged Elowen up and over her shoulder. Her body was surprisingly light, and though it was not a comfortable position, Kaede thought she could manage to carry her some distance this way. She trudged down the length of the throne room and through the door to the prison.

Every last one of the fay came to watch her pass this time. Some appeared sad; others eager; but none seemed interested in avenging Elowen's death. The sprite had already begun to unlock some of the cages, and those who had been set free started to follow Kaede and her burden out of the cavern.

It was a long, hard walk through the many tunnels of the

fortress, and several times Kaede thought she might have lost her way. Elowen's body, which had once seemed light, soon felt so heavy that Kaede wanted to weep with the strain of it, but she would not let herself stop, and she would not accept the help of the fay who followed her. She had killed Elowen, and she had a superstitious feeling that it was her task to bring this to its proper conclusion.

At last she arrived at the entry hall, and she went through the great doors and outside into the sunlit afternoon. She was almost surprised that the sun had not already set, for it felt as though she had been inside that fortress for a life-time. And then she wondered if carrying Elowen outside had been pointless, for she had been intending to build a funeral pyre, but there was no wood on the beach—not even a single spare piece of driftwood. She laid Elowen's body on a stretch of icy sand and sat near Elowen's head, her eyes squinted against the setting sun. She wanted to give up.

The sprite emerged from the fortress first, followed by one of the lithe, willowy nymphs with fingers like small branches. More and more of them came outside, blinking up at the blue sky, and many of them were carrying torches as though they had known what Kaede was preparing to do. They came toward her, and the first one set her torch down upon Elowen's body, the flames flaring up as they touched the fur cloak that served as her shroud. One by one, they set her afire, and in this way, Elowen's prisoners built her funeral pyre.

Kaede sat still on the beach, watching the flames grow, and she felt a thick, ashen despair settle over her. She had come to this island in the far north with the goal of murder, and she had done her job, but now she only felt like a killer. There was no glory in this. She had seen Elowen's face as she died, and she knew the memory of it would haunt her for the rest of her life. Kaede put her head in her hands and wanted to weep, but tears would not come. She felt split apart, broken, as frozen as the island that bore the weight of Elowen's ambition.

Kaede looked into the flames late into the night, and forced herself to watch as the cloth curled back from Elowen's face, as it ate through her furred mantle and burned away her flesh, until all that was left to see was an empty skull, blackened and charred.

"Taisin," said the voice again. It was Con. He was holding

Chapter XXXVIII

aisin heard the voice from very far off, dim and faint. It was comfortable where she was: Everything was dark and soft. Her mind was empty, quiet. She felt free for the first time in weeks, and she just wanted to linger there. A cushion of nothing at all. Blankness.

But the voice would not stop.

Gradually the sounds formed syllables. The syllables formed a word. Her name.

"Taisin."

She recognized that voice.

"Taisin! *Come back.*" It was a demand. There was dust in her mouth, the taste of ashes, gritty and dry. Her tongue was thick and swollen. Her head throbbed. Her shoulder ached—and that was what pulled her back into her body at last. The stabbing, twisting pain in her muscles, where she had wrenched her arm climbing down the glacier wall.

She gasped, her eyes opening to a star-strewn sky.

"Taisin," said the voice again. It was Con. He was holding

her head in his lap, and she looked at his face upside down above her, filling with relief as she blinked. "Taisin, what happened?"

The air was freezing, and it carried the smell of burning. The waxing moon was a sliver in the east. She said: "Elowen is dead."

❧

When dawn broke, Kaede rowed the little boat back to the mainland. A small wind had risen with the sun, blowing drifting snow over the smoking ashes. Elowen would never leave her island.

Taisin and Con had the camp half-packed by the time Kaede set foot on the dock. The dogs came running to greet her, barking loudly in the early morning stillness. Taisin met her halfway and put her arms around her, holding her tight. Kaede wanted to stay there forever, with her face buried in Taisin's hair, but she could still smell the scent of Elowen's funeral pyre, and she wondered if it would always be with her.

When they parted at last, she saw Con hobbling toward them. She embraced him, and he said gruffly, "Welcome back."

She gave him a weak smile, then glanced at their camp. The provisions were already packed up; they only had to strip down the tent, and they could go. She said: "We must leave this place."

Con nodded. "We're almost ready."

They reached the point where they had descended from the glacier by early afternoon, and though they were all exhausted, they had no intention of waiting another minute. It took several hours to make the climb back up. Con was wet with sweat by the time he reached the top, and for long minutes he simply lay there on the snow, looking up at the sky, his breath misting out above him as his leg throbbed.

The sledge was where they had left it, perched alone in a vast white landscape. There was no sign of storm clouds in the sky. The weather, in fact, had been still all day, as though it were waiting, testing out the new balance of power in the world. It put Kaede on edge. It felt like something was unfinished. Elowen was dead, but nothing had been made right.

Their journey across the ice field took less time than their journey out to the fortress, for the weather remained calm and the sledge was lighter now. They left the broken tent behind, and their supplies were mostly gone. Both Kaede and Taisin walked with a kind of dull determination across the snow. Taisin was so exhausted from their battle with Elowen that it was all she could do to put one foot in front of the other. Con watched them with an alert eye, for he was worried about them. At night he gave them more than their fair share of the rations, but they did not notice. They only ate what he handed over and slept so deeply he was afraid, in the morning, that they might never awaken.

They did not know that in the distance behind them, the fay had begun their own journeys home. The knockers— hardy mountain dwellers accustomed to the cold—carried those who would have otherwise frozen: some of the dryads, or the winged sylphs, whose bodies were limp in the wintry air. The asrai and the undines had slipped into the icy northern sea to head south for the mouth of the Kell, where they would swim upstream to their cool lakes and rocky rivers. The sprite who had attended Elowen that last day remembered the name of the one who had saved them, and she repeated it to every fairy she set free with those keys: *Kaede*. So the story of the girl who had defeated their tormentor was passed from one to another in languages that had gone generations without once uttering the word *human*.

Had Kaede known this, she would have told them that she had not acted alone, that both Taisin and Con had helped her. But she did not know the fay were speaking her name, so she was spared the burden of becoming their hero, when in fact she still felt like a murderer.

When they saw the ragged line of the Wood in the distance, Con felt like a sailor long at sea, finally sighting land. Relief surged through him; he hadn't realized how much he had feared that they would never leave that frozen wasteland behind. They quickened their pace that afternoon, the dogs running faster as though they, too, were eager to seek the shelter of the trees. Waiting at the edge of the Wood was the Fairy Hunt: the same riders who had sent them off across the ice field so many days before.

The Huntsman took stock of their bedraggled appearance and ordered someone to care for Con's leg and Taisin's shoulder, and then he came to Kaede and regarded her gravely. "You have done a good deed for us all."

She said dispiritedly, "Have I?"

"You have," he said, but she was not convinced.

The journey back to Taninli took several days. The farther they rode into the Wood, the warmer it became, until at last it was summer again, and they could strip off their furs and pack them away. But despite the warmth, a pall hung over them, and the sun remained hidden behind clouds. Kaede remembered how the Xi had seemed to glow the first time she had entered Taninli, but this time the whole world was muted. She wondered if there was something wrong with herself, for ever since leaving the fortress of ice, she saw everything through a film of ashes.

But as they rode through the streets of the Xi city, it became clear that the same miasma was affecting everyone. Few of the Xi came out to watch them pass, and the ones who did looked haunted. At the palace, a thin layer of dust drifted over the white stone. Their horses kicked it up when they rode into the courtyard, and it floated into Kaede's nose and throat and made her cough.

The Huntsman did not allow them to rest. He took them directly through the quiet, dim halls to the Fairy Queen's throne room. Kaede was shocked to see the Fairy Queen slumped over in her throne, her face as gray as the dust that drifted in ashy piles around their feet. The Huntsman seemed terribly affected by this; he went to her side and knelt down to take her hand, and Kaede realized by the way he touched her that he loved the Queen. When he turned back to them, his face was drawn with grief.

"What is wrong?" Kaede asked, stepping forward. She

put one foot on the first step at the bottom of the dais but hesitated to go farther.

"She is not well," the Huntsman said.

"Should we return at a later time?" Kaede asked.

The Queen stirred. "No." She pushed herself upright and looked at the three humans. "Which one of you killed Elowen?"

The question sent a chill through Kaede. Before she could speak, Con answered, "We acted together, Your Majesty."

"Which of you held the knife?" the Queen demanded, and Kaede flinched, for she sounded like Elowen. "Which one of you?"

Kaede bowed her head. "It was me, Your Majesty. I held the knife."

The Queen sighed. "Come here."

Dread filling her, Kaede climbed the low steps of the dais. The Queen extended her hand, and when Kaede took it, the skin was dry as paper. The Queen pulled her closer so that she had to kneel before the throne. The edge of the seat cut into her belly, and the hard stone floor bit into her knees. The Queen's cheeks were marked with unnaturally bright red spots; her burning golden eyes had the same fierceness Kaede had seen in Elowen. Her hair was white and brittle. She looked defeated; she looked ancient.

"This is what has become of me," the Queen whispered, "for ordering the murder of my own child."

Kaede heard the anguish in the Queen's voice, and guilt burned through her. She was the Queen's accomplice in this murder.

"You are not surprised," the Queen murmured. "Did she tell you that I was her mother?"

Kaede lowered her eyes to where their hands were clasped together, remembering the curl of Elowen's lip as she said the word *mother*. "Yes. She told me."

"I thought that removing her from this world would set things right, but I find that I was wrong. Her death has killed part of me, as well."

A droplet of liquid splashed down on their hands, and Kaede realized that the Queen was crying. Every drop was cold as ice: hard little shards pricking at her skin. Kaede watched numbly as tiny red marks erupted on her hands where the Queen's tears struck. She did not know how long the two of them remained there, the floor bruising her knees as the Queen wept. But at last the Queen drew her hand away and lifted Kaede's chin so that she had to look into the Queen's golden eyes.

She saw the world in them. The Wood around Taninli, the trees bowed down with the weight of the Queen's sorrow. The wind sighing over brown, broken grasses. The glacier, dry and frigid, spread all over with funeral ashes. She couldn't look away, even though the sight of it made her wither inside. Had she done this to the Queen? Was it all her doing—because she had killed Elowen? Kaede drew in a shaking breath. She deserved to feel all the misery the Queen was feeling. She wanted to taste the dust that coated the palace. She wanted to drown in the deepness of the Northern Sea, feel its gelid water seeping into her.

The Queen's fingers pressed against her cheeks. Her

341

nails scraped against Kaede's skin. "Listen to me," the Queen whispered, her voice rough with pain. "You can save me. You can save all of us."

The words floated into Kaede's mind as if from a great distance. She heard them, but she did not understand. She was engulfed in the enormity of the Queen's grief.

Taisin's voice was thin and sharp behind them. "How?" she asked. She took three quick steps toward Kaede and put her hand on Kaede's shoulder.

Kaede twitched. She felt Taisin's fingers, firm and warm; she drew another uneven breath. The Queen's face wavered before her, coalesced into the image of an old woman, lines cracking from the corners of her eyes and spreading down her cheeks.

"How?" Taisin asked again, her fingers digging into Kaede's shoulder bone, prodding her back to the reality of the throne room. The Queen's hands fell away from her face, and Kaede swayed. Taisin held her arm; helped her to her feet.

"There is only one cure for me," said the Queen.

"What is it?" Taisin put her arm around Kaede, steadying her.

The Queen ached with regret. She felt her energy leaking out of her. Her heart was punctured; she would become a hollow shell. "The water of life," she answered. "I must drink it."

"Where is it found?" Taisin asked.

"It is far from here. Through the darkest Wood and across the three rivers; beyond the red hills and within the trees of gold."

Con had been standing silent nearby, watching Kaede kneeling before the Fairy Queen as if entranced, and a sense of disquiet filled him. "What will happen if you don't drink this water of life?" he asked.

The Queen closed her eyes. "I will die," she said, her voice light as a dry wind. "And my land will die with me."

"Your land," Con said. "What do you mean?"

Kaede understood, now, what the Queen had wanted her to see in her bright yellow eyes. "She means that Taninli will crumble," Kaede said. "She means that the fay will die. And she means that the Wood itself will perish. The trees will fall; the rivers will dry up; the earth will become nothing but ash." As she spoke, the words uncoiling through her, she felt her heartbeat quickening. What would the world come to? It would surely spread to the Kingdom. The border between their lands was porous; the Queen's death would hover over their cities and villages, too. She had a terrifying vision of Cathair drenched in ash-gray rain, covering the red roofs of her parents' home in a choking sludge.

Taisin put a hand on Kaede's cheek. "Kaede," Taisin said. "Open your eyes."

Kaede blinked them open. She hadn't realized they were closed. She saw Taisin's worry-filled face.

"Are you all right?" Taisin asked.

Kaede rubbed at her forehead. She felt unbalanced, disoriented. "I don't know. I saw—I saw Cathair. It was dying, too."

Taisin looked the Fairy Queen. "Are you putting these visions in her mind?"

"She must see what will happen if I die," the Queen said.

"Why?" Kaede and Taisin asked together.

"You, Kaede, are the only one who can save me," the Queen said. "So you must know what will happen if you choose not to."

"Why only Kaede?" Taisin demanded.

The Huntsman said, "The hand that took Elowen's life is the only hand that can bring life to our queen."

Kaede was hot and cold at the same time. Visions, apparently, disagreed with her. "What do I have to do?" she asked. "How do I find the spring where this water comes from?"

"It is not a spring," the Queen said.

Taisin stiffened. She remembered, suddenly, Mona and that little sharp knife drawn along her skin.

"The water of life is the blood of the unicorn," the Huntsman explained.

Kaede stared at him. "The unicorn?"

He nodded. "You must seek out the unicorn and submit to its judgment. If it finds you innocent, then it will sacrifice itself to you and give you its lifeblood. You will bring it back to the Queen."

Kaede remembered the stories, of course. Everyone told them. But this was akin to asking her to hunt down a dragon, and though she had seen enough wonders for an entire lifetime in the short period she had been in Elowen's fortress, this was too much to take in. Besides, in those tales, no one ever survived the judgment of a unicorn. "What if it finds that I'm...not innocent?" she asked, and once again she felt the weight of guilt pulling her down. Her hand had been smeared with Elowen's blood. She had done it, had taken the Fairy Queen's daughter's life. She had seen it pouring out of her onto the ice.

The Huntsman said somberly, "If it judges you guilty, then it will kill you."

A thick silence blanketed the throne room. Kaede felt feverish. Everything seemed unreal. She wiped her hand across her brow, leaving a streak of dust over her skin.

Con's voice cut through everything. "This is mad," he objected. "Kaede, you can't go alone."

"We were there with her in the fortress," Taisin insisted. "Your Majesty, I helped Kaede kill Elowen. I share the burden with her."

The Huntsman looked terribly sad. "Your friends do you much honor, but in the end, it is your choice alone."

Kaede looked at the Queen, frail and aged. She looked at Taisin and Con, whom she might never see again if she did as the Queen asked. But the Queen's grief—and her own guilt—pulled her in the only direction she could go. She turned to the Huntsman and said, "I will do it."

He bowed deeply to her in thanks. "We will leave as soon as possible."

PART V

Those who love are clouds floating side by side:
Dewdrops bending blades of grass at sunrise.
Yet love is the rhythm of nature;
Love is oneness with beauty;
Love is the joyful revelation of the way.

—The Thirty Blessings

Chapter XXXIX

aede rode with the Huntsman out of Taninli later that day. He would not allow anyone else to accompany them. They traveled so quickly that the Wood became a blur of green and brown, moss and bark, but their horses did not tire. She ate the food that the Huntsman gave her, and she drank from the water skin he handed to her without question. The liquid burned down her throat, making her eyes open wide in momentary shock, and then they were riding again.

When they stopped to sleep, she dreamed of ashes, drifts upon drifts of them, covering the Wood in a stale scent of burning. She heard the Queen's voice: *Please hurry.* All around them, the trees were dying. She could feel it so clearly, though she did not understand how or why. Something had changed within her when she looked into the Queen's eyes; now there was a bond between them, Fairy Queen and human girl. Sometimes she would reach out along the length of that bond, and at the very end, she could just sense the quiver of the Queen's heartbeat. She still waited in her throne room.

Kaede and the Huntsman passed through a forest of giant trees, their trunks black with age, the sun obscured by thick, tangled vines. They crossed a narrow wooden bridge over a rushing river, and a bridge that swayed over a gorge carved out of a granite mountainside. Kaede held her breath as her horse picked his way across, seemingly oblivious to the precipitous drop beneath them. Far below another river churned, and above them birds with vast wingspans shrieked, their calls echoing down the rocky canyon.

On the other side, the trees were so densely packed together that their horses had to slow to a walk. From time to time sunlight shone in tall shafts through the foliage, and then there were stretches of shadow, or brief squalls of rain and mist. She saw deer in flight, white tails like flags. She saw crows with their darting black eyes, perched on branches above. Eventually they came to a river that ran sweetly over rounded boulders, and the Huntsman told her it flowed south to meet the Nir. There was no bridge here, and they waded across, for the water was barely higher than her knees. On the opposite bank, the trees began to thin out, and the next time they camped, the earth was the color of ocher and smelled of metal.

They climbed one hill, and then another, and the red soil covered everything until even her hands were tinged a rusty brown. At last they came to a spring that bubbled out of a tiny little cleft in the rocky red hillside, and the Huntsman dismounted and knelt down to it, cupping up a handful of water. When he had tasted it, he said, "We are near. We'll camp here tonight, and tomorrow you'll continue on your own."

"You're staying here?"

He nodded. "The rest of the journey is for you alone."

"But… how will I know where to go?"

He pointed up the hillside. In the distance she saw trees, their leaves as gold as the Queen's eyes. "You'll go that way. Through the trees."

She dismounted and watched as her horse drank from the spring. Her head felt fuzzy. The Queen's presence was much more distant now, and she felt almost unmoored. She wondered how far they were from Taninli. "The unicorn— will it be waiting for me?"

The Huntsman shook his head. "You must seek it out. It does not show itself to everyone."

"Is there only one?"

"I don't know. Once, there were many. But those days are gone."

"How do I seek it out?"

He bent down to unbuckle the saddle from his horse. "That is for you to discover."

"What if I can't?" she asked, and a bubble of panic rose in her stomach. "What if I fail?"

He set the saddle down on the ground and looked at her with a grave expression. "I hope that you won't."

❧

That night she slept poorly. She fell in and out of the same dream she always had: ashes falling over the land, settling into the crevices between tree roots, dusting over every unfurled bud, smothering each hint of life. She allowed herself to get up as soon as dawn broke, and she knelt beside the spring and splashed the freezing cold water on her face, gasping at the chill.

The Huntsman brewed a bitter, dark tea that morning that she had never tasted before. "It will give you strength," he said, noticing her grimace. "You should drink it all."

As the sun rose, she sipped the tea, feeling her body slowly coming to life. The daze that had cloaked her during their journey was lifting, like cobwebs being brushed aside. She looked over the red hillside, at the rocks and the soil and the scrub grass, and then at the arch of the sky, pink and gold in the east. A question that had been forming in her ever since they left Taninli finally found its way to her tongue: "Why is the Queen so tied to these lands? Why does the land fall sick when she does?"

The Huntsman considered her question for some time before he answered. "Our queen is the embodiment of our land. It has been this way since the dawn of time, and it will be so until our last queen dies."

"There have been many queens?"

"Yes."

"Then when one queen dies, why does the land not die with her?"

"She is not like your king. She is not born into her station. Each queen chooses her successor, and each chosen successor must undergo many rituals to prepare for her duties. It may take decades. When the chosen one is ready, her predecessor goes willingly to her death."

"But this queen is not ready to die."

"No. She is not ready. She has not yet chosen a successor, and without one…" He could not finish the sentence. His heart constricted at the thought of his queen being taken before her time.

Kaede dug her fingers into the ground, trapping the soil beneath her nails. It was already turning to dust.

⁂

The Huntsman gave her a horn cup with a leather strap affixed to it. The cup had an ingenious cap, carved also of horn, and it latched into place with silver hinges. It was made from the horn of a unicorn.

"After the judgment," he told her, "you must fill this cup with blood, and bring it back." He did not mention the possibility that the judgment might render her incapable of returning. "I will be waiting for you here."

She took the horn from him, feeling oddly calm. She thought she ought to be afraid—terrified, even, for she might be riding to her death. But instead she only felt ready. She had come so far, and in a way she felt as though she had been preparing for this her whole life. She buckled the iron dagger onto her belt and mounted her horse.

She rode toward the golden trees as quickly as she could, but it was noon before she felt the shade of the first tree on her back, and she paused beneath its limbs to eat a dry biscuit and get her bearings. She had never seen trees like this before: white bark and branches so delicate she could not understand how they supported the weight of those leaves.

They looked like gold coins, and when the wind blew through them, she heard a thousand tiny chimes. The trees sang.

She continued on, and the trees began to grow more thickly, until all around her were slim white trunks. Sunlight dappled the ground; afternoon slid into dusk; and shadows spread purple and blue across the golden forest. The wind grew cooler. As far as she could see were these golden trees. There was no end to this forest, and she did not know which direction to go. She dismounted from her horse and decided to make camp for the night.

Her horse was unusually skittish. She felt his muscles trembling as she unsaddled him, and he pranced as if he wanted to leave. "What is it?" she asked, her voice sounding strange in this wilderness. She tried to calm him down, but he continued to be nervous, and at last she had to tie him to a tree, afraid that he would bolt.

She tried to sleep, but the horse's anxiety and the keening of the trees kept her awake. She finally dozed off a little before dawn, only to wake up when she heard the horse whinny loudly. She scrambled to her feet, still half asleep, and saw the tail end of her horse disappearing through the trees.

"Stop!" she yelled, but the horse did not halt. She looked at the tree where she had tied it, and the rope was still knotted around the trunk. The end that had been tied to her horse's halter flapped loose in a slight breeze.

Cold slid down her spine, and her heart pounded. She bent over, hands on her knees, trying to calm herself. She was suddenly aware of how alone she was in this queer place, and she had the uncanny sensation that the singing trees had been singing about *her*. It was a chilly morning, but she felt perspiration rise on her skin. The direction of the wind abruptly shifted, and the melody that had been running through the leaves changed.

Something—or someone—was nearby.

She could not sense people's energies the way that a sage could, but this spirit or consciousness was so focused, so brilliant, that anyone would know it was there.

She straightened, glancing around, but she saw only trees. She tried to swallow her fear; tried to ignore the prickles of panic that raced along her skin. She told herself she was there for a reason, and it was an honorable reason. She clenched her hands into fists and turned into the wind, letting it stream over her head, loosening her hair. The sun was rising, shedding gray light over the golden forest, and in the shadows she thought she saw something moving in the distance.

"I am here for your judgment," she whispered. The shadows moved again, but they did not come closer. She raised her voice, bracing herself. "I am here for your judgment!"

She felt suspended in the wind. The music of the trees rang in her ears. She wondered how long she would have to stand there, waiting. The leaves shook like tambourines.

The unicorn seemed to step out of nowhere. It was a male. His head was small and perfectly formed, shaped like that of a deer, but with a gray beard growing from his chin. The horn, a speckled, ivory spiral, protruded from between black eyes that were undeniably intelligent. He was about the size of a mature buck, with fur that contained all the colors of the rainbow. From one angle, he might look like lichen or moss; but from another, he was as stunning as a phoenix, his coat sliding from gold to silver to fire.

She knelt down before him, her whole body tense, and asked for the judgment.

~

Though she had felt Taisin enter her mind in Elowen's fortress, this was entirely different. As his consciousness filled her, there was a sensation of perfect openness. All of her, heart and soul, was spread out before this creature, and he examined every last detail of her life.

He saw her memories of childhood—roughhousing with her brothers, running around their courtyard home, begging their mother for rock sugar. There was her first trip to the Academy; the time she had upset Fin by leaving the workshop a mess; the warm saltiness of the sea on a summer day. The moment, that morning in the Council chambers, when she truly noticed Taisin for the first time.

She felt the sway of the King's ship as she left the Academy behind. Shock as she watched the King's guards execute the bandit on the highway.

In Ento: the black eyes of the monstrous child as she plunged the knife into its belly. The horror that gripped her as she watched its funeral pyre.

The split second of sheer panic as the wolves came at her. The stretch of the bowstring as she shot arrow after arrow into their bodies, her stomach tight as a fist.

Taisin: the warmth and the smell of her skin; the pleasure of her kisses. Love, new and fierce.

And then there was Elowen, reaching for her throat. Blackness; everything snuffed out. She floated free, like a seed on the wind. Kaede wondered: Had she died? There had been a moment—she was sure now—when she had ceased to exist as a living human being.

She remembered opening her eyes to see Elowen's snarling face. Her knees skidding across the floor, her hand reaching for her weapon. The iron dagger, buried in Elowen's heart. Blood on her hands.

If she had killed someone who already killed her, did that still make her a murderer?

Her eyes flew open. The unicorn lowered his head. She looked into his black eyes, and though he did not speak in words, she understood him.

Harmony: This was the heart of nature. Every living being—plant, animal, human, fay—had its place in the cycle of life and death. In this cycle, countless creatures worked in tandem as well as against one another. All of these beings formed a complicated whole that shifted and changed in order to maintain that harmony.

Elowen had taken many lives in order to extend her own. Her stockpiling of power had wreaked havoc on nature. Her death was justified. But that did not mean that harmony was restored, for harmony is never achieved through murder.

And Kaede had to accept her part in that. Tears slid down her face. The experience of killing Elowen—of death on her hands—would be imprinted on her always. She had been given an extraordinary gift in Elowen's fortress: a second

357

life. She understood that now, and she knew she had a responsibility to live up to it—if the unicorn allowed her to.

He lowered his horn until the point came to rest lightly against her chest. The touch of it sent a shock through her. All he had to do was push forward, and she would be dead. But he remained still. He was not finished with her.

He showed her that although she may have held the knife, it was the Fairy Queen who put it there, and the Queen had acted out of desperation and self-hatred. She did not want to accept her own responsibility for the tragedy of Elowen's life. Now the Queen was paying her own price: She was dying, and so were her land and her people.

If the Queen died without an heir, the ash that had blanketed Taninli would spread, sifting into the cracks and corners of the Wood, sinking into the Nir until the river became thick and slow. There would be no summer; there would be no autumn or winter or spring—only this neverending grayness, as if all the color had been leached from the world.

This could not be allowed to pass. The Fairy Queen must live, so that her land could heal. Kaede knew that the Queen would never be the same again. Her time to die would come soon. But she needed to live—for now.

The unicorn lifted his head and gave Kaede permission to draw his blood with her knife, the same one that had killed Elowen.

With shaking hands, she slid the blade across his throat, holding the horn cup beneath it, and drop by drop, his life fell into her hands.

The Huntsman looked as if he had aged a decade when she returned to his camp. Her horse had found his way back on his own, looking none the worse for his experience in the unicorn's grove.

"Is it done?" the Huntsman asked.

She held up the horn. "Yes." She was drained, exhausted.

Relief flooded into the Huntsman's face, making him look almost human. "Then we must return," he said, and called their horses.

He pushed them hard on the journey back to Taninli. Every day that passed brought the Queen one step closer to her premature death, and he could sense the Wood already beginning to wither. The sun, now, was always covered by cloud.

When they returned to Taninli, they found the city much changed. The layer of dust that had fallen over the palace had spread to the streets. The scent of burning hung heavily in the air.

At the palace courtyard, they dismounted quickly. Kaede had slung the horn over her shoulder, and the knife slapped against her hip as she hurried after the Huntsman. In the throne room, the Queen still lay in her crystal chair, and Taisin and Con paced near the windows as if they had never left. But Kaede could not spare more than a glance for them, for the Queen was on the verge of death.

Kaede climbed the steps to the dais and knelt before the Queen as she had knelt before the unicorn. She unlatched the cap and dipped her fingers into the blood, which was as warm as it had been when it dripped from the creature's throat. She smeared it in long strokes over the Fairy Queen's sunken cheeks, and words came to her mouth as though the unicorn were speaking through her: "As life is in the blood, so you shall receive it, for it is blood that brings life." She lifted the horn cup to the Queen's mouth, and a great shudder ran through the Queen's body.

As the blood spilled over the Queen's tongue, Kaede's world lurched. The floor seemed to shake beneath her, and she clutched the horn cup, feeling dizzy. The Queen leaned toward her, and she was so close now that Kaede could see the Queen's pupils dilating. The Queen's mouth opened in a gasp. Kaede saw the smear of blood on her lips, and somehow Kaede, too, could taste it, metallic and bitter. She felt it traveling through her body as if she had drunk from the cup herself. She realized that iron was burning through the Queen—iron from the unicorn's blood—and it would kill her just like Kaede's dagger had killed Elowen.

The Queen's eyes were almost entirely black now; only a thin rim of gold encircled her pupils, and a chill was spreading over her skin like frost. She was dying. Kaede wanted to sob: This was not what she had intended. The Queen was supposed to live!

She closed her eyes; she did not want to see the Queen die. A memory rose like a ghost between them, and Kaede could see it just as the Queen did: a birth. A night of pain, horrible pain, followed by the sweetest dawn of the Queen's life. A baby girl with eyes of gold and hair the color of sunlight. Elowen.

Another ghost of a memory appeared: A hot summer afternoon in the Great Wood. A man alone, lost. There was something beautiful about him: the openness of his face, the strength of his hands. The Queen had no intention of keeping him for long, but he was so different from her many courtiers, with their elegant clothes and cool, appraising blue eyes. This man's eyes were the color of the earth, and his mouth was warm.

Kaede felt the Queen's heart pounding. Moments before she had felt the chill of death on the Queen's skin, but now there was a rising heat. Kaede opened her eyes and saw the Queen's face glowing as if she were lit by a fire within. The light grew until the Queen was bright as a star; she was the brightest, strongest star in a constellation, and every living creature was in orbit around her. But even the Fairy Queen was not invulnerable, for even she could be wholly changed by the smile of a handsome young man on a hot summer day.

The Queen was alive; she was reborn. Joy and relief swept through Kaede, and she took the Queen's hands in her own, discovering that the Queen was clutching Elowen's medallion in her fingers. The chain rustled as it slid between their hands; the stone warmed as the Queen's papery skin became strong and smooth, and her cheeks bloomed pink as a rose.

She smiled at Kaede, a smile that sloughed off Kaede's lingering doubts and sadnesses, and she said, "My huntress: You shall have your reward for what you have given me." She leaned close to her so that she spoke in Kaede's ear, and no one but she could hear.

"My name," she whispered, "is Ealasaid."

When she drew back, Kaede saw her for who she truly was, and she wept to see the Queen's love for her dead daughter, and what difference there was between fay and human was erased, for both understood the sorrow of loss.

Chapter XL

Afterward there was a great celebration, and Kaede, Taisin, and Con were granted free reign to go where they pleased within all of Taninli. Con spent many hours with the Fairy Queen, discussing the terms of a new treaty between their lands, for they both agreed that the time of isolation should end. He planned to present the treaty to his father as soon as he was back in Cathair, and if possible, he would bring the King himself to Taninli the next year.

Kaede and Taisin spent their last night in Taninli in the rooms they had been given during their first visit. Though they could have joined the revelry in the streets below, they were content to simply be near each other, for they both sensed that something precious was coming to an end.

It was Kaede who finally said the words, for she could not bear to pretend. "You're going back to the Academy, aren't you?"

Taisin looked away, but she could not deny it.

"I understand, you know," Kaede said resolutely, though it felt like her heart might break.

Tears trickled from Taisin's eyes. She covered her mouth with her hands as if that would hold the emotion inside.

Kaede got up and walked the few steps to where Taisin was seated nearby, and pulled her close. Taisin's shoulders shook as she cried, her face pressed against Kaede's stomach, her arms wrapped around her waist. It was a long time before she could speak, and Kaede knelt down and held her hands while she listened to her.

"It's the only thing I've ever wanted my entire life," Taisin said, her voice breaking. "I've dreamed of becoming a sage since I knew what a sage was, and I've always known what sacrifices it would require. There is still so much for me to learn, and I have so many questions to ask my teachers. But I love you so much. How can I give you up?"

"You're not giving me up," Kaede said, and she kissed her hands. "You'll always have me."

Taisin's eyes welled up with tears again. She dragged one hand free and wiped them away, drawing a ragged breath. "Kaede," she said, and she had never before realized how much she loved the sound of her name, the way it felt to say it, the look on Kaede's face when she heard Taisin call her. "Kaede, if I become a sage, you know what that means. I have to take a vow of celibacy. I will be with no one."

Kaede had planned to tell her that she should not give up her lifelong dream for her; that she had proven herself too gifted in her power to not continue her training at the Academy. But she also ached deeply to think that she might never hold her again. It was like someone was digging a hole in her and dragging out her heart, and she didn't know if she could bear the pain. "It's a ridiculous rule," she said bitterly, startling a laugh out of Taisin.

"There is a reason for it," Taisin said gently.

"What reason?" Kaede demanded.

Taisin stroked Kaede's hair back from her face, her fingers tangling in the black strands. "Every time I look at you, Kaede, I—" She stopped, breathless, her cheeks reddening.

"What?" Kaede said, the core of her quickening.

"Every time I—I—you know I can't think, Kaede. You make me stop thinking." She gave a brief laugh, and when Kaede's hand ran over her thigh, she shivered.

"You think too much," Kaede murmured, and she pulled Taisin's hand from her hair and kissed her bare wrist, pushing back the sleeve of her tunic. Her skin was warm and golden and unmarked.

Taisin sighed, her whole body coming alive. "I'm not a sage yet," she whispered, and they kissed, and kissed, and a few minutes later, they left the sitting room and went to the round chamber overlooking all the city lights, and they closed the door.

⟳

It was easier to say some things in the dark.

"When we leave here—"

"—things will change."

"It's better this way," Taisin said. "We'll have to get used to—to the way things are going to be." She felt as though she were kicking herself in the gut.

"You should change the rule."

Taisin smiled. "No matter what happens, I'll always love you."

"Taisin—"

"Wait," Taisin said, putting her finger over Kaede's lips. "Let me say this. I'll always love you, but I make no claim on you. You aren't bound the way I'll be. I know that. There's no reason for you to be alone—"

"Taisin," Kaede said, raising herself up on her elbows and looking down at her. "Stop it. I love you, and right now, that's all there is."

Chapter XLI

The Huntsman and several of his riders escorted them through the Wood as far south as the river Kell.

One morning, Kaede emerged from her tent to find a wreath woven from new leaves and perfect pink and white flowers. She stared at it, confused, until the Huntsman told her it was a gift from the wood nymphs, who had visited during the night.

"A gift? Why?"

"Because you saved them, and you saved their queen."

She blinked at the wreath; it was so lovely, a crown fit for a woodland princess. She gave it to Taisin, who blushed to receive it, and thanked her with words so formal that Kaede's heart ached. They did not know how to tread this new path they had chosen, and sometimes it hurt so much that Kaede had to turn her back on Taisin. When she stared out at the Wood, at the trees and the sunlight and the pattern of oak leaves against the sky, it helped, if only a little.

One night, Con asked her why things had changed between her and Taisin, and when she told him, he was saddened. "Are you sure?" he asked softly. Taisin had already gone to sleep, burying herself in her blankets so that she might not have to stay awake beside the person she had decided to be parted from.

"No," Kaede said, "and yes. How can I ask her to give up what she wants most?"

"She wants you."

"Not only me, and that's as it should be." Though it pained her to say it, she was beginning to discover that she believed it. "Her path is different from mine."

"And what do you think your path is?" he asked.

She looked at the Huntsman, who was standing with his riders some distance away. "I think...I think my path lies with them."

Con glanced over his shoulder at the Xi. "With the Fairy Hunt?" He was surprised.

"With the Xi. And with you." She looked at Con. "When you bring that treaty to your father, I want to be there."

He nodded. "The Queen asked me to bring you next year, when I come back with my father."

"Did she?" Kaede said, and she found she was pleased to hear it.

"Yes. So: Will you come back with me?"

"I will," she said immediately.

"We'll have to give you some sort of title," he mused. "We can't keep calling you the Chancellor's daughter."

She smiled. "A title. I'll think about it."

When they came to the river Kell, Kaede could hardly believe her eyes, for there was a bridge. It was obviously old, and barely wide enough for one rider, but it seemed sturdy enough.

The Huntsman walked to her side and said, amused, "Did you think there was no crossing?"

She glared at him. "You saw us that day—of course we had no idea! Where are we? Are we south of where you found us?"

He glanced up at the blue sky. "South, yes, I think a little bit. If only you had gone a bit farther."

"How would we know?" she cried, exasperated. "All the maps are inaccurate."

"Then it's certainly time to correct them," he said, and gave her a warm smile.

She was overcome with bittersweet emotion. "Thank you," she said, "for everything."

He bowed his head to her. "We are grateful to you. And you—and Con and Taisin, too—will always be welcome in our lands. Perhaps your kingdom has a need for a huntress, to tend the Wood south of this river. You might ride with us one day, and we could teach you."

"You are very generous," she said, and tears came to her eyes.

He seemed to struggle with some emotion of his own, and Kaede wondered if he had ever had a daughter, for she thought he would make a good father.

South of the Kell, the Wood was awakening from its long slumber. Sunlight streamed through the branches overhead, each one heavy with green buds. Flowers bloomed along the edges of the trail, pink and purple and white, and birdsong filled the air every morning. It was like an entirely different forest than the one they had traveled through on their way north. There seemed to be no sign of the malignant Wood that had taken their friends Tali and Pol, and nearly taken Shae, as well.

Con intended to stop first at Mona's cottage, in case she was still waiting for them, and the closer they came to it, the more quickly he wanted to ride. Kaede and Taisin understood his eagerness, and the three of them pushed their horses hard on the first day without the Xi. On the third day, they were startled when Con left them behind in a cloud of dust, galloping down the trail toward a horse they could not quite make out in the distance. As they drew nearer, Kaede recognized it, and she said to Taisin, "It's Shae." She and Taisin halted their horses some distance back, not wanting to intrude on their reunion.

Con pulled his horse to a stop and slid out of the saddle, but when his feet touched the ground he felt unexpectedly shy. Shae dismounted from her horse, but she left one hand on the saddle to steady her, for her leg was still not entirely healed. Her hair had grown so that it fell softly around her face, and though she was thinner than she had been before the journey, Con was glad to see that she had color in her cheeks, and some of that color, he hoped, was due to seeing him.

"Con," she said, and gave him a tentative smile. "Well met."

"Shae," he said, and before he could lose his nerve, he went to her and kissed her, cupping her face in his hands. She let out a little sob, reaching up to put her arms around his neck.

Kaede turned slightly away, not wanting to stare. She had worried that the sight of them might make her mourn what she couldn't have with Taisin, but instead, it awakened something warm and alive inside herself. She was only happy for them, and when she glanced at Taisin, she was glad to see that Taisin felt the same way.

"Do you think it will make a good story?" Taisin asked. "The prince and the guard, who fell in love on a journey to the Fairy Queen's city." The sun seemed to shine especially brightly on this part of the trail. It gave Taisin's hair a halo of deep, dark red; it made her face glow.

Kaede smiled, and though her heart still ached, the love she felt was stronger than the pain. "It will make an excellent story," she agreed. And after they had given the prince and the guard another few moments to themselves, Kaede and Taisin rode down the trail to meet them.

ACKNOWLEDGMENTS

Even though a writer sits at her desk alone, there are many people who stand behind her. Thanks to my wonderful agent, Laura Langlie. Thanks to my awesome editor, Kate Sullivan, who shares my storytelling vision. Thanks to my early readers, Sarah Pecora, Lesly Blanton, and Cindy Pon, for your feedback. Thanks to the whole team at Little, Brown Books for Young Readers who help to bring *Huntress* into the world: Barbara Bakowski, Kristin Dulaney, Alison Impey, Zoe Luderitz, Stephanie O'Cain, Ames O'Neill, Jen Ruggiero, Victoria Stapleton, and Amy Verardo. And last but not least, thanks to my partner, Amy Lovell, who witnesses good writing days and bad, and loves me anyway. This book is for you.